The Eliza Doll

Tracey Scott-Townsend

Wild Pressed Books

Second Edition
This is a work of fiction. Name, characters and events are the product of the author's imagination. Any resemblance to actual events or persons, living or dead, is entirely coincidental.
The publisher has no control over, and is not responsible for, any third party websites or their contents.

Contact the author through their website:
www.traceyscotttownsend.com
Twitter: @authortrace
Cover Art by Tracey Scott-Townsend

ISBN: 978-0-9933740-2-9
1st edition published by Wild Pressed Books: 2016
2nd edition published by Wild Pressed Books: 2020
Wild Pressed Books, UK Business Reg. No. 09550738
http://www.wildpressedbooks.com

*In memory of Dawn Annette Wilson 1959 – 2009
Sister, trailblazer.*

The Eliza Doll

1

Suffolk

18 September 2013

Ellie pricks her finger on the needle. The bead of blood mesmerises her, but she shakes herself free of the spell.

"Look at that, Jack. Silly me."

Jack cocks his head.

She tears a square of tissue off the roll by the sink and wraps it around her finger. *Don't get blood on the skirt.*

Her phone's been going off all morning. Lots of texts: *'Happy birthday!'*

The big 5-0. Birthdays used to mean homemade cards and inedible breakfasts.

But today she's glad to be alone.

It's Rosie's birthday, too. Ellie posted a card to her from Cley in Norfolk, a few days ago. Inside, with a shaking hand, she wrote *'to the best birthday present I ever had'*, as she always does. Rosie needs to know her mother still feels the same.

She threads the needle back into the fabric and turns the miniature garment over in her hands, trying not to let tears drop onto it. Jack whines, he pushes his nose against her knee. When she can speak again she says, "Yes, yes," absently.

The sun moves around the sky, warmth pours onto her through the window at her side and the glare hurts her eyes.

"Time to put this away," she tells Jack after another half hour. "I expect you're ready for a walk." He gives her an eager dog-grin, panting, anxious she might change her mind. There's often a long gap between saying it and the actual event.

Ellie opens the cupboard above her head, slips the fabric, needle, reel of thread and scissors into a wooden box. She runs her finger lovingly over the carved surface. Eliza brought the box back from, where was it? India. When she was only seventeen. Ellie had to send her some money to carry it on the plane. *You'll be pleased you did, Mum.* Her lovely, young daughter so proud of herself. It was the first thing Eliza brought home from her travels.

Ellie thinks of the other box, the silver one from Iceland, a decorated chest representing the legend of Skogafoss Falls.

She's been standing too long, staring at nothing. It would matter if there was anyone but Jack to notice. She snaps back into action, moving robotically. Bends to push the slide-out table away over the end of the bed, fastens the wooden cover onto the old-fashioned sewing machine and replaces it in the nook beneath the bed.

"We'll look for some wood while we're out, getting a bit low on supplies."

Keep on keeping on.

She rifles through the pile of kindling, the finely-chopped logs that slot into a metal frame beside the stove, decides the wood should last another evening.

"Yes, yes, I won't keep you waiting any longer." Jack makes the van rock with his capering. "Go on then."

She pulls open the heavy door and steps carefully down from the van, moving aside for Jack to jump onto the rough grass verge. Beyond it, cultivated fields stretch to the horizon but there's a patch of scrubland off to one side where she can exercise Jack. There is nobody, no house or vehicle for miles around. Jack's eyes burn telepathically into hers.

"Find a stick then," Ellie sniffs. Her eyes have been crying again and seem quite independent of her.

She makes her arm lift and throw the stick Jack brings, his body rippling with excitement. He's off before the stick leaves her hand he's nearly hit, but doesn't care. He grabs the stick as it bounces off the ground. Comes running back to Ellie, his paws flicking up mud. Ellie's phone buzzes in her shirt pocket but she ignores it.

Just give me a minute's peace. Funny she should think that when she has so much of it these days. Her thoughts need an uninterrupted trajectory: how many months has it been now? *Seven.*

The vibrating phone stills, and with it the beat of her erratic heart. She can't cope with conversation right now. Jack's leaping figure bounds in and out of view in the long grass, spelling *dog-joy* in a frenzied blur of black letters. Layers of sky overlap each other to the horizon. Somewhere, not far away, is the sea.

The stretch of Suffolk coast has a pebble beach. There's a strong smell of seaweed. She can see Felixstowe across a channel of water on her right, and straight ahead, nothing but sea. A thin mist, either light rain or spray from the sea, wets her skin and clothes, obscuring the view through her glasses. Having to wear varifocals is such a nuisance. She grabs a scrap of cloth from her pocket and wipes them repeatedly, but they only smear. She pulls the hood of her parka up over her head.

Jack doesn't feel the cold. He hurls himself into the waves, dips his head into the foam and comes out with a glistening pebble in his mouth. Back up the slope he races, the stone in his jaws. He drops it at her feet, shaking water all over her.

Ellie takes her sandals off and pushes her bare toes down between the pebbles, sending tingles through her body. Strands of hair like damp rope whip her cheeks. A sudden savage breeze slashes her long skirt against her legs. The van is parked in a layby just above the beach and she wonders if she'll get away with staying the night there. The spot is deserted; it'll be pitch-dark later.

"Take a risk, Mum," says a voice on the wind. "Do it. Nothing bad'll happen."

Ellie takes off her glasses. She wipes them again, this time with the hem of her skirt. Hair blows across her face and she pushes it away, replacing the glasses on the bridge of her nose.

She's here.

Eliza stands next to her, oddly luminescent.

A shimmer of raindrops or sea-spray coats the downy skin of her face. Her straw-coloured hair, which she has never cut, straggles and blows about in the wind. Eliza is wearing a long, striped coat.

"Where did you get that?" asks Ellie, fingering the coarse fabric, damp and heavy. She estimates the strength of needle she'd have to use to sew through such material.

"Oh, I think it was Éire," Eliza says breezily. She's been to so many places; Iceland the most recent. "So, I managed to find you on your birthday. What've you been doing?"

"Waiting for you, mainly."

Ellie tries to slow her breathing.

Cold spray from the sea makes her shiver and for a moment she's transported back to the icy ground by a waterfall, snow and crashing water soaking her then as she's soaked now.

"Are you all right, Mum?"

I should be the one looking after her. She nods and makes her mouth smile. "Are you warm enough?"

"Of course. Are you?"

"I am now you're here." The weight of the morning lifts. "It's been ages. I've missed you, where have you been?"

"In and out," says Eliza vaguely. "I'm here now. Have you got anything to eat?"

Inside the van, Ellie's afraid to take her eyes off Eliza. She stirs a saucepan with her body half-turned away. Eliza's prone to changing her mind at the last minute. She might decide to stay, or she might go. If she wants to stay there's plenty of room in the bed for both of them.

Eliza used to creep into her bed as a child. It was the only physical contact she'd allow. Ellie wonders what she can do to make staying more tempting.

"Shall we light the stove?"

Outside is dim already; a storm brewing. Ellie switches the light on but still shivers again with foreboding. Jack curls himself by the warming stove, steam coming off his black coat. Eliza laughs. She crumples herself next to him on the floor, laying her face on his neck. Eliza always got on best with animals.

If Jack was a cat he'd purr. Instead he lets out a long, contented sigh. Eliza shifts, moving her head so she is looking up into Ellie's eyes.

"It's a brilliant thing you did, taking to the road. My renegade Mum. I'm proud of you, you know."

Ellie's chest hurts. She slides a hand under her cardigan and feels her heartbeat. *Keep on keeping on.*

"I wish all my daughters were."

"Mum," says Eliza, as sternly as she's able with the high, girlish voice Rosie used to tease (*"you sound like Kate Bush."* She'd enrage Eliza by playing their mother's old records, waving her arms about). "Rosie will come round. She couldn't expect you not to follow your dream, just because she thought you should give her some money from the house. You're the one who struggled to maintain it all those years," Eliza giggles. "Dad was such an itinerant."

Her fingers make trails on Jack's sleek coat.

"I let Rosie down." Ellie closes her lips. She places the lid on the pot she's been stirring, turns the gas down and fits herself into the space behind Eliza. She sits on the bed, legs wedged against Eliza's spine. She keeps her own back straight and holds her breath, counting seconds.

Heat rises from the stove. Steam escapes from under the lid of the saucepan. Jack sighs deeply. Ellie's forced to release air from her lungs.

"She's still not talking to me properly, you know," she admits.

There doesn't seem enough oxygen in the van to replace what she's lost.

"Rosie's married," Eliza is saying. "Her and Rick are okay. Don't beat yourself up about it. Move on."

A log shifts within the stove. The sky at the windows becomes darker. Ellie fights panic.

Jack struggles up from the floor and shakes himself as best he can in the confined space, making the van rock. Hard rain is suddenly pattering against the window; it might even be hail. Despite this Ellie knows what Eliza's about to say. Like Jack, her daughter has pushed herself up from the floor. She's buttoning her coat.

No.

The past tumbles forward and crashes at Ellie's feet. *Don't go.* Events from a jumbled timeline converge. Why isn't it possible to take a huge step back and rearrange things?

"I'd better get off, it's getting late."

Icy feelings suffuse Ellie as Eliza makes preparations to leave. They stand close together as the young woman tucks her long, long hair inside the coat and pulls the hood up. Eliza gives her mother a smile.

"Sorry, Mum. Got places to go, y'know?"

The rain outside sounds like a waterfall, nothing will stop its relentless precipitation.

"You haven't even eaten," Ellie's voice is hardly there. "There's a storm outside. Eliza, please don't go."

But it's pointless to ask.

The wind buffets the van, it creaks alarmingly. Ellie wakes with a sob. Then panic overtakes her, a fear that the van will overturn. How far away is the sea? Will she be swept away? She can't help imagining choking on great gulps of water, so cold it would freeze her lungs before it drowned her. Her hands grip the quilt so tightly she has difficulty straightening her fingers. The van rocks. Jack whines in his sleep and stretches along the bottom of the bed. Her body is rigid but she forces herself to let the tension go, inch by inch.

She couldn't drive in this anyway.

Down will come Baby, cradle and all.

She tightens the layers of coverings more securely around her; draws her knees up and wedges her feet either side of the hot water bottle. *Give in to whatever happens. Nothing can be worse than. . .*

She's never been afraid of sleeping alone before now, in fact she's longed for solitude.

A few glowing embers survive behind the glass door of the stove, it can't be that late. Every now and then a particularly strong gust of wind screams down the chimney and lights the embers into fitful flames. Jack sighs and snores, his sleep unbothered by the storm. Ellie thinks of Eliza saying she's proud of her. I can do this.

She doesn't think she's slept at all but she must have done because sun streams through the gap in the curtains at the end of the bed, hitting her in the face. Turning her head to the side she meets Jack's eager eyes. He's on the floor, chin propped by her pillow. His tail wags fiercely as he gives her his most engaging grin. His breath gusts over her.

Ellie groans and pushes herself into a sitting position. The absence of last night's roaring gale means she can hear the swell and suck of the waves, a hundred metres away. She swings her feet to the floor and stands, reaching up to snap the roof window open. The scent of the sea floods in and she breathes deeply. Everything's blurry without her glasses so she puts them on, then pulls her dressing gown around her and shoves her feet into her slippers. Jack lets out a pleading whine.

"Go on then," she says, hauling the van door open. She ought to follow him with a bag. *Hmm.* While he races off she puts the kettle on. Bending to watch him through the small window over the sink, she sees him head unerringly for the sea. She'll have to have a towel ready for when he comes back.

Using the toilet, she tries to remember when she last emptied it. There's a hint of smell. She'll need a night on a campsite to stock up on water, empty the waste and make use of laundry facilities. *It will cost money.* But not having to worry about the amount of water she uses in a shower will be a luxury her body's ready for. *Call it a birthday present.*

In hooking up to electricity, she'll be able to plug in the sewing machine and get more work done, so maybe it will pay for itself.

Later, she'll get the map and work out where to go next. She has a stall booked at a craft fair in Leigh-on-Sea but it isn't for another week or so. She has time to complete a couple more dolls before that.

Her phone buzzes. After a search, she finds it in the pocket of her shirt, on the end of the bed where she threw it after her walk with Jack yesterday. Five missed calls show up on the screen.

"Hi," she says. "Jonah. Sorry I didn't get to talk to you yesterday." She keeps her voice guarded.

"No worries. How are you doing? Did you have a nice birthday?" He sounds far away.

"I'm okay. How are you?"

"I'm fine. Got back twelve days ago." (From America). "Made some money, you know, so if you need any help?" He's smoking; she hears the long suck in and the outlet of breath afterwards.

"Thank you."

There's a bump on the side of the van. Looking out she sees a seagull flying erratically away. Down the beach, Jack spots it and tears off like a greyhound.

She could do with money but doesn't want to admit it. This is supposed to be about independence. Maybe she'll be fine after the next craft fair – it's the run-up to Christmas, after all; people should buy.

The thought of the festive season sickens her.

"Are you crying?" asks Jonah.

There's a scratching at the door, Jack's polite way of knocking.

"Shit!"

The toast under the grill has burst into flames.

"Hang on a minute." Ellie bends and retrieves it then throws the charcoaled bread into the sink, runs the tap. *What a waste.* Jack's whining but she won't let him in until she's dried him.

The van smells of burning.

"I'm just. . . exhausted," she admits.

She thinks of the tasks still to be done: cleaning out the woodstove, making the bed; stacking the wood more securely and fastening it in. She needs to make sure everything is packed away so it won't crash about in the back while she's driving.

When all I really want to do is sleep.

But cars are starting to park on the verges on either side of the narrow road and she can see people throwing interested glances at her bright yellow LDV. She curses whoever painted it that colour.

"Ellie."

She presses the phone closer to her ear. *Pull yourself together, Ellie.*

"Tell me where you are," he says. "I'm coming to meet you. I'm taking you to a hotel for the night. Just one night," he persists, ignoring her protests. "Don't worry," he adds. "I'll get us separate rooms. But I'm going take you away from all this, just for one night. Tomorrow you can get back to your gypsy life."

2

Hull

June 1985

The ambulance rattled over bumps on the way to the hospital. Ellie screamed and refused to stop.

"Shush, now," said the helpful uniformed man in the back with her. "Concentrate. Think positive thoughts. Is this your first baby?"

"Of course not," she yelled. "Why d'you think he," she jerked her chin towards the driver, "wouldn't let my husband come in with me?"

He didn't answer, so she told him. "Because he's got to look after my other two, that's why." She moaned again.

Please make it go away. This isn't my baby, I don't want it.

"Oh dear." The young man's cheeks reddened. "You're going to have your hands full, aren't you?"

I'm twenty-two and my life is ov-er.

By the time she was deposited in a wheelchair at the hospital's entrance the contractions were overwhelming. Whisked past the reception desk, she glimpsed Jonah imparting her booking-in details, a sleeping Kester in his arms. Rosie sobbed nearby in the pushchair.

"Wait," begged Ellie.

She reached out to stroke Rosie's hair. Rosie grabbed her hand and took a shuddering breath.

"Where did you go to, Mamma?"

It broke her heart. Rosie wasn't even three yet. Ellie squeezed her eyes shut against another pain. A nurse came around the desk.

"We can find someone to look after the children if you want your husband in with you." The nurse squatted in front of Rosie and made comforting sounds. Ellie nodded miserably.

She resisted the birth as long as she could. Jonah's hair swung forward over her face and a midwife told him to tie it back.

"It's not very nice for her, is it?"

But Ellie didn't mind a screen to hide behind. She didn't want this thing inside her and she didn't want it out. It was too soon after Kester, a horrible mistake.

"Can you try and encourage her, Dad?" asked the other midwife.

Despite her best intentions to put the moment off, a baby was finally extracted. Ellie screamed as she split open.

The cord was around its neck.

I don't want to look. But she couldn't help herself, a powerful force gripping her head and wrenching it towards what looked like a limp, grey doll on the resuscitation table. The baby was completely silent. An answering hush fell over the room while the paediatric team worked.

Jonah gripped Ellie's hand, his eyes wet. She found that she was praying; *please, please, please,* but it was more for him than the baby. How would she face him if it died? A midwife rubbed harder with a towel. *"Come on."* Then there was a muted cry, which soon built up into a crescendo, filling Ellie's head until everything else was blocked out.

She lay on the hospital bed with the new baby in the crook of her arm. They gazed at each other. The baby gave her a level, scrutinizing stare.

"Who *are* you?"

She really wanted to know. This baby was a total stranger, how could she take it home and pretend she was its mother? Ellie's head ached. The skin of her face felt taut. "I don't know you at all." She started crying again. She'd been left holding someone else's baby.

Her nipples felt sore from the stranger's greedy tugging. Ellie longed to tuck her real baby, Kester, into his rightful place at her breast. She knew that if this baby hadn't been revived, she could have been persuaded by a long, healing sleep that the whole event had never happened. *It could have all been a dream.*

"Stop looking at me like that," she sobbed. "Please, go to sleep."

The baby stared a moment longer and only closed its eyes when it was good and ready.

"We have to give her a name," said Jonah. He was walking up and down the living-room with the baby over his shoulder. This was the most hands-on he'd ever been as a father.

Ellie only fed the baby grudgingly. Now she curled up in the armchair with Kester; the boy's blue eyes fixed on her face, his fingers touching her chin. He was so much gentler than that other one.

"Ellie."

Jonah was fed up with her. But it wasn't *his* life that had been ruined.

The TV blared in the corner, keeping Rosie happy. It wasn't how Ellie had imagined bringing her older daughter up. Watching the screen blank-eyed, one or the other baby sucking at her breast, seemed to be all Ellie ever did. When the news came on it cemented her depression. A passenger jet had disintegrated in the air, reminding her of the dreams of falling planes she'd had the previous year. The police beat up the Peace Convoy at Stonehenge. She cried again because it evoked poignant memories of the summer she went there with Jonah. It was all about violence and endings now.

"I need the loo," Jonah said. "Here, take her for a minute, will you?"

Ellie tensed, causing Kester to tighten his grip on her rolled-up shirt.

"Put her in the carrycot."

Kester pulled away from the breast when Jonah left the room, struggled to get down on the floor where Rosie was playing with her dolls' house. The plump one-year-old toddled over to the baby's carrycot, grasping the rim with his fat hands.

"Babba, Mamma, Babba?"

She was afraid he'd pull the carrycot over and then Jonah would be furious; that was the only reason she got up and steadied it. She stood away slightly, not wanting to meet that scrutinising gaze. But the impassive little face caught her eyes anyway, and stared unflinchingly back.

3

Iceland

February 2013

They wait for their turn to get off the bus. The guide is smiling, reeling off a string of Icelandic anecdotes for their entertainment. She has a personal word with each of the passengers as they disembark, as if they've been friends for a long time; she lays a hand on their arms.

"Is it your first visit here?"

Ellie grips the handrail, biting her lip, nodding. She can't think of anything to say. Placing her feet carefully on the rubber treads, she hears Jonah's gravelly laugh behind her in answer to a remark the guide has made to him.

You were always able to compartmentalise your emotions, Jonah.

A powerful gust of wind grabs her and hurls a pebble-dash of snow into her face. She's nearly taken off her feet by the force of it and she can't believe the bus made it along those icy mountain roads in one piece, the driver laughing and chattering with Kristi, their guide. Once again, she marvels at the Icelandic propensity to take whatever is thrown at them in their stride.   While the driver steered one-handed around a twisting bend to the beep-beep of an alarm warning of ice on the road, Kristi taught the passengers how to say something that sounds like *'theta reddast'*, meaning 'it'll be fine'.

But it isn't.

It feels like the landscape is spinning. On each trajectory, Ellie glimpses the blackness of a river, blue-white mountains, and wide, white spaces dotted with troll-shaped rocks. Dread lodges in her gut. A weight of grey hangs low in the sky. Snow blusters and twirls. Ellie has to hold tight to her soul; it longs to plunge into the open void.

She closes her eyes, the earth is sucked from beneath her feet.

She gasps. Jonah is beside her, grasping her arm. She tilts her face up to his, catching snowflakes on her glasses.

"I hope we see the Northern Lights while we're here..." She has to say something, he's looking concerned.

It doesn't matter whether they do or not, but it's a solid goal to fix on. *Eliza wants us to see the Aurora.*

Eliza planned their trip for them; specific about the details. They should see Iceland together before meeting up with her in Reykjavik when she could greet them as the *'Mum and Dad I used to have.'*

> Dear Mum,
>
> I want you and Dad to come and visit me together.
>
> I'm going to write the same thing to Dad. Forget any differences you have and remember that you're both my parents. You've drifted apart, I want you to become friends again. I think you owe it to me. I've got a right to see you both, I want to tell you things.

It's rare for Eliza to express need.

Ellie thinks she's going to be sick again.

"There're some toilets over there," Jonah points out a wooden building near some information boards. "Do you want me to come in with you, hold your hair?"

She manages a scathing look before crunching across the hard-packed snow, grasping her middle. Vomiting makes her feel better.

Jonah should try it.

On the walk to the glacier, Ellie's new boots will rub, breaking open the blisters she already has. She could have put on more plasters, even bandaged her feet. But she needs the pain.

Buy snow boots well in advance and make sure you practise walking in them before your visit. You want to be able to enjoy the scenery, not spend your time moaning about sore feet. I know what you're like.

A razor-edged laugh rises in Ellie's throat. She comes out of the toilet and scans the snow for Jonah. He's standing alone, off to the right of the information boards. From the corner of her eye she sees the rest of the group gazing at the river. Small icebergs sit like fat swans on the grey water.

When she looks at Jonah's face she sees his closed eyes. He's meditating. A spear of envy pierces her heart; he'll probably walk in a state of heightened consciousness while she, on the other hand, will feel every energy-draining step.

She doesn't really want to do anything, but she must keep on keeping on. The kids used to laugh at her favourite saying.

Cold bites through her gloves. The few patches of ground that show between occasional gaps in the snow are gritty; dark, volcanic.

This island is created from volcanos. Every now and then one of them goes off, hopefully not when you're here though.

This land of ice and fire. She wishes one would.

Fine grains of snow sting Ellie's cheeks. She leans forward, hands on her thighs, aching from the walk. The glacier hunches like an extinct dinosaur before them, or a black and white tortoise, head hidden in its shell. Dead and cold. Far away on its surface, a group of glacier-walkers resemble brightly-coloured ants.

Kristi tells them that the glacier has changed more in the last year than in the five years between 1990 and 1995. The prediction used to be that it would be gone in ninety-five years, now it's expected to melt completely within the next sixty.

Kristy gives them a moment to absorb this, then bends to collect samples of volcanic rock for them to examine. Passing the rocks out, she explains their different colours and textures in relation to their age and the kind of eruption that caused them. Ellie spots something in the dark grit. She bends to pick up a piece of fool's gold.

"Jonah."

He's not beside her. For a minute she can't spot him amongst the other tourists and her heart knocks uncomfortably in her ribcage. Her eyes are blurry. She removes her glasses clumsily with glove-bundled fingers, wipes them on her scarf. When she replaces them on her face she sees him, talking to a woman with blonde hair that sticks out beneath her pink ski-hat. Is that a pang of jealousy she feels? *Maybe Eliza's plan is working.*

Jonah's shoulders are hunched in the grey down jacket he bought on eBay. His jeans hang loosely on his wiry frame. More than wiry now, she wonders when he got so skinny.

He ought to be next to her. *We're supposed to be doing this together.*

"Jonah," she calls again. Why is she thinking of the particular thing she wants to tell him now?

He gives the woman a smile and comes to stand beside Ellie as she beckons him with a crooked finger.

"That doll I made for Eliza when she was little. Remember?"

I've been thinking about her a lot recently. Rainbow, her name is, because of the dress you made her from those coloured scarves. Can you bring her with you?

"Eh? Uhm. . ." Jonah and she haven't spoken for a while. Since they stopped at the glacier, he's been chatting to other bus passengers, but she can't bring herself to talk to anyone but him.

"Not sure what you mean." His mind's elsewhere. His mouth is full of a chunk of caramel bar. He talks through it. "I'm hungry, aren't you?"

"No." She wants to share memories, before they reunite with Eliza.

Jonah carries on chewing. Ellie's sinuses prickle. "You were always so preoccupied. You didn't notice anything going on under your nose."

She struggles to pull off her glove, attempts to dislodge the tightly-fastened lid of her water bottle. She would like to walk down to the foot of the glacier but the slope is steep and she worries she might slip on the loose rocks.

When did I become so afraid of everything?

Far away, a rider on one of those tiny Icelandic horses moves slowly across the expanse of white plain. From this distance, the horse and rider are in slow motion. The valley is so vast, broken by the silver breadth of river, reflecting the sky, and its floating icebergs. The quiet, the majesty of the landscape makes her well up.

"Come on now, what do you mean by that, saying I never noticed anything?" Jonah's fishing in his pockets for more snacks. He can't find any, so he takes a swig of his own water instead.

Ellie decides not to answer. She locates a tissue in a deep pocket of her coat and wipes under her eyes, careful not to dislodge her glasses, and then her nose. When she stuffs the tissue back in she discovers a packet of nuts and hands them silently to Jonah, a peace offering.

A fresh sprinkle of snow flurries down out of nowhere. The guide is gathering her flock together, ticking them off on a list. A feeling of anxiety makes Ellie's insides twist and she finds herself pressing her arm against Jonah's. She needs to be close to him.

Jonah, finally managing to open the packet, pops a nut in his mouth He gives Ellie one of his sideways grins and proffers the bag at her but she shakes her head, trying to remember when she was last able to eat.

The sky hangs even lower, laden and grey, obliterating the tops of mountains.

"Two people are missing," Kristi calls out, checking her list again. "Does anyone know where they are?"

The anxiety pushes higher into Ellie's chest. *Has there been an accident?*

A second group of tourists from another bus is mingling with theirs, making it harder to see. For a moment she holds her breath. *Something bad has happened.*

But no. The young couple, both in bright orange North Face jackets, are scrambling back up the slope towards Kristi, who is wagging her pen at them and telling them they're making everybody late.

Ellie and Jonah have agreed not to get off the bus with the other passengers when it next stops. Waterfalls are the most important thing on Eliza's itinerary.

You don't have enough time to really get the feel of each place on those coach tours, Mum. I suppose that'll have to be the way you see Gullfoss because the Golden Circle tour's worth doing in itself, but I want you and Dad to hire a car for your trip to Seljalandsfoss and Skogafoss. Please do. Skogafoss is my favourite. I've hitched there loads of times. I want you two to appreciate it the way I've had a chance to.

Kristi is chivvying her flock back along the path to the bus, telling them they won't be able to spend as long at the next stop because they're running behind schedule.

Ellie breathes deeply. The air is so pure it makes her dizzy.

"Anyway, the doll." She consents to a single nut, chewing slowly. Dropping the fool's gold inside her bag she zips it up, pulls her gloves back on and fastens them around her wrists.

"Rainbow," Jonah says without seeming to think about it. Ellie smiles, though it hurts. "That's right, Rainbow. You do remember. The first ever doll I made."

"It was an ugly bugger," Jonah says after a pause. "Looked as if it'd come straight out of a horror film."

"Jonah!" He's right, though.

"C'mon, Ellie, you can't deny it." He tweaks one of her plaits, sticking out from under her hat like the blonde woman's hair. She can't believe he's almost making her laugh.

Kristi is encouraging the group to hurry along the narrow path. Ellie falls into step beside Jonah. They're walking quickly and their breath comes out in puffs.

"But Eliza loved it," he belatedly adds, apropos the doll. "Didn't she?"

Ellie tries another smile.

"Yeah, she did. Anyway, she wanted me to bring it over. But I couldn't find it anywhere." Her voice trembles. "I'm worried I might have thrown it out." She takes another deep breath.

Jonah's adjusting the straps of his rucksack. He pulls her against him with one arm and gives her a quick squeeze as they walk. When he lets go she has that sensation again of spinning above the world.

"She won't mind," he says, evenly.

4

Hull

January 1982

Ellie forgot to take her contraceptive pills home at Christmas. She spent the holiday in a fog of withdrawal from Jonah. They'd only been together two months, and it was physically painful to be apart.

It didn't occur to her that taking the missed ones all at once when she got back would render them ineffective.

Shortly after the start of the spring term, Ellie and Jonah left their university accommodation and rented a flat on Park Grove. They were now a proper couple with a real home. After they'd been living in the flat a month, they adopted two cats from the RSPCA; a black-and-white mother and her grey son. She thought of herself and Jonah as the parents: the cats their children. Ellie smiled to herself. *One day, maybe.*

But she was already pregnant by then.

March 1982

Ellie stood in a telephone box by the park. The streetlight next to it wasn't working. Wind whipped the surrounding trees into a frenzy of accusation and disappointment, a chorus to her mother's pronouncement. *You're a stupid girl, a stupid girl...*

Don't listen to her, thought Ellie to the baby. She was three months pregnant.

"What's the father doing about it?" Vivian's voice cracked on the line.

Jonah was *OK* with the pregnancy (that's what Ellie was telling everyone, anyway). Shocked but not angry. Not really angry. Not after his initial fury had died down. He'd promised that he'd never frighten her like that again.

In her head, Genesis sang about dust settling. It wasn't Jonah's fault, the news was bound to take a while to sink in. She loved him so *much...*

Wind rattled the glass panes of the telephone box. Ellie shivered.

"The father is Jonah, as you well know," she said testily. "The father is being loving and supportive, as ever."

Some of the time.

She wouldn't give her mother any more ammunition to attack her with.

Another gust of wind rattled the window and she jumped, nerves in shreds.

"You've only known him five minutes," Vivian pointed out.

That's kind of true.

But her mother was too old and definitely too unfeeling to understand about the ancient recognition between Ellie and Jonah. It was strong enough to carry them through any crisis.

Still, the shocking realisation of an end to everything she'd planned for herself kept hitting Ellie with devastating finality.

"What about university?" Vivian must have read her thoughts.

"I'm finishing the first year." Ellie swallowed. "Getting my credits. Once the... after I have the baby I'm going to look at other courses. I was thinking of changing, anyway."

So there.

"Oh, you'll never be able to do anything for yourself, now." Her mother sounded satisfied to be informing Ellie of this fact.

———

Ellie's mother visited the flat only once, when Jonah was out, bringing Ellie's younger sister with her. Deborah turned her nose up at the cat hairs on the furniture and shook her Pre-Raphaelite mane like a pony. Ellie pictured her stamping a hoof.

She was jealous of Deb but not because of her sister's looks: it was something magnetic in her character, people were either attracted to her or repelled. Nobody ever failed to notice her like they did mousy Ellie.

"When *I* have a baby," Deb announced with a look down her nose at Ellie, "I'll be married and have a decent home."

Where does she get her confidence from?

Before they left, Vivian surprised Ellie by unwrapping a hand-crocheted shawl.

"It's from your grandma."

Grandma Maud was in a residential home with dementia, hardly able to remember who she was. It was hard to understand how she could retain such skill with a crochet hook and delicate, silken yarn.

"We must take the baby to see her when it's born," said Vivian. "She really perked up when I told her about it. She loves babies."

For a minute, Ellie felt they were a proper mother and daughter, handling the soft folds of the shawl together.

Deb stuck her tongue out at Ellie as she dragged their mother off to 'hit the shops'.

"I can't pretend to know what it's like having a bad relationship with your sibling," Jonah said later. He'd been at a band rehearsal all afternoon and so was in a good mood. "Because I don't have one. I've only got you."

She felt sorry for him then. His hand stroked her belly. The baby arched its back, or she imagined it did. The skin over her stomach tightened and Jonah breathed harder. He slid his hand down lower and she pressed her thighs together on his fingers. She felt as if she was poised on a precipice, about to plunge.

"God, Ellie, you've no idea how much it turns me on, you being pregnant."

A deep, sensual ache pulled at her insides. "I think I do," she said.

June 1982

They hitched down to Wiltshire for the Stonehenge festival. It was the second time for Ellie, the previous year she'd gone with her ex-boyfriend Mal. They'd spent two days at Glastonbury festival and arrived at Stonehenge in time for the Summer Solstice. It was the summer before she started university. At the time she knew her relationship with Mal was coming to an end, but the excitement she felt at her impending student-hood overrode her sadness at a friendship splitting apart.

Now being a student was coming to an end, too. She refused to consider the state of her relationship with Jonah. They were having a baby; that *made* them solid.

They travelled down-country by lorry, truck and car and the power of Ellie's thumb. She was six months pregnant. Jonah hated hitchhiking but they were short of money and couldn't afford either bus or train fares. Both had student overdrafts. Ellie tried not to worry about how they would pay them off once they were living on a couple's allowance of Social Security.

As she stood at the side of the road with her thumb out, Jonah slumped on the verge behind her, complaining first about the heat and then about the rain when it started to fall. Ellie tried to keep positive. It was only that he was depressed, he'd had a massive row with his parents over his own decision to leave university. But he still loved her and that was all that mattered.

The day dragged on with one short lift after another. Sometimes a vehicle stopped for Ellie (her pregnancy obscured by a loose cardigan) but moved off again when the driver noticed Jonah rising from the grass behind her.

Ellie had plenty of time to think. She wondered if it was too late to change her mind about leaving university. Was there a way she could manage with a small baby? Other students managed it. Maybe she'd acted too hastily in choosing to leave.

But everybody had been telling her it would be so difficult to continue her studies. She didn't know what to do.

They spent a whole day and most of the evening on the road. Jonah was in a seriously bad mood by the time their last lift, a farmer in a Land Rover, dropped them outside the festival field. It was getting dark and the lights of what seemed like a city stretched into the distance, streets of tents and stalls with lights strung up along them. It looked like Fairy Land.

They trudged deep into the temporary town, walking between rows of stalls, moving deliberately apart every time their tired frames bumped into each other.

Jonah's eyes widened like a child in a toyshop as he absorbed his surroundings. The smell of weed was strong. Vendors offered speed and acid. Ellie placed her arm protectively across her belly. She hadn't realised how pregnancy would alter her perception of this magic city.

They emerged from the tightly packed stalls into a kind of clearing, crowded with transient dwellings. Candles flickered in the branches of a circle of trees and it looked like there were makeshift beds up there as well. Benders made from curved poles with polythene stretched over them surrounded a fire.

A woman breathed music from a flute and a man played a fiddle. Someone sang in a low voice. Moving shadows behind the fire circle indicated a group of dancers.

There were two women crouched over the fire, cooking. One was also breastfeeding a toddler. Her breast was exposed and the bare-bottomed toddler held it in both hands while the woman got on with stirring a pot. Firelight flickered on the uncovered skin of her chest and shoulder and on her tattooed arm, repetitively stirring. She looked like a character out of *Mad Max*.

The second woman glanced over at Ellie and got to her feet. She asked if she could give Ellie's baby a blessing. Ellie shrugged the backpack from her shoulders and stood still while the barefoot woman in a long (grubby) white dress placed her hands on Ellie's stomach and chanted some words she didn't understand.

The people around the fire then invited them to stay for supper. Ellie wanted to but Jonah at first hesitated and then said they had to get on. He was still tight-lipped and not looking at Ellie. He explained that they were meeting friends and they needed to set up their tent first. Ellie was disappointed, she was more interested in the tribal way of living she was glimpsing than the career opportunities that Jonah anticipated.

Jonah was meeting his friends at the main stage, sometime that night; the arrangement was only vague. The sky was a deep turquoise colour as Jonah pulled Ellie by the wrist through the packed, restless bodies towards the front. The air was thick with pungent smoke and Ellie worried she might cause harm to the baby.

Amazingly, John-Paul and Martin turned out to be standing directly behind them in the mass of people, just as Hawkwind tuned their instruments and the crowd shifted with expectation.

Jonah's friends had weird, fast-moving eyes and made odd jerky movements with their hands.

Jonah was laughing for the first time that day. *I shouldn't have come*, Ellie realised.

The baby had woken up, kicking and prodding her while Jonah snored, packed tightly beside her in the small tent. She could barely move and was uncomfortable on the thin mat, unable to turn over. Her hip hurt.

Sounds and shadows loomed around the cramped camping area. The nylon walls were so thin. Every now and then someone tripped over a guy rope and fell against their tent. How would she get through a whole night of this – several nights? She shouldn't have come.

Her mind was still filled with the green and red of the stage lights, the ragged chords and wailing guitars of Hawkwind. Stoned faces from the crowd loomed on the screen behind her eyes and she couldn't sleep for worrying.

As they'd shuffled into their sleeping bags, Jonah expressed his eagerness to take speed for the first time the next day. *No. I need you to be an adult, Jonah.*

Another worrying thing was the rumour that trouble was expected on site from the Hells Angels.

She mustn't continue trying to live the way Jonah still wanted to. He couldn't absorb the magnitude of the responsibility they had, whereas it was beginning to weigh on her. When Ellie closed her eyes, it felt like she was being sucked backwards.

July 1982

Jonah and John-Paul's band The Travelling Man were playing at the university's Summer Rock Ball.

Summer term had ended and with it Ellie's spell as a student. Heavily pregnant, she'd taken her first-year exams and done well. But she hadn't plucked up the courage to approach her personal tutor about the possibility of staying on as a student-mother. He was quick enough to sign her off when she told him about the pregnancy. "I'm disappointed that you've thrown away your opportunity, Ellie, you could have done quite well," were his exact words (as if she'd never have the chance again). She couldn't go and tell him she wanted to stay on now.

The event looming at the end of the holidays was completely out of her control. *I'm scared, but I don't know who to tell.* Being pregnant was embarrassing when all her friends were obsessed with exams and parties. She felt like some kind of freak.

Jonah hated the physical attention Ellie got. People wanted to touch her bump and ask her questions. She was a novelty; that was all. But it grated on Jonah.

"It's not as if you have to have *talent* to grow a sprog inside you."

He was subsumed by his own impending importance to the world.

He marked his place with one finger while he gave her a withering look.

"Maria goes on and on about how amazing you are, it's getting boring."

Ellie's friend had just left.

Ellie held her hair back with one hand while she rubbed circles on her belly with the other. What could she say to connect with Jonah again?

The grey cat jumped up on the table and tried to sit on Jonah's pages of notes. "Fuck off," he snapped. Turning back to Ellie he demanded, "Why did we get these cats anyway?"

Nothing could make him happy, apart from the musical recognition he sought. He pushed the animal away and continued working down his list of record producers.

Jonah was engrossed in his new band and the songs they were writing. Having decided it wasn't worth finishing his own degree because he was no longer interested in History, he'd dropped out too. His decision caused multiple fall-outs with his parents. In a letter they blamed Ellie. Apparently it was inevitable a *northerner* would bring a *southerner* down.

She'd never even *met* them.

On top of the announcement of Jonah's impending fatherhood he couldn't now be certain of the financial support for his musical career they'd promised to give him when he finished university, so he was putting his energy into getting it kick-started before the baby was born.

Ellie could understand his need to prove himself. His career as an adored only son seemed over as surely as hers as a potential high-flying historian/anthropologist was. And she admired and supported his drive to succeed as a musician. But she had a secret fear; *I don't want to be a single mother.*

Ellie was feeling sorry for herself. She felt sharp pains in her forearms and looked down to discover she was gripping them, digging her fingernails in. What was left of her fingernails; she'd taken to biting them. She felt too bulky to go out on the dancefloor with Maria, still a teenager swinging her ponytail, swivelling her hips in her bright green dungarees while she bellowed the lyrics at the top of her voice.

Maria was going abroad for the summer to visit family in Spain. When she returned, university would begin again and Ellie wouldn't be there. Ellie's old friends from Beverley also had their own, more youthful concerns. She had no-one, except a boyfriend far more engrossed in his music than her and their baby.

The life Ellie was meant to live, whatever it was, had been ripped out from beneath her feet, while Jonah was still heading for his.

The DJ announced that the band would come on in five minutes. This was the moment Ellie was supposed to feel proud. But she couldn't swallow her nausea.

"You okay? It's not the baby, is it?" Maria panted from her exertions on the dancefloor. She bent forward with her hands on her knees. "I'm sweating like a pig."

Ellie clenched her hands, fighting the urge to hit somebody.

"What is it?" Maria examined her face. "Have you been crying?"

The band were getting ready on stage. A tall youth bumped Ellie in the back as people crowded in, jostling for space.

She whipped round. Maybe this was the person she could hit. But he looked so young, and she felt so old.

"Sorry," he apologised. "Wow, you're pregnant, that's amazing, man." He pointed her condition out to his friends as if she was the star attraction in a freak-show.

Ellie felt the baby startle. *You must have recognised your daddy's drum intro.* Sometimes Jonah practised at night in the living room. Either the drumming woke her (and the baby) or it was the neighbours, banging on the door.

Jonah justified the disruption when she complained: "My work's important, you can sleep whenever you want." But she couldn't, unless the flat was empty of his friends. "I need to make it big," he emphasised, "so I can support you and the baby."

People around Ellie joined in with the lyrics. She hadn't realised The Travelling Man had a fan club already. She rubbed her arms, wishing she'd worn a cardigan.

Jonah came out from behind the drums at the end of the song, replaced by the second guitarist, Martin. There was a pause while Jonah tuned his bass. When he came to the front of the stage, shaking back his long hair, a girl let out a scream.

Ellie's womb contracted, and the baby kicked back.

She put her arms around the burden that was weighing her down, and fought the feeling she had regularly of the ground being sucked out from under her feet.

5

August 1982

John-Paul had been to visit a communal household in a village near the sea.

"It's a really cool place," he told Jonah and Ellie at their flat.

The living room was narrow: two or three of Jonah's friends' long legs stretched across it made it impassable. She envisaged having to pass the baby (in those moments when she could actually comprehend the reality of the baby) from one person to another across the cramped space, dim from the always half-closed curtains, ever-filled with a haze of smoke. You had to go through the bedroom to get to the bathroom and there were always people around to disturb you.

"I'm gonna do it."

"Do what?" asked Jonah.

"I'm gonna go and live there."

"What for?"

Jonah was distracted from his conversation by the sudden dramatic movement of Ellie's stomach. He placed both hands on it and cocked his head on one side as if listening for messages. He occasionally showed interest in the baby and it gave Ellie hope that things would be all right. The bump was turning over.

Ellie pushed her cardigan aside and they watched the thin material of her summer dress ripple and inflate with the movements.

John-Paul stuck two fingers in his mouth and made a retching sound.

"Ow," Ellie complained. It was horrible, that tugging feeling. "That's the head I think; quick, feel it."

"Wow," Jonah said. "Cool, man. That's amazing. Every time he does that I think he's gonna make a break for it."

"Fuck, no." John-Paul turned slightly green, either from the thought of birth or from what he was smoking. "Not yet, I hope."

Ellie shivered at the look in his heavy-lidded eyes.

Why couldn't she and Jonah ever have any privacy? A renegade thought escaped; maybe she'd be better off living alone. *Just me and the baby.* No! She *loved* Jonah.

"She," she corrected, lifting her chin. "It's a girl, I know it is."

Jonah lost interest. "Cheers, man." He accepted the joint John-Paul reached over Ellie to pass. A glowing flake dropped from its end onto Grey Cat's back, he was snuggled between the sofa arm and Jonah's elbow. The cat scrambled up with a yowl, streamed himself over the arm of the sofa and snuck it behind to lick his wounds. Jonah and John-Paul giggled and Ellie worried about what kind of father Jonah was going to be.

The Grateful Dead played on the stereo. Jonah closed his eyes, nodding his head; breathed smoke in. Letting his breath out again, his voice had a high edge to it when he returned to the topic of their child.

"It's a boy, you wait and see. Daddy's right, eh, kid?"

He gave her belly a friendly pat. She felt so lonely.

She wrinkled her nose as the room filled again with pungent smoke. The smell was starting to get to her. She wished she could go and lie on her bed but if she did she'd soon be disturbed by someone passing through on their way to the toilet.

"No thanks." She spoke directly to the joint, proffered to her face.

Jonah didn't get it. Their child was probably imbibing far too much passive smoke as it was.

We can't even look after a cat properly.

Jonah passed the joint back to John-Paul.

"Anyway," John-Paul steered the conversation again. "I'm gonna go and live there coz it's a brilliant place, yeah? You could come and live there as well."

He looked only at Jonah. Ellie and Jonah looked at each other, Jonah with an *'I bet you're going to say no,'* expression on his face. *"You never back me up,"* he'd said to her recently. *"It's got to be your way or nothing."*

In the kitchen the kettle Jonah had put on, for his precious friend, whistled. Nobody moved. Unable to stand it any longer, Ellie tried to haul herself off the sofa. Jonah helped by pushing from behind.

She stepped over John-Paul, who carried on talking.

"There're gonna be about ten residents. All, y'know, creative types, that's what the guy who runs it's looking for. Best thing is, there's a barn, or maybe it's a garage, something like that anyway, at the back of the house where we can practise."

In the lobby, Ellie kicked John-Paul's rucksack aside. *Fuck him.* She was trembling.

"Who owns the place?" she heard Jonah ask.

"Some guy," said John-Paul. "This guy I spoke to. He wants to set up some kind of arts project. Y'know, involving young offenders or something. The residents of the house have to help on the project. You have to go for an interview to get a room there."

He sounded vague.

Ellie stood in the kitchen doorway waiting for the tea to brew. She resented having to use milk she got with her DHSS tokens to sustain John-Paul. *This milk is supposed to help the baby grow.* No, he wouldn't have it. She scraped the last of the powdered milk from a tin that Jonah had chucked in the bin into John-Paul's tea instead.

"But won't they mind that I'm pregnant?" she said, coming back to the room.

They both looked at her in surprise, and then at each other. She couldn't be interested in the 'project'. She wasn't an artist or a musician, simply an inconveniently pregnant girl.

She didn't know if John-Paul was even including her in the invitation, or if he thought he could persuade Jonah to leave her behind.

"Dunno..." John-Paul sighed and moved his legs to one side to let her through, struggling to carry three mugs. He flicked her a disinterested glance. "You could ask, I s'pose."

"We'd have to get a car," Jonah said unexpectedly. She resettled her bulk amongst the sagging cushions next to him. "If we went to live there." He put his hand on her thigh without looking at her. She leaned into him and wound a strand of his hair round her finger. John-Paul had stirred Jonah's curiosity, but the thought of another extreme change in their lives made Ellie nervous.

"Ellie," Jonah said. "It'd be pretty amazing, actually."

He still wasn't looking at her. She watched his leg jiggling. He breathed out a wraith of smoke, tapped ash into the glass bowl on the table.

"John-Paul says the house is right between the river and the sea." His head bobbed in the direction of his friend. "Think how much the baby would like it."

She was touched. He was thinking of his child, at last. She felt a rush of adrenaline and the baby, in the new position it'd gotten itself into, gave her a hard kick. Maybe it was saying yes.

"A car, yeah, man, that'd be cool." John-Paul had a gleam in his eyes. "Or a van, maybe. Y'know, to put the drum kit and everything in."

"And the baby," Ellie said.

They both looked at her.

18 September 1982

Maria was back from Spain. Ellie gave her an emotional hug when she arrived at the flat on Ellie's birthday.

"I was so worried when I heard about that plane crash in Málaga on Monday," she blubbed. "Isn't that the day you left Spain?"

"Yes, but it wasn't my plane, as you can see."

Maria spread her arms wide, demonstrating her intactness. She seemed more sophisticated than when she'd left. Opening her bag, she handed Ellie, appropriately, a set of embroidered handkerchiefs edged with Spanish lace. She frowned when Ellie immediately blew her nose on one.

Maria said, "I got something for the baby, as well." It was a fine woollen shawl with tassels. Ellie already had the one from Grandma Maud. *I could use this one for myself.* It was pretty and very Spanish. There was also an embroidered nightdress and a bonnet, (for the baby).

"You can use them for either a boy or a girl, don't worry," Maria assured her. "Everyone does in my family's village in Spain."

She stepped between the packed boxes and packets of nappies; the carrycot on wheels Ellie had insisted Jonah allow her to save up for from their dole money.

"Oh my God, Ellie," Maria took her first proper look at her friend. "You're enormous. Are you sure you're okay? You look pale."

"Tired," Ellie explained. "I never realised how tired I'd get."

To her relief, Jonah had gone to Martin's for a practice. The band had a gig that night at a club on Beverley Road and the flat was for once mercifully quiet.

Ellie planned to celebrate her birthday by going to the gig with Maria, (who knew if she'd ever get another chance?) They were having a takeaway at the flat first.

"Can I feel your tummy?"

Everyone said that but they usually recoiled when they felt the baby move. Maria kept her hand in place though. The baby arched and rolled inside.

"Crikey. It must feel incredible to have a baby inside you. When exactly is your due date?"

"Two weeks today, it feels like forever."

"Oh dear. You're really all set to move to this back-of-beyond place? I can't understand it. You'll be so isolated."

"I'm isolated here, Maria. You'll all be back at university in a week or so, and my life's going to be so different from yours. At least I'll have a room there that nobody but me, Jonah and the baby can come into. It's a big room, bright and sunny." She paused, chewing her lip. "Jonah's getting his own room as well, and there's plenty of communal space. I'll have a lot more privacy than I have here with the band always coming round."

Maria took in the subtext of what she was saying. Ellie saw the concern on her face.

"It's not because we don't want to sleep together."

She didn't let on that they hadn't had sex for ages. "We're having separate rooms so I have a dedicated space for me and the baby. If we only had one room I couldn't guarantee it wouldn't end up full of his mates all the time."

Maria sighed. She concentrated on another part of Ellie's stomach. A foot or hand skittered about beneath her palm.

"That makes sense, I suppose. So were the DHSS alright about paying your rent?"

"Yeah. We had to say we're splitting up so we can have two rooms." Again she bit on her lip. "But it'll work out cheaper than staying here anyway. And we'll both get an allowance for helping on the arts project. We have to declare the allowance though, so they'll cut our benefits. Jonah's all for not declaring it but I can't risk having my benefit cut off, not with a baby."

"So, uhm, you and Jonah aren't claiming as a couple any longer?"

"No. . . " Talking about it caused a weight in her chest. Brief thoughts of freedom passed through her mind on their way to somewhere else, but there was no freedom for her now.

Maria advised me against dependency on Jonah in the first place.

"The guy at the place didn't mind about you being pregnant then?"

"No. He said some of the kids that come out to do the project would find it very calming, having a baby around. That was nice of him, wasn't it?"

The carriage clock Ellie's grandma had sent as a present ticked loudly on the mantelpiece above the unlit gas fire. Every second took her closer to meeting a new little person. She picked up the baby clothes Maria had brought, held the pure white cotton against her cheek.

Talking about the baby with someone else made the prospect of motherhood feasible.

"They're not young offenders, like John-Paul said," she told Maria. "But they have been expelled from school or something. They just need a focus." She imagined herself being a calming influence, especially on young girls.

"What do Jonah and John-Paul think about this project?" Maria asked, looking dubious.

"They're getting funding for a practice room in the barn so they're happy. In return they have to offer coaching to the youth groups, but only for a few hours a week."

"Hmm." Maria pushed a wave of dark hair over her shoulder. "Tell me about the place, then, *Running Hare House*, you called it in your letter."

"OK."

Ellie tried to settle herself more comfortably but it was difficult because she had a backache. "It's a cool name, isn't it? Apparently, hares play on the fields opposite in the spring." She thought back to her visit. "There're two sections of the house, an old part and a new extension. The owner, Ted, lives in the original part with another guy we think is his, you know, partner."

"Partner *like that*?"

"Yeah, we think so." Ellie shifted her weight. A beam of light caught a million dust-motes hanging on the air.

She grunted as she reached to the low table for her mug of tea.

"Here, let me," said Maria, handing it to her.

"Thanks." Ellie jammed a cushion onto her lap and balanced the tea on it. "One of the girls who already lives there says Ted has a girlfriend as well. What d'you think of that?"

"Oh. Well, it takes all sorts, I suppose." Maria made a face. "So where's your room, in the old house or the new?"

"In the annex. Jonah's is about two rooms down from mine and John-Paul's is across the corridor." She kept her voice level.

Maria narrowed her eyes. She'd fallen prey to John-Paul's intimidating charisma during her first term at university, just before Ellie started going out with Jonah. Now she didn't trust him.

"Hmm. Let's hope John-Paul gives you and Jonah a bit of space. Don't think he's quite grasped the idea of you two becoming parents."

Parents. Ellie's heart thudded. The baby gave an answering kick.

"Ouch, that hurt." The pain seemed to last a bit too long.

Ellie rubbed a finger across the bridge of her nose. She needed to stay friends with John-Paul to avoid conflict with Jonah, and sometimes she got on okay with him, but she shared Maria's concerns. He was possessive over Jonah, jealous of her.

"Hopefully he'll get used to it when the baby comes," she mused, after thinking about it. "It seems abstract at the moment, even to me. After all, John-Paul and Jonah have been friends a long time." Much longer than she and Jonah had.

What a strange feeling it was when her womb tightened the way it kept doing. When the false contraction ebbed she said, "John-Paul still thinks of Jonah as a boy, the same way he thinks of himself. When the baby's a real person it'll be a shock for us all."

The ache was moving lower down her back. She finished her tea and unfolded her legs carefully.

"Pins and needles." She swivelled her ankles. "Lord, I need a pee, can you help me get up? Thanks." She stretched, rubbed the base of her back. The ache strengthened. At the same time a flush of energy went through her. She must tidy up, make sure everything was clean.

"Here, pass me those mugs," she said. "And the two over there. Thanks. Oh yeah and there's a cereal bowl in the corner by that chair. Bloody John-Paul came over for breakfast this morning, he never tidies up after himself. I'll take these into the kitchen and put the kettle on again on my way to the toilet."

"Don't overdo it," Maria said. She had a nervous look. "You're behaving oddly. Let Jonah do the washing-up when he gets home, or if it must be done now, let me do it."

But Ellie was already running water in the sink.

"I wish you were coming to live at Pottersea as well."

Ellie bent carefully to place fresh mugs of tea on the table and found it difficult to straighten up again.

"It's hot in here, isn't it?" She looked at her friend, cool and composed in a red sundress.

Something in her body popped.

"Ah," she said.

Dampness soaked into her pants. *How embarrassing.* The ache deepened. She stood, rigid.

"Are you sure you're alright, Ellie? You're looking odd," Maria said. Ellie looked at her across a great distance.

"Is your back hurting you?" Maria stood up, fussing with the cushions on the sofa. "Come on, sit down."

"Yeah, a bit." Ellie's voice sounded light in her head. "I get this backache a lot, but it's worse today. Oh dear." She leaned over the back of an armchair. Her legs trembled. "It'll pass in a minute." She breathed heavily. "I'm sure it will. Anyway, did you know Martin's decided to join us out at Pottersea? You like him, don't you. . . "

Her voice caught in her throat as the hole in the dam broke completely open.

"Oh shit."

"What's the matter? What's that? Oh bugger, I think I know. . . "

Maria stood up again, flapping her hands. Water gushed onto the floor at Ellie's feet.

6

18 September 1982

Maria called the ambulance, which took them to the maternity hospital on Hedon Road. The ride was the worst part. Between the vice-like grips of the pains Ellie registered the look of horror on her friend's face.

While Ellie was being admitted, Maria went to use the telephone in the corridor.

"Did you get hold of him?" Ellie forced the words out through gritted teeth.

"No, I tried everyone I could think of, sorry."

"Arrghhh." The contractions came so close together Ellie could hardly draw breath in between.

Maria was the one who was with Ellie when Rosie was born.

"I knew it would be a girl." Ellie had a faraway feeling. Every now and then she snapped into herself though, into full realisation of what had just happened. "I knew it. I told Jonah." She floated away again on another wave of euphoria. She came back on a wave of after-pain.

"Arrghh. Thank *God* it's over. I never want to do it again, Maria. *Never.* Make sure you remind me of that, if I'm ever stupid enough to say I want to do this again." Her cheeks felt hot.

"Where the fuck is he anyway, that bloody Jonah?" Maria clapped a hand over her mouth. "Sorry, nurse."

Midwife Jane straightened her plastic apron and resumed swabbing Ellie between the legs with a damp sponge. "It's alright, lovey. I'll forgive you a bit of bad language for being such a star. Although it's usually the mummy who has the dirty mouth." She dripped fresh water onto Ellie's thighs. "Don't know what this young lassie here would've done without you."

"Oh my God, Ellie," Maria lifted a corner of the towel to examine the small person she was holding. Ellie saw its starfish hands waving. "I've just realised, this is actually a *baby*. Oh no, my arms have gone too weak to hold it, take it off me, somebody."

Barbara, the other midwife, came around the bed and took the baby. "You want her back now, Ellie, or shall I get her dressed for you first?"

"Get her dressed first. Please." Ellie wasn't ready, and probably never would be.

Jane opened the slatted blinds. Late afternoon sun streamed in, glittering on metallic objects, offering sliced portions of light to the cotton blanket on the bed. Ellie was mesmerised. She raised her arm and hand, thinking it looked like the neck and head of a swan. In places, light seemed to shine right through it.

Then she remembered something else. "It's my birthday today, I'm nineteen years old."

The others in the room raised their eyebrows and chuckled.

"You've only been saying that all afternoon."

Barbara murmured in a low voice to the baby as she checked her over. The sound that came out of Ellie's daughter was primeval.

"What a birthday present you gave your mummy, eh?" Proffering the bundle at Ellie, Barbara asked, "Do you want to have another go at feeding her, lovey?"

Ellie shook her head. "Not yet." Her nipple was still sore from the last try.

"Hang on a minute anyway," said Jane. She changed her latex gloves for a fresh pair and dipped a clean cloth into a fresh bowl of warm water, dabbing at Ellie's face and neck, lifting her hair.

She emptied the water into the sink. "Let's get this place tidied up a bit then."

Loading things onto a trolley, she pushed it towards the door.

Barbara finally handed the baby over. As the warm weight sank into the curve of her arms, Ellie's giggles with Maria turned to tears.

"She's so beautiful, I don't think I'll be a fit mother."

"Oh, don't." Maria went red in the face. "You'll have me going as well."

Jane and Barbara rolled their eyes.

"Right, young ladies," Jane said in a businesslike way. Soon she'd move on to another birth and Ellie would be left to do motherhood all on her own. "I'm just going to dispose of this lot, then I'll be back to take your temperature again. Ellie, maybe we can even manage a birthday cupcake for you, eh?" She gave them a wide grin. "Can you get the door for me please, Barbara, chuck?"

"I can indeed my dear. Oh look," Barbara opened the door with a flourish. "Who's this coming in now? Could it be the famous *Missing Dad*?"

Jonah stood in the doorway, arms hanging loosely at his sides.

"Jonah," sobbed Ellie. "Look what I did."

Vivian brought Deborah but not Ray to the hospital with her. Ellie wished she could have some time with her mother alone. Surely for once, Vivian could have left Deborah at home.

But maybe not.

She could have at least visited while Deborah was at school though.

They brought a set of sleep suits in pale yellow and cream, and some knitted bootees from Grandma Maud.

"I mustn't hold her, I'm sorry." Vivian's nose was red from a cold. She peered at the baby across the bed. "Deborah?"

But Deborah was studying the view of gardens from the window.

You jealous cow. Ellie had never hated her sister more.

She couldn't stop crying when they'd gone. Rosie's face wrinkled up in empathy.

Her final visitors at the hospital were Jonah's parents.

"It's lovely. . . "

The christening shawl (*christening?*) was shop-bought. The nightgown for Ellie was an old lady one with ruffles at the neck.

Jonah hadn't arrived yet.

"Thank you, Mrs Whitefern."

"Call me Sarah, dear."

Ellie made her face into a smile. Her daughter's grandparents studied her with snatched glances.

"Please," Ellie said. "Would you like to hold Rosie?"

Colour rose in Sarah's cheeks.

"Oh, yes. How wonderful."

When Jonah breezed in, just before visiting hours finished, Ellie noticed his father hand him a cheque. "Make sure our granddaughter has everything she needs."

The older man didn't say much to Ellie.

Jonah didn't tell her how much the cheque had been for. Ellie asked him to pay off the weekly payments on the swinging cradle and she gave him a list of clothes and nappies to buy, hoping there'd be some money left for later.

But it wasn't long after that, a portable recording studio appeared in Jonah's room at Running Hare House.

7

Running Hare House

September 1982

Ellie lifted Rosie out of the carrycot. She had the now-familiar sense that the objects and people around her were getting further away.

I can't get all the parts of me to connect... Once she snapped back into alignment, she realised the fellow residents of her new home were crowding around to look at the baby. Everyone introduced him or herself. Hayley was the plump black girl with a headful of plaits. Jennifer was tall with a thin, pale face and fine, pale hair.

"Oh, hi, Martin." Ellie was surprised to see he had arrived already. John-Paul must be around, too.

She was trying to remember all the new names when the door from the annex opened and a lad with light brown hair, almost golden, came in, restraining a dog by the collar. He spoke with an Irish accent.

"Hi, I'm Greg. This here is Stan. He won't hurt you or the baby, I promise."

While cups of tea were distributed, Ellie found herself being chatted to by the light-haired lad. She heard the words 'reclamation sculptor'. When she looked agog he said, "Ah, sorry. It's just a fancy way of saying I'm a junk-artist. What do you do?"

As if she wasn't merely someone with a baby.

She moved her lips experimentally. Up to now she hadn't been required to speak.

"Textiles, sewing, that kind of thing," she heard a voice similar to hers saying, and he was nodding, so it must have been her.

But sewing was only really a passionate hobby and she hoped she could live up to the claims she'd made to Ted, the owner. She wondered if the repairs were done on her sewing machine yet, hoping it had been delivered while she was in hospital.

The dog was mostly Labrador. It gave Ellie a goofy grin, panting.

Netty and Grey Cat were already here. Netty slinked in from the doorway to the kitchen when she heard Ellie's voice, but stopped when she saw the dog.

"They've become sworn enemies already, I'm afraid," Greg chuckled. Netty leapt up onto the back of a chair and hissed, fur stuck up straight. The dog ignored her. But the cat moved higher onto a ledge above the sofa and stayed there, glaring balefully. *Poor Netty.* Ellie's first baby.

On Greg's advice Ellie sat in a chair and let Stan have a good sniff of Rosie. Rosie kicked her legs and flailed her arms, meeting the dog's gaze squarely.

The large living room was bright and open with windows on two sides giving views of fields. The light hurt Ellie's eyes; she'd been living in a cave all those months in the flat.

Squeezing her eyes shut and opening them again, she noticed a high shelf above a serving hatch into the kitchen. Red and brown pots crowded the shelf.

"You like them? They're Vincent's." A huge guy appeared, towering above her. "Mike," he added, lowering himself to one knee as if about to propose. He offered his hand to be shaken after stroking it lightly over the now sleeping baby.

"Hi," said Ellie. She checked the pure white vest covering Rosie's tummy, in case the ingrained paint on his fingers had rubbed off on it.

"Vincent's a ceramicist. He's away for the rest of the week so you won't meet him yet."

Mike, Vincent, Jennifer, Hayley, Greg. Ellie ticked the names off in her head, weight loading her eyelids. Time seemed to jump. Mike had moved off across the room. Where is. . . ? There was Jonah, in an opposite corner, talking to John-Paul.

The floor was a wide expanse of patterned carpet. Ellie tried to picture Rosie crawling over it in a few months' time but it was impossible. She couldn't believe she really had this baby for keeps.

Voices buzzed like a swarm of bees.

The dog established himself in a comfortable position on her feet, lifting his head to check the baby every now and then. Pinned down by the two of them, she couldn't move.

Her heart pounded. It was all as surreal as Mike's painting on the wall, a huge hare running along a motorway, straddling a line of miniature traffic.

Rosie made squawking sounds, swivelling her head from side to side. A woman appeared in front of them.

"I'm Bonnie." A face with crinkles around the eyes, leaning into the mother-and-baby bubble. "I noticed you struggling to get the baby latched on. Let me help you."

Fetching a sheet from the carrycot, Bonnie draped it over Ellie's shoulder and across her chest. "That better for you?"

Ellie struggled not to close her eyes with relief at the let-down as Rosie sucked.

"Thanks."

"I bet you're tired, aren't you?"

Ellie nodded again. Her eyelids were heavier than ever. She forced them to stay open a bit longer. She'd have to get up soon, go for a rest in her new room. She was looking forward to seeing her own things. The thought of the peace to come released a fresh tingle of woozy hormones. Rosie gulped contentedly at the new rush of milk.

Bonnie stooped across her, reaching to tap Martin on the shoulder.

"Budge up, will you, mate?"

Bonnie squeezed into his place while he moved to a padded bench under the back windows.

"Got babies of my own," Bonnie said. Close up, she must be in her mid-thirties at least. Sleep threatened to overwhelm Ellie. Rosie's mouth was loosening on the nipple and she promised herself she would get up when the baby finished feeding.

"Where are they, your babies?" Ellie was now uncertain whether the warm, buzzing room, the faces blurring around her, the intermittent tugging on her breast as Rosie drifted off and briefly re-awoke to resume feeding, were dream or reality.

"Live with their dad, don't they?" Bonnie said mournfully. She began to hum a bluesy tune.

Someone started to pick out notes on a guitar. Ellie couldn't find the energy to lift her head and see who it was. Next to her Bonnie's voice strengthened as she about how her words were from the heart. Another guitar joined in; a hand strumming chords. Someone closer to Ellie; Martin, she thought, drummed out a slow beat on the furniture. Bonnie was now singing about pouring herself sympath. Ellie forced her eyes open again.

Rosie had slipped off the breast and lay in the crook of her elbow, face flushed with milk-drugged sleep. Under the cotton sheet, Ellie clumsily tucked herself back into her bra and then wrapped the sheet around Rosie, lifted her up onto her shoulder. A sweet, sharp pain ran through her, echoing the lyrics to someone's baby, from the heart.

On her second day there, Ellie was called to a meeting in Ted's office. His pursed-lips expression worried her.

"How about a few months' maternity leave, Ellie, before you start working officially with us?"

He eyed the fidgeting baby, in a sling across her chest. "You must have your hands full."

Her status had been reduced, yet again. Ted must have seen the look on her face.

"What I was thinking." He stood up and shifted a pile of papers off the chair opposite his desk, beckoning her to sit down before resuming his place behind it.

"We could convert the dining room of this house, which is never really used, you see, into a sewing and craft room. You could lead your workshops in there. But we need to get more funding in first."

"Of course, I understand." She felt herself going red. She pinched the top of her nose against the threatening prickle of tears. It would probably never happen.

It's amazing how strong a new-born baby is. As Ellie sat down, Rosie strained against the sling, bashed her head against Ellie's chest. Her hormones were all over the place and she got hot and bothered so easily. She hoped she wasn't going to make a fool of herself. Rosie struggled more, mouth opening to let out a wail, and in desperation Ellie inserted her thumb. The baby sucked on it hungrily. *Ted's right, I can't possibly run workshops just yet.* But she had the sense chances were slipping away.

Ted continued to eye her.

"I wondered, would you be willing to help with the funding applications in the meantime?" He sorted around on his desk and came up with a folder which he slid over to her. Opening it with one hand, she saw it contained leaflets and brochures, lists of figures and spreadsheets. She turned the pages slowly, trying to force her baby-brain into some sort of understanding of what she was looking at. All the time she kept her thumb in Rosie's mouth.

"Is that something you think you'd be able to do?" Ted asked anxiously. "I need someone to find out exactly what's available – you might need to go to the public library to do that..." He eyed the baby with trepidation. "I'm willing to lend my car to project workers, seeing as we're so far from town."

Ellie had passed her driving test when she was seventeen. But she wouldn't feel confident to drive with the baby. Maybe Jonah would drive her... Or someone.

"I want someone with literary skills who can put in a good case for us and write the proposals. You have an A-level in English, don't you?"

Ellie took her time searching through the papers. They contained testimonials of other projects that had successfully launched funding bids.

I need to feed the baby. She wasn't comfortable in front of Ted just yet.

"Yes," she said. "I'll do it."

At the sound of her voice, Rosie spat out her mother's thumb and resumed head-butting Ellie's collarbone.

"Ouch," Ellie said. "Sorry, Ted."

She got up ungracefully. "Thanks. I'll get onto it as soon as I can."

"You'll get your allowance for the work, of course," Ted said, scrambling to get up and open the door for her. "The same as the workshop artists."

Ellie's breasts prickled but her heaviness of heart had lifted. She got out quickly, before wet seeped through her shirt.

October 1982

The sewing machine soothed Rosie. Ellie set the cradle rocking with her foot and got a hem of one curtain finished before it stopped moving. There were four windows along one side of her room, looking out onto the garden. She'd already completed curtains for two, practising skills for the workshops she wanted to run. Ted said she could have two sewing machines for the project (eventually).

Her own sewing table butted up to one of her windows. Across an expanse of paving bordered with a kitchen garden and a rose garden were the studios and the barn. Ellie watched the artists coming and going. Smeared with paint or with plaster-dust in their hair, they carried armfuls of wood or bags of clay. The band members came in and out of the barn, releasing music outdoors in intermittent bursts.

A small party of children who weren't in school for one reason or another was at Running Hare House that day and the whole of The Travelling Man had come out to assist on the project. Whenever the barn door opened, Ellie heard the uneven rhythm of inexpert drums and faltering bass and guitar notes. Wavering singing voices gained confidence as Bonnie worked with their owners.

Jonah and John-Paul enjoyed their duties a lot more than they'd expected to, especially since they didn't have to use their own instruments with the youth groups.

They'd planned a Christmas concert in the barn, featuring The Travelling Man with Bonnie on guest vocals and the kids who came out for workshops. Local villagers were going to be invited, in an attempt to diffuse rampant suspicion about what the 'cavemen' got up to (Vincent reported having heard a woman at the post office refer to them as such).

"You should get out and about more with the baby, Ellie," Vincent suggested. "Go knocking on doors. Those little old ladies couldn't fail to be won over by our Rosie."

8

Iceland, February 2013

The patchwork of colours in the immediate landscape reminds Ellie of a coat she once made for Eliza.

Steam rises from the turgid, soupy mud, bubbling and grumbling beneath the wooden footbridge.

"Only yesterday, late in the evening," says Annie, today's guide, "there was an explosion at a geo-thermal hotspot just like this one, on the other side of the mountain." She grins at her tourists' visible dismay. She whips out a phone and shows them all a photo. They crowd around her. "Blew the footbridge and viewing platform completely apart, see? Boiling mud everywhere." She presses a button on her phone and slips it into her pocket again.

Someone asks if anyone was hurt.

"No, the last tourist had just finished taking photographs. He was hurrying to catch up with the others on their way back to the bus. Bit of mud on the back of his coat, that was all."

"Isn't it dangerous to be here, then?" a nervous Asian woman speaks in a halting accent.

"It is if you're in the wrong place at the wrong time, if you want to look at it that way," responds Annie. "But it could be dangerous anywhere, for one reason or another. You can never know, can you?"

That laid-back Icelandic attitude again. "It's just the way things are."

Ellie grips the rail tightly.

"Feeling dizzy again?" asks Jonah.

"A bit, it'll pass."

Jonah gives her arm a pat. "Amazing here, isn't it?"

If only she could give the landscape her full attention the way he is. She promised Eliza she would.

A gust of wind blows the sulphurous stench of the mud their way. It's overwhelming. Ellie presses the side of her hand to her nostrils. The rest of their group have moved away, forming a crocodile up the winding path.

"Are you ready to go on?"

Jonah's being unexpectedly solicitous. *This is about you, as well, not just me.* But he seems to be coping better than her.

"OK." She forces her other hand to let go of the rail.

Jonah is like a different person than the husband she remembers; rock-steady as the huge boulders they saw on the journey here, the ones that have tumbled from the tops of mountains and lodged themselves firmly into the ground halfway down the steep slopes. They nestle behind barns and houses built in the foothills and no-one is ever afraid they will be crushed in the night by the weight of stone.

The vibrant contrasts in colour in this area are striking after the different tones of monochrome Ellie's become used to. On the south coast where they went yesterday, the cliffs and beaches were startlingly black in the patches between snow and pointed rocks like needles pierced the surface of the slate-grey sea. And the land above and the mountains beyond in many shades of white, so many shades.

On their journey here they took a gritty road up into the mountains. Ellie has stopped being afraid of the precarious bus journeys, even when the road is loose and unmade and the bus's alarm warns of ice. The drivers are obviously experienced, despite the youth of some of them, like Annie. She took them to a vast lake with a wide, black shore on which the snow had only part-settled. The shore went on forever and the lake seemed to have no boundaries. Ellie felt she was glimpsing Heaven.

"Ellie, you okay?"

Boiling streams snaking through ochre-coloured mud are blue, reflecting the brightness of the sky, clear for once. The steam rising from the ground is white, ghost-like and transparent. Vivid green shows itself below the patches of snow laid on the mountainsides.

"Look, Ellie, over here."

Her glasses have steamed up again and she has to take them off and wipe them once more. Jonah's pointing to a huge crater. Creamy foam and thick yellow liquid swirl around the edges of a broiling cauldron at the crater's centre. The mud heaves and sobs, breathes in and spits out repeatedly. The dread soaks into Ellie again.

Danger lurks in the ground, waiting to claim an unsuspecting life such as hers, or Jonah's. Or anyone's.

9

November 1982

Ellie walked along the fence behind Running Hare House, carrying Rosie in the sling. *Bird World* was on the other side, with its visitor centre and small café. Ellie pointed out the kestrels, owls and other birds of prey and Rosie squealed and kicked her legs.

There was also a vulture, tethered by a long rope to a post at one end of the enclosure area. Now two months old, Rosie was inflamed with excitement at the sight of the huge bird taking giant leaps along the ground as far as his rope would allow him.

An oil slick washed up along the East Yorkshire coast. Mike contacted the local bird rescue organisation and all the Running Hare House residents volunteered to help with the clean-up operation. A guy called Ian arrived to give the house members some basic training, explaining that the birds could be as easily killed from incorrect care procedures as from the oil on their feathers. He then dished out long rubber gloves, aprons and boots for them all.

Noticing the baby sleeping in her pram, he asked whose she was. He explained that Ellie had to be especially careful to avoid contamination from the oil if she was breastfeeding.

"You'd be surprised how easy it is to end up ingesting splashed fluid if a bird is well enough (we hope) to become agitated and kick up a fuss. Also you may have traces of oil on your hands, which could transmit to the baby." He looked disapproving that she would even consider the job.

"Are you sure you should be doing this?" Vincent asked worriedly.

Ellie swallowed annoyance at being singled out yet again on account of her motherhood. But she bit back a sharp reply and looked at Rosie instead. The baby's cheeks were flushed, she had sleep-dampened hair plastered to her forehead. What was really more important? So she agreed to help by watching over the cleansed birds instead.

The rescue organisation brought boxes into the house and barn and all the outhouses. Each contained a sick seabird. Then a whole load of plastic tubs were delivered for the birds to be washed in. The cleaning solution consisted of diluted detergent in warm water.

Under the supervision of Ian, the house members worked in pairs; one holding a bird, the other gently washing oil from its feathers with a very soft toothbrush. They had to move the bird from tub to tub until the water was clear of oil. Finally, all traces of detergent had to be removed so that the bird would be able to keep warm and regain its flight capabilities.

Ian said it was likely that most of them would never be able to fly again.

"But we do our best. Now, after cleaning, the birds need to be dried with air blowers, we've borrowed some from a pet grooming salon."

He held one up and looked around to check all were paying

attention. "Then you will feed them via a tube, with a special nutritious liquid."

This was one job Ellie was allowed to help with. But only a few birds reached that stage.

The weight of helplessness lodged in Ellie's stomach over the following weeks as she watched the doomed rescue attempts. The birds seemed a symbol of the mess people had made of the world.

The mood in the house was sombre and workshops were temporarily suspended while the rescue operation went on. A much larger percentage of birds died than recovered. In the end, the effort they'd all put in seemed pointless.

We saved so few.

Tucking Rosie into her crib at night, Ellie tried to lose herself in the internal universe the two of them created. Even Jonah didn't seem a part of it.

Three times she took Rosie on the bus to the library in town, a satchel laden with papers tucked into the carrycot. Rosie spent most of the journey sleeping or feeding under Ellie's voluminous jumper. In the reference room at the library she lay in her carrycot for a surprising amount of time staring up at the lights. If she cried Ellie tried feeding her. But on two occasions when she thought she'd have to leave because Rosie wouldn't settle, a kind lady at the enquiry desk got up and offered to walk Rosie around in the pram, once asking if it was okay to take her into the private office. Yes. A chance to throw herself into the work, arms-free. *I feel valid again.*

Ellie investigated the availability of public and private arts grants. Then she sent off for forms. Going through them, she focussed on ticking the relevant boxes: who the project would help, how it would benefit the local community, how it might become self-funding in the future.

She got the Running Hare Committee, (all the residents) to check over her proposals at a special meeting, making slight alterations according to advice from the others. When she had finished she sent the completed bids off from the Post Office in the next village. She wrapped Rosie up warm and walked all the three and a half miles there and back with the pram. The women who worked in the shop were always delighted to check on Rosie's progress.

<hr>

After the bid, Ellie had a week of twiddling her thumbs.

"I never see you," she said to Jonah in the corridor.

"Sorry. You know I love you and Rosie, but I'm trying to get my career together, man."

"I think you're confusing me with John-Paul," she dared to say. If he got angry there were people in the other rooms who would hear. "I'm not your man. I was supposed to be your woman." She muttered the last part under her breath, but just before she turned away she noticed the sudden blaze in his eyes.

"It's a pity you can't be just a *little* bit proud of me," Jonah threw at her retreating back. "I'm doing my best for you and Rosie. I never *chose* to become a father this young, you know."

They hardly spoke for several days afterwards.

"Look, Rosie, that's your daddy." She held her daughter up to the window while Jonah crossed the yard to the barn. His long hair was tucked into his jumper at the back. "Remember him?" A sob surprised her throat. She had an intense memory of the time she and Jonah spent together at the beginning of their relationship.

If she didn't make an effort, Ellie would end up spending her whole life in the room with Rosie. She mapped out her days with 'instructions to self'. *Sit down for a feed, change baby's nappy. Bundle baby into snowsuit and go out for a walk. Remember to eat. Endeavour to have conversation with someone who isn't Rosie.*

She needed another professional challenge.

"Billy," she asked Ted's live-in friend, who hovered around the edges of their community. "Would you be willing to let me borrow your SLR camera?"

Billy smoothed back his Shakin' Stevens-styled hair.

"I don't think so, ducky. The baby might get her sticky fingers on the lens."

"She won't, I promise." Ellie shifted Rosie into an upright position on her chest. Dribble poured from the corner of Rosie's mouth down Ellie's neckline and she mopped at it with a tissue. "I won't let her."

Billy was still shaking his head when Ted entered the hallway of the main house. He glanced from Ellie to his partner and back again.

"Anything I can help with, Ellie?"

"Erm, I err, do you have a camera I could borrow?" Ellie didn't want to get Billy into trouble. Already Ted's expression was darkening, everyone knew Billy had the most up to date model. Ted gave Billy a lengthy stare but Billy held his ground.

Ellie shifted from foot to foot and Rosie let out a piercing shriek, displaying the inside of her wet mouth.

"I only have one of those instant ones," Ted eventually said. "It's crap, but of course you may borrow it if you wish. Is there a special reason?"

Rosie grabbed a handful of Ellie's shirt at the neck and held on with a surprisingly strong grip. Ellie struggled to release herself from imminent suffocation whilst maintaining dignity in front of the two men.

"I had this idea," she got out. Rosie was grizzling and she'd have to go and feed her soon. "I thought I could make a brochure for the workshops." She swayed from side to side as she spoke, mesmerising her daughter temporarily. "I'd need to photograph everybody about their work, and maybe the surrounding landscape. You know, to attract people to book with us."

Ted tapped his chin with his long forefinger.

"Hmm. What an inspired idea. You certainly do earn your keep, Ellie. But of course you'll need to use a professional camera for such an undertaking. Don't want to let the side down, do we?" He laid his hand on Billy's shoulder, pressing rather hard, Ellie sensed.

With Ted's encouragement, Billy reluctantly agreed to lend her his prized possession. She tucked the camera securely into the bottom of the carrycot, out of range of Rosie's vigorous feet. Billy watched from the window as she wheeled it away, mouthing and gesturing that she should only use the camera with the strap hanging around her neck. She nodded and made a thumbs-up sign. *Poor Billy.*

Freedom. The river beach and mudflats, the sea marshes, the crumbling red cliffs that spewed concrete war defences into the sea; they would all make atmospheric subjects.

She returned to the property and took pictures of the Running Hare artists at work in their studios and practice rooms. The following day she captured some charming images of visiting children participating in workshops.

She took the films to be developed at Boots during her weekly visit to town. As she rifled through the images when she got them back an hour later, hot excitement rose inside her coat. *They're good. I could do this as a job.* Then she went home and wrote copy to go with the pictures. She worked during the evenings when Rosie was tucked into her crib.

She managed to get Jonah to look after his daughter for an afternoon.

"Martin'll come with me," he said after deliberating. "We'll take her for a walk down the road to the pub."

Ellie would have to hurry: the minute Rosie cried he'd probably come rushing back. She sat at the dining room table and did some cutting and sticking.

Ted will be really pleased with my work; maybe I can get a permanent job, with proper pay.

The following week she borrowed money from the cash box to take her ideas back into town to a printing shop. She explained how she wanted it to look.

The brochures would be ready the week after that, they said.

When she'd collected the finished brochures, she took them into the office to show Ted.

"We could advertise private workshops," she explained her idea. "Parties, family days, stuff like that. We wouldn't need funding and it would bring in income for all of us. You take a percentage for the venue, the artists get full pay for their work. What do you think?"

"Ooh, I say, Ellie. You are good, aren't you?" Ted was at his most camp when he was excited. She almost expected him to flap a wrist. "What a brilliant idea of mine it was to employ you in this manner. Go on, *please* do; carry on as you were."

10

Greg Mulligan

December 1982

Winter was a good time for work. Driftwood had washed up on the main beach and Ellie allowed him to use her carrycot transporter, an old fishing net slung across its frame, to bring it in.

"I'll be gentle with it, I promise," he joked.

She seemed a bit lost. He guessed it was hard getting used to being a young mother, so he asked her if she wanted to come out foraging. And after that she mostly accompanied him on his walks. He admired the way she wrapped herself in a thick coat with a fur-lined hood and tucked the baby inside. She wore cute mittens and a long knitted scarf. Her nose always turned endearingly red.

He loved listening to her chatter, her soft murmurings to the baby.

She looked like a child herself, yet she'd more than proved her worth to the community they'd become. Thanks to her successful funding bids they all had jobs for at least another year.

Sometimes he pretended the three of them were a family.

Rosie's father was a bastard, in his opinion. If Greg had a kid of his own, a wonderful baby like Rosie... but it was none of his business. All he could do was be a friend to Ellie.

He was planning a Madonna and Child sculpture from the strange, twisted pieces of wood they were collecting. He'd spoken to a gallery owner in Manchester who was interested in commissioning a piece for a show called *Iconic*. Greg was plucking up the courage to ask Ellie to model for him.

The sea wind was vicious on the beach under the cliffs, but there was something exhilarating about it, made you want to scream at the sea, especially being out there with her. But as he got to know her, Ellie's growing listlessness worried him. The music workshops were the most in-demand at the house, but when he wasn't involved with those, her boyfriend was always practising or just hanging out, smoking, with his bandmates. The smoke sometimes filtered through into Greg's room. Anyway, Jonah never any time for his girlfriend. Or the baby.

The Travelling Man had gigs further afield now and Jonah let it be known he was convinced a record deal was at the band's fingertips.

Greg bumped into him in the corridor.

"We might have to move back into town if we get it."

Greg wondered if the selfish bugger had spoken to Ellie about it. "Even to somewhere like London..." Jonah's lungs must've been full of that stuff he smoked: Greg got a blast of it in his face when the twat breathed out.

"The A&R man at *so-and-so* records wrote back and said he might come and see our next gig. Fucking exciting, isn't it?"

Maybe for you, mate, but not for her.

Ellie and Jonah never spent the night together. Greg knew because his room was between their two. Jonah worked late into the night with Martin and John-Paul, composing and recording songs on the portable studio Greg suspected was purchased with the money Rosie's grandfather had given the couple (just something Ellie let slip).

Sometimes Bonnie would join the band in Jonah's room, contributing a guest vocal. Greg wasn't sure how he felt about that.

He encountered Ellie standing outside Jonah's room with a sleepy Rosie on her shoulder one night, evidently hesitating about whether to knock on the door.

Greg looked at Jonah's closed door and back at Ellie, scratched his head, tried to ignore the pull in his stomach muscles.

Keep it real.

He ought to give her a smile and put a closed door of his own between them. But he didn't.

"Fancy a hot chocolate with me in the lounge?"

His feelings were more caring than sexual, honest they were.

Ellie glanced back at Jonah's door, sighed deeply.

"Thanks, that'd be nice."

"Even better," Greg proposed as they walked down the corridor together, "How about you let me have a cuddle with that baby and *you* make the hot chocolate? Aha, see, there's a forfeit to me offer."

He waited while she went and got a shawl for the baby. When she wrapped Rosie in it her hands were trembling. For some reason he imagined Rosie was giving him a knowing look from her sleepy, long-lashed eyes.

He took the child in his arms and lay back on the sofa. After a while, Ellie brought in the mugs of hot chocolate. She placed them on the table and went over to the windows to draw the curtains. He couldn't help admiring her reflection in the black glass, a slim girl wearing a tattered jumper. Her jeans hung low on her hips. When she reached up to pull the curtains together he caught a glimpse of white belly. There was a twitch in his groin; he crossed his legs; shifted Rosie further up his chest.

"Lost a lot of weight, haven't ya?"

She lowered herself into the chair next to the sofa, the one she'd sat in the first day she arrived. He pictured her then, with Stan at her feet.

"Not really." She tucked her chin into the neck of her jumper. Her reddish fringe obscured her eyes. "This is what I used to look like, that's all. Just me being normal again."

He kept on looking. Her skin reddened, even on her hands. She fidgeted with the hem of her jumper.

"OK?" Greg asked, feeling mean. *Leave her alone, won't ya?*

She raised her chin.

"Yeah, I'm fine, thanks. You?"

Reaching forward she grasped her mug with both hands. She lifted it up to her lips and took a sip.

"Ah yeah," Greg said. "I'm good. Nothing like a sleeping baby to mellow me out." Rosie's warm weight anchored him to the sofa and to that moment. The feeling of comfort wasn't going to last. *If only it could.*

Ellie looked directly at him.

"You're good at this baby stuff. Do you have younger brothers and sisters?"

"Nah," Greg said, too quickly. "Just an older one of each."

"Nephews and nieces, then?"

"Nope."

He'd have to tell her the reason soon, the reason he was so good at this baby-stuff.

"This is so nice," she said, licking the chocolaty moustache from her upper lip. "I buy the really cheap brand but it never tastes as good as this."

There was his opportunity. He smiled at the baby as a bubble appeared between her lips, and took a breath.

"Ah well, but Bonnie likes that one." He tried to make it offhand. *Me and Bonnie, y'know?* "I tried the cheap stuff on her, and she didn't like it one bit."

Ellie visibly stiffened.

"Bonnie?" She took another sip, hid her face in the mug.

Shit. He'd blown it now.

"Yeah. We take it in turns to buy it. We're both fans, y'know?"

"Oh."

Me and Bonnie.

What a joke.

Ellie gulped noisily, moved the mug away from her lips, she was embarrassed.

Damn, she was more than that; she was upset. *Change the subject.*

"Where is everyone tonight, anyway?"

Holding Rosie firmly so she wouldn't wake up, he leaned forward to get his mug. Ellie looked away. She didn't say anything. So he answered his own question.

"Your musician folk are working on a new song, aren't they?"

She just looked at him.

"I can hear it through my wall, sounds good." *As if.* "And Mike, Jen and Hayley, they're down the road at the pub, they have a meeting there with Ted, that's right." He was babbling. "Vincent," he went on. "Well, he went over to his mother's in York, I think."

Pausing at last, he took a gulp of the hot drink, keeping the mug away from Rosie. His foot tapped. He cleared his throat.

"And Bonnie's spending the night in Hull, gone to see her babies, she has."

He was a prick for not making it clear about Bonnie before now. He'd thought she must've realised, but at the same time maybe hoped she hadn't.

Placing her empty mug on the table with a decisive clack, Ellie reached for her baby, avoiding his eyes.

"I should put Rosie to bed."

He checked her face for signs of emotion but she had a good poker-expression going on by now. "She'll be cranky in the morning if I don't."

A cold place was left on his chest... in his chest, when Ellie and the baby had gone.

11

Ellie

December 1982

Jonah's parents came to visit when Rosie was three months old.

Jonah and Leopold walked down the sea road with Rosie in the pram while Sarah took Ellie aside. They went into Ellie's room and Ellie could see Sarah giving it a visual inspection. Ellie almost stood to attention. Winter sunlight lit up the dust fairies. *She'll think I don't clean.*

"Shall we sit down?" Ellie indicated the desk chair. Sarah glanced at it before positioning herself.

"It looks as if you're making a go of things here. Rosie seems very well and happy, developing normally, is she?"

"Of course she is."

She seems surprised. If she was that bothered, if she wanted to help, she should have visited sooner.

"The health visitor's very pleased with her. Rosie's quite advanced for her age."

"That's good, dear. And is everything alright between you and Jonah?"

Ellie shifted on the edge of her bed.

"Fine, yes. We both love it here."

"Hmm." Sarah dipped her head.

What is she thinking?

Sarah opened her handbag, took out a handkerchief and dabbed at her nose. Then she pulled something else from a pocket inside the bag.

"Leopold wanted to make this out to Jonah, but I thought you'd have a better idea of what Rosie needs. She must be growing out of her clothes by now and I thought you might want to buy a baby-walker or a sturdier pushchair, something like that."

She handed over a folded cheque.

"Oh my God, thank you so much." Ellie nearly burst when she saw the amount. "I really appreciate this. A pushchair, I think. Rosie likes being propped up when I take her out in the pram. She'll appreciate a pushchair so much more."

A smile floated across Sarah's face. Ellie got the strange feeling the woman was drugged.

"How much did Mum give you?" It was the first thing Jonah asked when they were alone. He was sitting next to Ellie on the bed, Rosie on his knees. She liked to be held upright under her arms so she could bounce.

Rosie gripped his thumbs, displaying her gums. Dribble poured from her mouth.

On the outside windowsill, a crisp layer of snow had built up. A twittering flock of sparrows took turns alighting on the bird feeder.

"Enough to buy a proper pushchair for Rosie."

She reached over and wiped the dribble off Rosie's chin. Rosie paused to give her an indignant glare before resuming her bouncing.

Ellie felt the space tightening between her and Jonah.

"Say Dadda," Jonah said to the baby. He glanced sideways, waiting for Ellie to explain herself.

I haven't done anything wrong.

"She thought it would be better if I had the money."

Jonah gave her another sideways glance. The mole on his neck seemed to throb.

"Yeah, I know that, Dad told me. He was a bit annoyed about it but he reckons she doesn't think I'm responsible enough." He chewed his lip. "So how much was it, anyway?"

His voice stayed level but the flaring nostrils gave his anger away.

Ellie folded the muslin in her lap and looked down at her hands.

Once during her pregnancy he'd hit her around the back of her neck with a towel. She remembered the shock, that she'd thought he was leaving the room and she was safe. So she hadn't been expecting it.

But he was holding the baby now. Surely he wouldn't?

"About the same as your dad gave you when Rosie was born, I should think."

What had Rosie got out of that? A cheap cradle she was already growing out of and a few nappies.

The groove on Jonah's forehead deepened.

He kept his feelings so much under wraps, until he couldn't control them any longer. She sensed a similar quality in his father, remembered the drugged air of his mother. She didn't want to be like that.

"Is your recording equipment working well?"

He stood up abruptly, making the smile fall from Rosie's face. She clutched his shoulder as he carried her over to the window. Ellie could see her digging her delicate fingernails in. He pointed out the birds taking off into the trees behind the barn.

Ellie sat still, watching Rosie's wide-eyed excitement. Then Rosie started grizzling. She grasped Jonah's hair, tied at the base of his neck with a shoelace.

"Don't do that," he said irritably, but she carried on. Twisting around to see Ellie, she pulled harder. His hair had got caught in her fingers. "I said, don't," Jonah snapped.

He swung around, marched back across the carpet, thrust the baby at Ellie. "Go to Mamma."

A strand of hair pulled across the baby's palm and she screamed.

"Bloody hell, Jonah. Be more careful, won't you?"

Ellie leant over Rosie, expecting an apology from Jonah. But when she looked up, he'd gone.

Hayley was taking orders for Christmas dinner.

"We're staying, I think." Ellie sat cross-legged on the lounge floor. On her blanket, Rosie practised seal impressions, jerking her head and flapping her arms.

"Watch it, Stan." Greg came through the door from the annex, making a grab for the dog's collar.

"It's okay," Ellie said, not looking at him. "She loves Stan."

Stan flopped down on his belly too. He crawled carefully across the floor towards Rosie and touched the side of her face with his nose.

Rosie chortled.

"She's a happy little thing, isn't she?"

"Yeah, she is." Ellie smiled but she kept her head down.

On the face of it, she got on well with Bonnie. The older woman was helpful with Rosie. But Bonnie had the kind of magnetism that was a lot more attractive to men than women. All the guys in the house were affected by it and it pissed Ellie off that Jonah spent so much time with her.

Vincent was the house member Ellie was closest to – they ate their meals together because of Jonah always being busy. Vincent told Ellie that Bonnie was thirty-six. Much older than the rest of them. She'd applied to live at Running Hare House first, then Greg moved out to join her.

"But what about these *babies* that Bonnie's always going on about?" Ellie sprinkled more salt on her food. The pot fell off the edge of the table, knocked against Vincent's ankle. She took her time coming back up, knowing she'd been unfair: Bonnie hardly mentioned them (Ellie couldn't imagine never mentioning Rosie).

Vincent shrugged in his expressive way.

"Dunno. Apparently she left them with her husband when she moved here. I don't think they're actually babies, as such."

Ellie shovelled the rest of the noodles off the plate and aimed them at her mouth.

"So... Bonnie and Greg... How did they get together? Bit of an age difference, isn't there?"

She closed her mouth on the last of the noodles. Snow fell steadily outside, obliterating the fields opposite. It made the sky look thick and impenetrable. Vincent, soft brown hair falling in waves over one eye, tilted his head. She kept her expression bland.

"A bit interested in Greg, aren't you?"

"No I'm not." Heat on her cheeks. "It's not that. It's just, we used to chat a lot and we hardly do anymore. I just wondered how two people from different generations get together like that."

"Bonnie was Greg's mother's best friend. The two women aren't speaking anymore, for obvious reasons. Glenda, that's Greg's mum, found him in *her* bed with Bonnie."

"Oh my God."

"I don't think Greg really knew what he was letting himself in for. Bit of a *Mrs Robinson* situation. He probably didn't realise she'd leave her husband and four kids for him."

"Four?" She hadn't asked Bonnie many questions about her children for fear of upsetting her.

"Yep, four."

Ellie couldn't imagine having that many.

"I do know Greg's a bit intimidated by that," Vincent said. "He's told me he feels trapped. But he felt he owed it to her to move out here and give it a bit of a go since she, you know, left her husband."

He took his final bite of burger, gazed amiably at Ellie, his jaw working ruminatively.

Ellie pushed her plate to one side and picked up her orange juice. She wondered why her pulse felt so erratic.

"Bloody hell," she said. "What's he let himself in for?"

The tingling beneath her ribs was annoying. She left the table and went over to peep at Rosie, still half-asleep.

"Here, let me get these plates," she said into Vincent's silence. "Thanks for cooking *again*; you're a star, Vincent."

Vincent got up and followed her into the kitchen. She noticed the redness of clay in his fingernails; in the lines on his knuckles.

"No probs," he said. "It's your turn tomorrow, unless you plan on eating with your boyfriend for a change."

The boiler on the kitchen wall choked into life. Ellie plunged her hands into the suds. She didn't like complaining about Jonah, but she sometimes couldn't help it.

"It's not really down to what *I* plan, is it?"

Vincent plugged in the kettle, then picked up a reasonably clean tea-towel and started drying the pots.

"It's not very fair on you though, is it?"

They could hear a volley of drums and the steady thrum of a bass from the barn, but only just. Jonah's world, going on as usual with no place in it for her. She wondered if she even cared. She put another plate on the draining board, gazed out at the twirling snow in the yard.

Through the flurry Ted came out of the woodshed with an armful of chopped logs, stepping carefully around icy puddles in his wellies. He went into the other house. Light fell onto the snow-covered ground from the back door. She saw him shake off his wellies on the mat and then close the door and the dark settled around the buildings again.

She turned back to Vincent.

"What isn't fair on me?"

"Come on. You're interested in Bonnie and Greg; I'm interested in you and Jonah." He gave her a brief pat on the shoulder. "You're the one that matters to me."

She swallowed a lump in her throat. *If things had been otherwise. . .* It could have been Vincent or Greg. *If I was still at university, only in my second year, I might have been out with lots of other guys by now.* With the back of her arm, she pushed hair off her face. Vincent tucked the stray lock behind her ear for her.

"Thanks. Anyway, what d'you mean, it's not fair on me?"

Vincent stacked plates in the cupboard. The kettle boiled and he poured the water.

"You know what I mean. He spends every minute of the day with those other guys in the band. That's once he's even deigned to get out of bed. You know what I'm talking about. He's like a Victorian father to Rosie, having her brought to him for maybe half an hour a day so he can remind her who he is and that's only out of a sense of possession."

She was surprised at his vehemence. In the pram on the other side of the hatch Rosie whimpered as if she'd understood. Putting the last fork in the drainer, Ellie dried her hands on a ragged towel. By now Rosie's lungs had opened into a full-on cry.

Here I go again.

"You go and get her sorted," Vincent said quietly. "I'll bring you your tea in a minute."

12

Christmas 1982

Ellie glanced around the table. When she was growing up the clink of cutlery and glasses was always the background to tension, fear of saying the wrong thing. But this was her family now.

They were eating in the annex lounge. Ted had gone away for a week with Billy but most of the residents had stayed. Most of them.

If only Greg was here. *Stop it, Ellie.*

Late in the afternoon Hayley put her arm through Ellie's and led her into the kitchen.

"You might want to make sure Rosie won't be hungry for a while."

Hayley was shrugging her shoulders into a vivid orange jacket, printed with silhouettes of giraffes. The colour contrasted so strongly with Hayley's dark skin it made Ellie's eyes go funny. She blinked and tried to pay attention.

"Jen and I have organised a surprise for you and Jonah in the main house. Nobody'll disturb you, I promise."

Ellie saw Vincent smiling at her through the hatch. Her skin prickled. *Why didn't you warn me?*

"We were all in on it," Hayley grinned. She patted Ellie's arm. "We thought you could do with some time to yourselves. I'm just going over there to put some finishing touches to it. Do you need to feed Rosie? Jen and I will be on babysitting duty for the evening, we can do nappies and all that stuff."

Ellie felt sick at the pressure. *Don't I have any control over my own life?*

The fire was lit in the living room of the old house. Hayley had laid the table with a white cloth, some holly and a candelabrum. Jonah and Ellie sat down. The candlelight glinted on Jonah's forehead, turned the hairs on his upper lip golden; enhanced the bone structure under his eyes. He met hers with a hint of a smile and she tried to smile back but it hurt somewhere inside her ribcage.

She was wearing a new dress, a Christmas present from her mother. It was made of green velvety material with buttons down the front. Ellie wondered if Vivian had chosen it because she was breastfeeding, touched that she might have.

———

Her family had visited the house on Christmas Eve, including Ray. It was the first time he'd seen his granddaughter.

"I can't understand why you're not coming home for Christmas," her mum kept harping on about it. "It would have been nice to see our granddaughter on the day." She reached over and straightened the bib Ellie had taken to putting on Rosie to soak up the constant stream of dribble. "Come with us now, Eleanor, just you and the baby if Jonah's busy?"

No Jonah to spoil your happy family picture, you'd like that, wouldn't you?

"We'll come on Boxing Day. Will Grandma be there?"

"Yes, your father and I are collecting her in the morning. Are you sure you won't come with us tonight?"

Her mother seemed twitchier than usual, glancing repeatedly at Ray.

"I can't, Mum, sorry. We've agreed to stay here. Dinner's all arranged." She added, "Everyone here loves Rosie, she'll have a great time."

She threw a challenging glance at her father. He had a deep frown between his eyes, sitting stiffly on a straight-backed chair in a corner of the lounge. He'd recently had his hair shorn and it made him look more sergeant-major than ever.

He couldn't look at the baby, not to mention Ellie.

Every now and then someone walked through the lounge. At each new person Ray cast an unbelieving up-and-down stare. Vincent was the first to be struck with it, his soft floppy hair and delicate way of walking eliciting a curl of Ray's lip.

Ellie was surprised the chill in the air didn't freeze Vincent on the spot.

"When did you become such a hippy?" her father hissed through his teeth. Mike, all dreadlocks, beard and ripped jeans was passing through on his way to the kitchen. "Bloody commune: why the hell is a granddaughter of mine living in a place like this?"

Ellie turned away, not liking his claim on Rosie. She watched emotions running over Deborah's face. What was she thinking? The girl had hardly spoken. Normally exuding such confidence, her face was tight. It must be lonely living with Ray and Vivian; no Ellie anymore to shoulder Ray's scorn.

Vivian shushed Ray, keeping her eyes averted. She bounced Rosie gently on her lap.

"Who's Nana's girl, then? Say Nan-nan; go on, say Nan-nan."

Ellie took a deep breath. Maybe Vivian would feel things for her granddaughter that she'd never felt for her. Rosie made an indistinguishable burbling sound and Vivian's eyebrows shot up. "See," she said to Ellie, "she said it."

"She can call you that. Jonah's mum calls herself Grandma, but that's ordinary. Nan-nan is different."

When they were ready to leave, Ellie tried to give Deborah a hug. But she stepped smartly aside.

"You look lovely." Jonah hardly ever paid her a compliment.

Mike, an apron around his waist, had served them with turkey sandwiches and varieties of cheese and pickle, along with a flourish of white napkins and paper hats. He left via the kitchen door. Through the window Ellie watched him walking across the yard to the annex.

Jonah's paper hat fitted neatly on his head but hers kept sliding over to one side. Christmas songs played on the stereo.

"Thanks, you look good too."

She popped a crisp in her mouth. For the past months most of their contact had been to do with Rosie. She couldn't remember when they last slept together.

The others should have given me a script and a list of directions if they wanted me to play this part.

Bonnie crashed into her mind. Bonnie wouldn't sit here pressing her legs together under the table, dabbing her lips primly with a napkin. She'd most likely have ripped the tablecloth off, pulled Jonah up out of his chair by now. With shame but also excitement, Ellie envisaged Bonnie straddling Jonah on the table. But before the vision melted it became Bonnie and Greg she was seeing.

Her crunching of crisps sounded excessively loud to her inner ears.

She took a long drink from her wine and it went straight to her head. What could they talk about?

"Are you having a good time?"

"I am. It's good to relax for a change – spend some time with you."

The thing about Jonah, by the time he showed his emotions they were so intense she was in danger of drowning in them.

He offered her his hand. She put her fingers tentatively into it.

The gesture soon began to feel limp so she turned his hand over, ran her finger up the veins and over the freckles on his skin. She'd once learned every mark on his body like she was taking an exam.

I remember the night we got together at the university rock disco. We went down to the union bar afterwards and talked until closing time. Every time you touched me it felt like electricity. I turned your hand over in mine just as I'm doing now and I traced the landscape of marks and scars on your skin, with the rivers of your veins running through them.

She heard his breath catch. When she looked up he had moisture in his eyes, illuminated by the candles. It made her chest tighten so she closed her fingers over his hand. He slid it around within hers so they were palm to palm.

I remember you, she thought again. Her skin recognised his.

OK, how to progress from here? Just because they hadn't been intimate for a while didn't mean they couldn't be. She may have been on the point of finishing with him but they had so much to stay together for, she ought to try.

She pressed her palm more firmly against his, wondered if the door was locked. *Don't worry; you won't be disturbed.*

If they were going to... now would be as good a time as any. She'd almost forgotten how to do it. Instead of meeting Jonah's eyes, she focussed on different parts of his body: the delicate veins on his wrist, the vulnerable fold in the bend of his elbow; the mole on his neck, just beneath his ear.

White Christmas came on and a flurry of snowflakes danced beyond the window like a chorus. Her head buzzed. Still holding Jonah's hand, she wondered if the vague relaxed feelings would deepen into something more meaningful.

She was a different woman from the one he'd last made love to, now with the soft body of a mother. The part he'd enter might have stretched and loosened. She'd had no interest in sex since Rosie was born.

He ran his fingers around the inside of her wrist. It sent a small electric shock up her arm and down her body where it seemed to settle in a warm pool in her belly. The belly that had cradled their daughter. She remembered him stroking it during her pregnancy, how it had turned her on.

At the end of the song the tape stopped. The crackling and spitting of wood in the fireplace seemed louder now. The room was dark apart from candles, Christmas lights on the tree, the firelight. It really was magical.

"It's snowing again." Jonah's voice had that gravel-note which always turned her on.

She cleared her throat; slipped her hand out of his.

"Hang on a minute." Unsteadily, she got up and closed the curtains. She placed another log on the fire, keeping her back turned, a pause of one, two, three, four, five beats. Then, taking a deep breath she came back to the table, finished the wine in her glass. She ought to follow through on the plans so carefully laid out on her behalf.

"Have you got. . . ?"

He studied the question in her eyes, smiled, patting his pocket.

"Hayley didn't forget anything."

She owed it to him to try, he was making an effort. He hadn't mentioned The Travelling Man once. He hadn't smoked or looked at his watch. He'd left John-Paul and Martin playing cards in the other lounge. Rosie was being well looked after. It was just the two of them. That's what they'd needed, she realised it now. That's what they'd had at the beginning. It would all work out fine as long as they kept making time for each other.

13

January 1983

Jonah was sleeping in her room at nights now. Both of them squashed into the single bed. If Rosie cried, Ellie lay down with her on a mattress she kept beneath the bed. In the morning she could leave Rosie with Jonah and steal some time to herself.

Stan slept on a cushion in the corridor outside Greg's room, guard of all residents. He expected to go with her when she left the building in the mornings.

On the river beach, mudflats mirrored the morning cloudscape. They followed a path winding around the outer edge of the estuary, through tall-grassed marshes that belonged to both the land and sea. The sky curved over the landscape like a dome. Out here, she was in a world within the world.

Stan bounded ahead, knowing instinctively where to land on the marshy ground. Ellie picked her way carefully for fear of the boot-swallowing mud. Birds crashed upwards from the bog, silhouettes against an opaque sky. She and Stan crossed more boggy fields via creaky wooden bridges over narrow dykes, finally arriving at the sea.

Ellie stood on the bank, wind-whipped face numb with cold, the sky thick and white. Grey waves lashed pebbles onto the sand in a resonating crescendo of booming music.

She'd arrive back at Running Hare House exhilarated, fresh and new, a wet, tired dog at her heels. Rosie would have woken Jonah by then and the three of them could spend some time as a family before Jonah was reclaimed by his music. The arrangement satisfied them all.

———

In the early months of 1983, the Project was resumed with vigour. They would see the full benefits of Ellie's funding bid in April and there were more committee meetings than usual, to establish the finer details of how to allocate the money.

It was late January, a Saturday afternoon, low sun seeping orange into a violet sky. Both colours tinted the snow, striped the field across the road. A line of skeletal trees was sketched in charcoal on the horizon.

The residents sat around the table in the main house, the same table at which she'd sat with Jonah on Christmas evening. Ellie caught her boyfriend's eye. As they smiled at each other, she noticed John-Paul's resentful sideways glower from Jonah's other side.

"So, Ellie," began Ted. "I've got something to ask you."

He was going to say they no longer needed her to work on the promotion. . .

Ellie bit the end of her pen.

Ted pushed his glasses up his nose, his strongest feature on a sharply defined face which bordered on gaunt. His eyes were like black beads. Two wings of silver streaked his black hair, curving back from a heart-shaped hairline, low on his forehead. His gaze was compelling. He could be a vampire.

"It's about the sewing workshops you wanted to do."

But then Billy interrupted by poking his head into the room. He made a gesture at his mouth with thumb and little finger protruding from his curled hand.

"Phone for you, ducky."

"Strange, I didn't hear it," snapped Ted. He shuffled his papers on the table, looked around at everybody before getting up to go into the porch with Billy, closing the door behind him. There was the murmur of voices from the porch, Ted's low and steady, Billy's starting to rise. Then the stifled thud of the other door closing. Ellie met Vincent's eyes across the table and they both shrugged. Jonah cast a sideways glance at Ellie. Greg, on her other side, tapped his foot. She made a point of stroking Jonah's hand, slipping her finger underneath, tracing circles on the inside of his wrist, their secret signal. He smiled. She could feel Greg's eyes on the movement of her hand.

Ted came back in.

"Sorry about that, folks." A muscle twitched near his left eye.

"Everything alright?" enquired Mike.

Ted made an eloquent gesture with his hands. Ted and Mike were mates; Ellie had often seen them chatting.

Rosie sat on Jen's lap. She'd grasped a handful of Jen's fine blonde hair. Hayley, next to Jen, was attempting to disentangle it.

"Just keep still," Ellie mouthed.

She mimed how to open Rosie's tight little fist without either of them getting hurt.

She turned her attention back to Ted.

"So, as I was saying, Ellie. . . how would you feel about not doing those workshops at all?"

A jolt went through her.

"What? Err, you never said anything about that."

Tears flooded the backs of her eyes. After all her hard work, she was going to be pushed out of the Project. She was only nineteen, *written off already.*

It's not fair.

Being a father wasn't stopping Jonah doing what he wanted to do, why should she stop just because she was a mother? She felt the familiar heat rising up her neck.

And yet. I'm not really qualified to run sewing workshops, am I?

It was true. All the others had some training or practice in their field – something to show for their skills... they were proper artists and musicians...

"I could go on a college course," she offered before Ted had a chance to say anything else. "Even an evening class would be a help, give me a simple qualification..."

"Ellie," Ted said firmly. "Shut up, yeah?"

It shocked her into silence.

Ted spread his hands out on the table in front of him. A sheet of paper slipped to the floor and Bonnie, on his right, leant down to retrieve it. She stretched forward in such a way that her freckled cleavage was revealed in the open neck of her cheesecloth shirt (In January – the rest of them were dressed for the cold weather). Ted looked away and cleared his throat, pushed the glasses up his nose again.

"The craft room will definitely be converted as planned, Ellie. I thought your idea of running children's workshops as a créche activity while parents were paying to attend one of the arts or music classes was brilliant, and you would be the best person to run it, because of course, Rosie could help."

He reached across Hayley to tousle Rosie's (sparse) hair and she grabbed his finger, jamming it in her mouth. He laughed rather uncomfortably.

"Ah, is that tasty, Rosie?" With some difficulty and a restrained grimace he managed to retrieve it. He wiped his finger on his trouser leg.

"Perhaps we could get you a childcare qualification, Ellie, to make it more legitimate?"

Ellie hoped he'd washed his hands recently. At the same time she was thinking, *great, childcare, that's all he thinks I'm fit for*. She bit her lip.

"And the sewing machines can still be bought," Ted continued. "If you do think you can get something going along those lines." (he clearly didn't). "But what I really wanted to tell you is how valuable your work on the funding side of things has been."

"Hear, hear," Mike grinned through his beard.

"Bravo, Ellie," Martin added.

She nodded gratefully. A spatter of applause broke out around the table.

"Couldn't have done it without you," Bonnie said in her raspy voice, as if her pronouncement was the one that mattered. She beamed Ellie a wide smile. It seemed genuine.

She thought she felt Greg's shoulder pressing against hers. When she looked up, John-Paul was leaning forward, his hooded eyes studying her from under his frizzy black hair. She felt she'd done something wrong.

What was it with John-Paul? He was either overly friendly, or he was cruel, but in a succinct way that nobody would notice. For example he'd try and catch her out and make her feel embarrassed at the same time. Once he asked her if she knew what Jonah was doing and when she answered that he was in the barn getting the amps set up for the workshop that afternoon, he said he'd just remembered, Jonah was actually in Bonnie's room in the other house, but she needn't worry about it, he was sure there was nothing going on between them.

Ellie picked at her fingernails.

"Order," said Ted. Snippets of unrelated conversations were starting up. He tapped his pen on the table.

"Can someone put the light on please? Just that lamp over there... Vincent?"

Vincent got up and switched on the wall lamp. He smiled at Ellie as he sat back down. Rosie reached out for him from Jen's lap and he took her, cuddling her against his chest. She got him in a vice-like grip around the neck and started head-butting him.

"I think she wants feeding, Ellie," he laughed.

Ellie got up and went round the table to collect Rosie. The baby immediately started rooting, tugging frantically at Ellie's clothes.

"Wait a minute, Rosie."

She was embarrassed. But she sat down, pulled up her t-shirt and jumper as discreetly as she could. She was mostly comfortable feeding Rosie in front of them; it was less attention-grabbing than trying to calm a distressed baby any other way.

"OK?" said Ted, looking off to one side of her.

"Yep, all set." She pulled her jumper down so nothing could be seen. *Alright, you can look now, Ted.* She didn't think he was that comfortable with babies in general. Mike's sister had visited recently with hers and Ted acted pretty similarly even when the twins were handed their bottles.

"OK, here goes."

What, what is it?

"Would you be willing to take on the position permanently instead of running sewing workshops, Ellie?"

"The position?"

"Funding Officer, Administrator, whatever you want to call it?" Ted paused to let it sink in. "We really need someone to take proper charge of this stuff, especially if we're going to be running private workshops as well. What do you think?"

Ellie's heart flipped. He was asking her to do a proper, official job. He didn't think of her as only suitable for running childcare.

"Oh my God, Ted, yes please. Administrator? Wow, that's cool."

Rosie broke away and stared up at her mother, moist mouth open in a grin of empathy. Milk dripped down her chin. Ellie pulled her top down hastily.

Ted tapped the table with the pen again.

"Everyone agreed that Ellie should become the Running Hare Project Administrator?" Ted asked. "Show of hands?"

All hands went up, even John-Paul's, Ellie was relieved to see.

"Excellent," said Ted. "Meeting concluded then, unless anyone has any other business."

14

Summer 1983

The old dining room in the main house now consisted of white plastic surfaces and curved-edged furniture, all wipe-able and safe. Helena helped in the créche. She lived in the village and was doing the same childcare course as Ellie at the village hall in nearby Restingham.

The closest Ellie got to teaching sewing was helping little ones pull wool through coarse fabric using blunt darning needles. But she was exhausted at the end of the day. Her book of patterns for children's clothes had hardly been opened and she hadn't yet gotten around to making anything for Rosie, apart from the crazy overalls she dressed her in for créche.

———

Bonnie had brought her kids out to Running Hare House for the day. It was Ellie's morning off but she was in the créche getting some activities ready for the next day when Bonnie turned up with her two youngest.

"You don't mind, do you?" She pulled their hands off her and was already halfway out the door. "Stay there, you two," she added as the little ones tried to follow her. "I really want to take the older ones to a music workshop," she shot back at Ellie.

The door was closed and the youngest had opened her mouth to cry before Ellie had time to answer.

"I'm sorry." Greg rushed in about an hour later. "I didn't know. Come on, sweetie." Bethany cried again when she saw him. He picked her up.

Ellie watched as the child wound her thin arms around Greg's neck.

If he isn't trapped by Bonnie, he is by the children.

Putting her down at last, Greg said, "Let's give Ellie a hand with the cleaning-up, will we, kids?"

"Oh, you don't have to. . . " Ellie started but he cut her off.

"Of course we do. We mustn't treat you like a skivvy, must we?"

She pressed her lips together, stopping herself from crying (Greg had recently returned from a one-month placement with an environmental artist in Scotland. It had been easier not to think about him when he wasn't there).

All the windows in the house were propped open, admitting the mingled buzz of insects and farm machinery. Scents of cut grass and roses drifted through the building. Outside, seagulls circled in an ultramarine sky.

Ellie's windowsill was crowded with pot plants, leaves trailing like Rapunzel-hair onto her desk. A bunch of entwined stems dangled all the way down to the carpet.

Someone knocked on her open door.

"Yeah, come in," she shouted over the rumble of the sewing machine. She'd finally got around to working on a dress for Rosie from one of the patterns in her book. Jonah had taken Rosie to the beach for the morning. She'd come back babbling about 'ice-beam' and in a sticky mess which Jonah would expect Ellie to clean up.

"Phone call for you." It was Greg. "She asked for Eleanor."

"It can only be my mother, then." Ellie switched off the machine, letting her fingers linger over it.

Precious time of my own eaten into.

Ellie and Greg walked down the corridor together.

"Hang on there, Ellie," Greg stopped her. He plucked a twist of sewing thread from her hair. She watched him wind it around his finger. "Are you disappointed you never got to run your sewing workshops?" he asked as they continued towards the lounge.

"I don't mind, really," she said, holding the door open for him. He gave a little bow and she smiled. "I'm enjoying the administration side of things. I still intend to go to college and study textiles, though, when Rosie's a bit older."

She wondered why her mother had telephoned.

———————————

"This is a nice surprise," Ellie tried. Deborah, holding a mug of hot-chocolate in both hands, gave her a withering look.

"All right," Ellie said. "I won't speak until you do."

Her mother wouldn't say why she needed Deborah to stay with Ellie.

"It's a simple request, Eleanor," she'd snapped. "Will you have her, or not?"

Ellie parked Rosie's pushchair next to Deb at the Habitat café and went off to order tea for herself.

Back at the table, she poured juice into Rosie's plastic feeder cup. Deborah watched with her new sullen expression. Where was the girl who tossed her hair and stuck her nose in the air as if she was better than everybody else?

Rosie was flushed-cheeked and irritable.

"Can I get her out?" Deborah asked unexpectedly.

Ellie thought Rosie would yell. She watched (*"Call me Deb, now,"*) struggle with the catches on the pushchair straps, then swing Rosie onto her knee. Rosie twisted her head around and fixed her auntie with a hard stare, bottom lip pushed out. Ellie waited tensely but the child settled quickly, reaching for her cup. *Deb* fed her bites of biscuit. Rosie crunched the broken pieces with her new teeth and let her mouth hang open, exposing its mashed contents.

Deb laughed out loud.

This is what it's supposed to be like, Ellie thought, *Deb and me together; sisters.*

"Ready to talk, yet?" she asked.

Deb's face closed again. When it reopened she had an expression of charming innocence.

"Talk about what?"

Expressions skittered across her face like flickering lights.

"Nothing in particular, or anything you want. I'm not fussed. Now, the bus back to Pottersea is at four o'clock, so we want to be finishing up here soon. I see you've got quite a big bag, we can hang that on the buggy if you like; it must have been heavy for you to carry."

She stood up, all bustling and business.

"Would you mind giving Rosie's face a clean with one of these?"

She handed Deb some wipes.

After a long sleep on the bus home, Rosie was awake and tearing around the lounge in her slippers that evening, pulling herself from one chair to another by holding onto human knees, chair arms, sofa cushions and Stan's ears.

Mike was trying to watch a Sci-Fi video. His face and exaggerated sigh on Rosie's third trip around the room jolted an exhausted Ellie into action. Even Rosie noticed Mike's temper coming to the boil. She quietened, gazing up at him, drool-mouthed.

"Come on, Rosie, bed."

Ellie lived in fear of being asked to leave the house. She couldn't bear it.

At least she had her own room to take Rosie to; her noise from there was no worse than the tape decks and record players of the other residents. And on particularly bad nights, Ellie wrapped Rosie in a blanket and went for a walk in the dark.

Now she dragged a screaming Rosie away. Stan barked in empathy. Mike put the video on pause and remained set-faced. *Shit*, thought Ellie; *they're all going to get pissed off with me at this rate.*

("Don't worry about it," Hayley said later. "Mike's a funny bugger: one minute he's your best mate and the next he's taken against you for no reason that anyone can see. It'll be someone else he's annoyed with tomorrow.")

It was true, but Ellie found it hard to be that relaxed; she was the only one with a baby. Except for Jonah, of course, and it didn't seem to bother him.

The plan was for Deb to sleep on the mattress in Ellie's room.

"Won't Jonah mind?"

They gazed at Rosie, finally asleep in her cot. She hadn't gone down without a fight.

"No, he won't be bothered, he'll be up half the night writing songs or playing Dungeons and Dragons. He has his own room, you know."

Ellie saw Deb's sly smile.

Ellie and Jonah's relationship was on another downward slide. If they hadn't had Rosie they'd have split up long ago. They should have done when she was pregnant, Jonah never wanted to be a dad. She was tired of all the thoughts constantly going around her head.

<hr>

Deb was playing a game of Scrabble with Jen, who she'd attached herself to. Jen had promised to take Deb on one of her salvaging walks the next day.

Ellie was so tired. She hadn't seen either Vincent or Greg that evening and she missed both of them. She just wanted to shower and then sink into bed, and hoped Deb wouldn't disturb her later.

On her way to the shower she met Martin in the corridor. The thrum of a bass and a muted vocal came from behind Jonah's closed door at the end.

Reddish light poured into the hall from the window of Martin's room, door open to reveal a mess of clothes and books, tapes scattered everywhere, guitar on a stand just inside the door.

"Hey." He rocked himself from foot to foot. A faint musty smell came off him.

"Hey." Ellie liked Martin. Both Jonah and John-Paul bossed him around.

"You alright?" Martin tucked his hands under his arms, his eyes shifting behind his glasses.

"Yeah, thanks. I'm fine. Is everything okay?"

"Cool," said Martin, shuffling his feet. "Stuff's going good. Ellie. . ."

Greg's door opened and he came out, Stan at his side.

Ellie held her breath.

"Oops, sorry, Ellie." He brushed against her as he passed, flashing Martin an enquiring glance. Stan stopped and fixed his eyes on her, nudging her with his nose.

"Sorry, Stan, Rosie's asleep."

"Tomorrow, Stan," Greg told his dog. "Later, Ellie, Martin." He went out the side door into the garden, glancing back once.

"What's up, Martin?" Ellie's gaze wandered through the glass in the door.

Greg and Stan crossed the yard and Greg opened the gate to the road. Ellie imagined walking with them, the evening breeze that would blow through her hair. She thought how she would match her pace to Greg's, remembered their walks when Rosie was a tiny baby in the sling.

Reluctantly, she turned her attention back to Martin.

"Oh, I just thought I'd mention, err, Jonah. Bit down, I reckon. Wondered if you'd noticed?"

Ellie inspected her feet. They were bare and getting cold. She pulled her dressing gown more tightly around her.

"No," she said, "not more than usual. Not that I get to see much of him these days."

Jonah had probably put him up to this.

Bloody Jonah, sympathy-mongering with those too weak to resist him. But it still hurt.

"Oh, err, sorry," Martin muttered. "Bit insensitive of me, I suppose. Not much good at. . . you know."

Ellie put her hand on his arm. "It's alright, Martin. I don't blame you. But it's not just my fault, either. Jonah needs to decide where his priorities lie. . ."

Hot water streamed down her face and body, hair hanging like heavy ropes over her shoulders. She soaped herself and thought about what Martin had said. Maybe Jonah was confiding in his male friends because he thought she wouldn't listen to him. To be fair, he'd indicated that he felt overwhelmed by the intensity of her symbiosis with Rosie. She should have listened to his deeper feelings.

She lathered one armpit and began shaving carefully, unsure of the sharpness of the razor she'd grabbed from her dressing table drawer. True, he'd expressed himself in a way bound to put her back up, but she realised that like him, she'd considered things only from her own perspective.

The razor didn't seem too blunt. She started on the other armpit.

The hot, streaming water helped her thoughts to flow freely, resentments trickling with soap down the plug hole. Whether she sometimes wished to be free of the relationship or not, the existence of Rosie meant she never could be, however much she thought about someone else. . .

She came back into her room full of resolve. Tiptoeing so as not to wake the lightly snoring Rosie, curled towards the wall in her cot, Ellie felt in the wardrobe and slid a cotton sundress out, holding the other hangers still. She pulled it over her head and smoothed the folds down over her stomach. As she glanced at herself in the mirror in the dimness, the peace of the sleeping baby and a sudden surety of who she was suffused her. Her hands, skimming through the underwear drawer, paused and withdrew. She closed the drawer carefully.

She bent over Rosie's cot. The temptation to touch her was almost too strong to resist, the smell of sleeping baby drew her in, but she didn't want to risk waking her. So she backed away and pulled the bedroom door shut once she was in the corridor.

Self-consciously she went, without bra or knickers, to Jonah's room. *What if Greg walks back in right now?* The thought excited her. Cotton fabric brushed her nipples, air wafted between her legs as she took the few steps between rooms. Ellie didn't give herself time to think, knocking firmly on the door and pushing it open straight away.

Inside, it was stuffy and stale-smelling, curtains pulled across the closed window, reminding her of their old flat on Park Grove. The room was just as smoke-filled as the flat had been. She glanced around and noticed a tower of used teabags that had toppled sideways off their saucer and been trodden underfoot in one corner of the room. Tea stains sullied the yellow paint on the wall. Crusted cereal bowls were piled up in another corner.

Jonah was still living the same life but in a different place.

Outside his window: a view he was blinded to, the breadth of the river stretched a mile and a quarter to the horizon, to the banks of north Lincolnshire. Just metres from his fog-filled haze, mudflats gleamed in the evening sun that streaked the sky orange; fishermen crossed the mirroring surface in their thigh-high waders, digging for worms. Seagulls wheeled across the sky. From just out there, the fresh tang of salt would blow in if Jonah would only open the window and smell it.

Her chest was tight, but she kept her chin up.

John-Paul moved towards her, glaring in a 'what are you doing here?' way, but she noticed a small smile on Martin's face. Jonah swivelled around from his synthesiser keyboard; hands paused above the notes, a far-away look in his eyes.

Stoned.

He was buried in this musty pit, darkness and stench representing dreams of a record deal, stuck on a turntable like one of his beloved records.

She had to remind herself that dedication to his music was one of the things that had made her fall in love with him. It was she who'd changed, not him. But they had Rosie now; it was her duty to make an effort to reunite the baby's parents. *See,* she could hear Jonah saying inside her head. *It's still Rosie you're thinking about, not me.* Well, that was what being a mother was about and he'd just have to deal with it.

She stopped herself from straining on tiptoes to catch a glimpse through a crack in the curtains of someone who might be walking on the river beach with their dog.

The smell of cannabis was thick in the room. The ashtrays were full of roaches; tobacco and papers and a sticky, dark block of resin were strewn on a record cover.

Ted had already warned them once, banned it from the premises.

"I have the reputation of the Project to think about, lads. If you want to do stuff like that, do it elsewhere, not on my patch."

So for a while they'd taken their habit down to the beach, huddled under the cliffs between the caravan parks, or gone to a favourite sheltered spot under a hedge on the edge of the fields between the river and the road.

Ellie was disappointed now and scared to find they'd broken their promise to Ted. The Project would never be granted funding again if there was a conviction for possession. She made an effort to bolster up her resolve to connect with Jonah again. Maybe she could get through to him if they spent some time alone.

"Fancy a walk?" She moved in front of his unfocussed eyes. Leaning over to the window she grasped the edge of one curtain and tugged it open. John-Paul and James, the other band member, tutted, but Martin stood back with an encouraging smile. She pushed at the window and managed to open it, despite its stiffness.

"What the?" mumbled Jonah.

"It's beautiful outside. We could walk along the bank above the mudflats."

Jonah didn't seem to comprehend what she was saying. She should flush his stash down the toilet, give him an ultimatum. But she'd try this way first.

"We're busy here, Ellie," John-Paul said pointedly. His black eyes reminded her, as always, of a vulture. His voice was like one as well. And his black hair and clothes. *Flap your wings and fuck off*, she wanted to say. He'd always been a barrier to her relationship.

She placed herself deliberately in the gold-coloured light that illuminated the smoky haze. It gave the piles of clothes, the ashtrays and pouches of tobacco and rolling equipment, the musical instruments and records with their sleeves off, the mess of tangled bedding on his half-obscured bed, a filmic look. It also shone right through her dress, silhouetting her body within the thin cotton, and she didn't care that all the others could see.

"Just you and me." She finally caught his eyes. "John-Paul and Martin will keep an ear out for the baby, won't you?"

Martin nodded. John-Paul rammed a record on the player and turned up the volume.

15

Two weeks later

In mid-August Ellie's mum arrived to collect Deb. She was taking her home to pack for a holiday.

"Tenerife," Vivian said offhandedly, "for a fortnight."

"On your own, just the two of you?" asked Ellie. "No Dad?" Her mind was turning somersaults.

"That's right, just Deborah and I."

A barely imperceptible exhale from Deb.

Now that Vivian was there, Deb had clammed up again, though she had seemed happy tagging around after Jen during her stay. She sat tensely next to Ellie in the garden.

"Not a bad set-up you've got here, actually, Eleanor." Vivian attempted to break the verbal impasse.

Skylarks hovered in the blue sky, trilling notes reminiscent of childhood summers, lying in the long grass on Beverley Common. A deep rumble came from an ocean-bound ship on the river. Rosie bounced on Vivian's knees, pointing excitedly at the vulture, head bobbing on its scrawny neck, beyond the fence. Netty, the black and white cat, stalked some creature in the uncut grass by the barn. Grey Cat hadn't been seen for a while and Ellie worried that he might have moved out for good.

I should've had him neutered.

The tide was in and you could hear the slosh of water over mud and stones.

"I'm glad you've got employment," Vivian continued. "Mr Riche tells me you're doing a very good job with the business accounts." (*Mr Riche: Ted. At what point had Vivian spoken to him?*) "Funny, maths was never your thing, was it? Anyway, it could have been so much more difficult for you, getting pregnant as young as you did."

As young as you did as well.

Vivian was the same age when Ellie was conceived.

"No. It hasn't worked out too badly at all." Holding Rosie with one hand, Vivian leant forward to pick up a floppy toy the child had dropped on the floor. Then she turned to her younger daughter.

"Now, Deborah, have you told your sister about Sam?"

"Sam?"

Ellie looked at Deb but her sister kept her head down, fiddling with the thin silver ring on her little finger.

"Deborah's getting married, didn't she tell you?"

What?

"What?"

"Getting married in September. Deborah, why haven't you told her?"

The back door of the barn opened and James, the band's singer came out. He stood in the doorway for a few moments, still talking to those inside. Snatches of conversation reached the three women on the benches against the wall of the house and Ellie felt frozen in time, trying to pick out words.

Eventually James closed the barn door and walked towards them.

"Hi, Ellie."

He smiled enquiringly at her mother and sister.

Ellie introduced them and after a few pleasantries he went on his way. The musicians had been in the barn all night.

When James had gone Rosie stopped bouncing and looked from one to the other of her female relatives.

"Deb-deb," she said.

Ellie breathed again.

"She said your name, Deb. Clever girl, Rosie."

Vivian gave Deb a poke between the shoulder blades.

"Sit up straight, Deborah. I can't believe you've been here all this time and not said anything to Ellie about Sam. Have you two been talking at all?"

She handed Rosie over to Ellie so she could stretch her back.

Ellie put Rosie on the ground. The child took a few toddling steps across the grass towards the fence. Looking back at Ellie, she let out a triumphant laugh, but the force of it propelled her backwards. She landed on her bottom with a shocked gasp. Her lower lip protruded, saliva dripping off it.

"Mamma," she wailed.

"Leave her, Ellie," Vivian instructed. "You're alright there, Rosie, aren't you? Now, tell Ellie about Sam, Deborah."

Deb slowly straightened her back.

"Tell her yourself, if you want her to know." She flicked Ellie a miserable look.

"Oh my God, this is worrying." Ellie felt her stomach cramp. "What the hell's going on here? Tell me, Mum, if she won't."

"Deborah is getting married in September," said Vivian with a bright smile. "Next month. The young man in question is called Samuel."

"Sam," Deb said. "His name's Sam Martin."

"Getting married?" said Ellie. "Deb's getting married... what the...? How the hell did this happen? Why didn't I know anything about this?"

"You haven't exactly been a regular at home, Eleanor, that's probably why you didn't know."

"Oh well, that's true for sure. Certainly, I haven't been a regular at home. I wonder why that is? Maybe it's something to do with the fact that my partner's not welcome there."

Not to mention I can't stand the sight of my father, or he of me.

"Now, Eleanor, I was merely pointing out that the reason you hadn't heard Deb's news was because you two haven't had much to do with each other recently. However I did think that with her staying here for two weeks there might have been an opportunity... I was hoping you two could become closer."

Was her mum's voice trembling?

"It's none of your bloody business anyway, Ellie," Deb said. She stood up and backed away. "You always have to make everything about you."

How the hell have we suddenly come back to this? Deb at my throat again just like always.

"Calm down," Vivian said to no-one in particular.

Ellie walked over to the fence where Rosie stood, holding onto the wire.

"Bos-Bos," Rosie said. She pointed to the vulture.

"Yes, Boris," Ellie said listlessly. She picked Rosie up and patted her bottom. "We need to go and change your nappy."

Anything to get away from them.

Rosie struggled in her arms, twisted to face her grandmother.

"Nan-nan?"

Vivian gave her a thin smile. Ellie wondered how much sun cream her mother had to apply to stay so white.

There was something bad going on. Out of the blue Vivian had announced Deb's extremely imminent wedding whilst Deb looked miserable as sin. Not only that, but two weeks earlier, Vivian had begged Ellie in tears to have Deborah at the house to keep her 'out of the way'.

And who the fuck was this Sam?

Try again, Ellie.

"Where did you meet Sam?" she stood a short distance away from Deb, kept her voice neutral, played finger-games with Rosie so Deb wouldn't feel the force of her attention.

Deb moved slightly back towards Ellie. With her chin down she shot Ellie a quick glance and then looked out to the river where the ship was motoring into the open sea.

"At youth club." She raised her chin. "You know; the one you used to go to."

She looked at her mother.

"That's right," Vivian took up the thread. "He's a nice boy, goes to the grammar school, well, he's just finished actually. Just got his A-level results. Deborah; I forgot to tell you. He did very well indeed, according to his mother."

This is insane, thought Ellie. *Two schoolchildren about to get married.* Why hadn't Sam himself told his future wife about his excellent exam results? To Ellie's knowledge Deb hadn't been on the phone to anybody since she came to stay.

"Wow." Ellie put Rosie down again and she toddled uncertainly back to the fence.

"Bos-Bos?"

"Yep, Boris." She followed her, felt the warmth of her daughter's head under her palm.

"So what does he look like, this Sam? The man who's going to marry my sister, what kind of person is he?"

Where are they going to get married? If it's next month, they must have made plans for it already. What do his parents think about it? How are the two of them going to earn a living?

"He's, well... nice," Deb said. "He's got brownish hair. He's friendly, you know?" She was warming up to her theme. "He was really polite to Mum, wasn't he?"

She looked to Vivian for approval.

... Great reason to get married.

"His mother is an old friend of mine," Vivian explained. "I'm sure Deborah will be very happy. They'll be living with Sam's parents at first, until Sam takes up his apprenticeship at an engineering works in Bedford next year. That's right, isn't it Deborah?"

"Yes." Deb gave Ellie a defiant look. "That's right."

Ellie felt like a pawn in Vivian's scheme. Her mother had been determined to keep Deb out of Ray's reach until she could get her away on holiday, then she planned to marry her off straight afterwards.

Ellie felt sick. Her face burned, not from the sun. Suddenly she needed to pick Rosie up again and give her a cuddle, feel their cheeks pressed together. She needed to sense the blood pounding through Rosie's veins, pumped by the small heart that kept her alive.

September 1983

You are invited to the marriage of Deborah Elizabeth Payne and Samuel Kevin Martin. . .

The wedding was at Hull Register Office, everything Ellie thought Vivian wouldn't have wanted for the golden girl.

Rosie was a bridesmaid. In the preceding weeks her sparse hair had thickened and seemed to be getting darker. She wore a pretty, ruffled dress that Vivian bought her and a flower-hairband the colour of her blue eyes.

Deb's dress was very simple. *Nothing like that awful puffball of a gown Princess Diana wore.* Two years on from the royal wedding, Vivian was still recovering from the shock.

Ellie guessed (correctly as it later became apparent) that Deb was pregnant, but it occurred to her (also later) that neither Deb nor Vivian could have known her condition for sure when the wedding was decided on, secretly, back in August.

When she could, she watched her father's face during the ceremony. His expression was clenched. Ellie got a shock when he suddenly turned his gaze on her, and she couldn't breathe.

16

Christmas 1983

Since the summer Ellie's mother seemed less intimidated by the residents at Running Hare House. Maybe it was because Deb had left home. She started visiting once a fortnight or so and got to know Rosie better.

"You and Jonah are both welcome to spend Christmas with us," she told Ellie. "I'm even thinking of inviting Jonah's parents. Deborah and her new family will be there as well, of course."

Of course.

A few days before Christmas, Vivian collected Ellie's grandmother from the care home and brought her over to Pottersea. When they walked in, Vincent was putting the kettle on.

"Can I make you all tea?"

Maud's face lit up.

"Michael," she said. "Michael, I haven't seen you for such a long time."

She took his face between her gnarled old hands.

Vincent stood very still but Ellie could sense him trembling.

"She thinks you're her son," she explained. "He died when he was twenty."

Vivian turned white. Michael was her twin. She took her mother's bony elbow and led her away from Vincent. "Come on, Mum, let's go and sit down."

Ray had been signed off sick from work. "He's been behaving very oddly," Vivian said to Ellie on the phone.

"Like how?"

"Oh, just silly things such as wanting to know what I'm doing every moment of the day. Getting angry more often. But he's usually fine in company."

During drinks and dinner on Christmas day Ray was quiet, so much so that Ellie wondered if her mother had slipped something in his drink.

Deb's pregnancy was announced by Vivian in the late afternoon, shortly before Ellie and Jonah planned to leave. Her mother pinged a teaspoon on a cup.

"Genevieve and I," (Genevieve was Sam's mother) "are thrilled to announce that we are to be grandmothers to Deborah and Samuel's baby. Due in June, I believe. . ."

She gave Deb a sharp look.

"June the fourth," Deb provided her line.

Ellie's stomach took a violent turn. She pressed her hand to her mouth Please don't be sick. Then the thought came: due in April, more like. Even with the sudden arranging, they hadn't been able to get the wedding in soon enough to prevent a premature-seeming birth. But Ellie's nausea was on account of something else.

". . . But I wouldn't be surprised if it comes earlier," Vivian continued. "Both of my babies came early," (only Ellie had, due to her mum already being pregnant when she got married), "and so did my pre-existing granddaughter here, little Rosie" (only by two weeks).

Well, that's all neatly tied up. Deb has got married and is having a baby without a whiff of scandal.

And it looks like my dad has been drugged.

Beverley Minster loomed over them as they drove past it in Ted's car. The towering church was illuminated more brightly than all the lights of Christmas put together.

"Ding-ding!" Rosie crowed.

She crinkled wrapping paper in her fists, probably eating it.

"Well. Our parents seemed to get on all right," Ellie said. She caught Jonah's eye.

Now we're tied more tightly together than ever.

"I'm glad we went." Jonah negotiated the cramped streets around the Minster, mounting the curb more than once. "It's time we accepted we're all family."

That's true. We'll need to.

Her stomach dipped.

The journey back took an hour. Ellie studied Jonah's face as he drove: the tapering nose, the well-pronounced cheekbones, the long, sandy lashes and thick eyebrows. His hair was, as always, drawn back from his face and fastened at the base of his head. He sensed her looking and gave her an annoyed glance.

"Is there something you want to say?"

She could tell him. . . *but no, I don't want to spoil a nice day. Or get him mad while he's driving.*

"Just thinking it was good for us all to spend time together. I'm looking forward to lunch with your parents tomorrow as well, before they drive back to Luton. Maybe we can visit them there this year?"

Jonah took his hand off the wheel and patted her leg.

"Thanks, Ellie, I'd like that."

Arriving back at Running Hare House felt like the real homecoming.

She remembered Christmas the year before when she and Jonah had made love for the first time after Rosie's birth. Since then they'd had several fallow periods followed by a month or two of loving and closeness. The last of these had ended in September, just after Deb's wedding. But it had left her with something as irrevocable as Rosie.

"You take her in," Jonah said, hauling Rosie out of the car. "And can you manage this lot? I'll bring the rest in a minute. I'm just gonna have a quick smoke outside."

Ellie's mind was still elsewhere. She thought back; had she and Jonah been careless and forgotten to use a condom? Or perhaps one they did use was damaged. How was she going to tell him?

There's still time. But she knew she wouldn't do anything about it. *This isn't what you planned for your life, Ellie.*

She didn't know if she'd be allowed to keep living here with a second child; and what would Jonah do if she couldn't? His precious John-Paul and Martin were here.

Greg flitted across her mind, a stab of sweet, painful sorrow.

She carried Rosie into the crowded living room. They were watching a film on TV, the companiable buzz of conversation filled the muggy air. It reminded her of the afternoon she'd carried her newborn in. A cheer rose up when they entered.

Rosie struggled to get down. Wrapped presents were retrieved from behind sofas and given to her. Ellie left her to it.

She hung back by the door, hot in the new coat from her mother.

"We missed our baby girl," Vincent said, appearing at her shoulder. "Not you, Ellie, you twerp. I mean Rosie. Christmas ain't no fun without a little one in the house."

Rosie toddled over to show them a glittery toy, jiggling from one foot to the other while she waited for Vincent to pull a string. Tinkling music erupted and she crowed along tunelessly to the nursery rhyme.

"I didn't see you this morning before you left," Vincent continued. "I missed you."

"This afternoon," Ellie corrected. "We didn't leave until noon. I'd been up for hours."

He picked Rosie up and followed Ellie into the kitchen. Ellie put the kettle on.

"Wanna cup?"

"Go on, then."

He set Rosie on the counter and got mugs for them both from the cupboard.

Through the hatch she surreptitiously searched for Greg. There he was, wedged on the sofa between Hayley and Mike. Ellie couldn't see Bonnie anywhere.

Vincent saw what she was doing.

"She was here with her kids earlier."

"Ma?" said Rosie. "Down."

Vincent put her on the floor. She toddled into the lounge and went in search of Stan.

"So, was she not staying, then, Bonnie?"

"Ellie," Vincent said regretfully. "I don't know why you do this to yourself."

His face grew pinched as he explained. "Bonnie was hoping to stay but there was a veto on all her kids. She'd been planning to leave the two older ones in her room and have the little ones in with her and Greg, but since her room's right next to Ted's in the main house he wasn't keen on having unaccompanied kids up there. So he told her, a flat-out no."

He got the milk out of the fridge. "An old row started up again. She hadn't even informed him she had any kids at all when she first moved here, apparently."

The kettle boiled and clicked off. Ellie poured hot water onto tea bags.

"She had to get her mother to come and pick her and all the kids up," Vincent added. "She was well pissed off. Greg didn't seem that bothered, though."

Ellie was hardly listening, worrying quietly about something else. It took Vincent a moment to notice.

"No need for you to worry, Ellie, you were already quite obviously pregnant when you accepted your place here. Rosie's one of us, we all love her, even kid-phobic Ted."

But he, or for that matter the rest of you, might not love my new baby, thought Ellie.

17

January 1984

"Okay, order everyone," said Ted. "Now just so you all know, my girlfriend, Barbara, is moving in with me next week, so if you see a strange lady wandering about – not that she's much of a lady, ha ha," he beamed round the table. "Although I have to say, she is a bit strange – that's probably who she'll be. I'll introduce her to you all personally so don't worry about it."

He coughed into his curled hand.

There was an uncomfortable silence, furtive, surprised glances from everybody.

Ted jolted suddenly in his chair.

"What?" Looking down, his face melted in relief. "Oh, it's you, Rosie, phew." He flashed a smile over the table at Ellie but it was combined with a small frown.

"Girlfriend... but I thought..." Ellie heard someone mutter. But she couldn't concentrate on what Ted had just said. Her stomach was flipping somersaults. She had to tell everyone today.

Ted looked trapped.

"Alright, Rosie, yes, that's very nice, thank you, but we need to get on with the meeting now." His eyes sought Ellie's again. "Could you. . . er. . . "

Ellie stood up, knocking Rosie's beaker of juice on the floor. "Shit!"

"Don't worry about it," Vincent said, "it's fine. You get Rosie, I'll clean this up." He went into Ted's kitchen for a cloth. Ellie ran around and snatched up Rosie. She slammed her down rather hard on her lap, trembling. Rosie said, "No, no, no!" She shook her head, wagging her finger at Ted. Ellie felt sick.

"You need to sit quietly and behave yourself while the meeting's on," she snapped.

How would she ever manage two children?

Rosie stopped saying no. Her bottom lip trembled.

"Ellie? That's a bit harsh." Jonah stepped into the picture. He opened his arms. "Come to Dadda, Rosie."

"Can we have. . . ?" Ted tried.

"Yeah that's right, let *Dadda* play the hero," Ellie found herself shouting across the table. She thrust her child towards him, then felt guilty and burst into tears.

". . . Order?" Ted finished.

"I'm sorry, Ted."

Ellie sniffed.

Nobody would look at her and it was worse than being stared at. Rosie climbed into Jonah's lap, her small body relaxing against him. Vincent sat down and put his arm round Ellie. Jonah gave Vincent a fierce look.

Ted looked perplexed; one black eyebrow rising up his forehead like a furry caterpillar.

"I have something to say before this starts properly." Ellie found her public speaking voice. "It's important. You all need to know."

"If it *ever* starts," John-Paul muttered.

"What is it, Ellie?"

"Well. . . you may as well sack me now." She pulled a tissue from her jumper sleeve and blew her nose. Silence finally fell around the table.

"Ellie. . . what?" Jonah stopped playing *two little dickybirds* with Rosie. She grabbed his hand back, bending the fingers.

"I'm sorry I haven't told you first," Ellie turned to him. "I really should have. But let's face it; we haven't had much chance to talk."

"You know I've been busy with this new recording," Jonah started. "It's important for my future – for our future. I wish you'd have a bit more sympathy for my side of the story."

"Oh, for goodness' sake, can't you see she's upset?" Vincent shouted. "Think about Ellie, for a change."

"Bloody order!" Ted banged the accounts book with his fist. "Now, for fuck's sake, Ellie, tell us what the problem is?"

"I'm pregnant," Ellie said quickly.

There was a further hush, everybody waiting, holding their breath.

"So that probably means you won't want me here anymore. I know you find Rosie a nuisance as it is."

"Ah now, Ellie, c'mon, don't cry." Greg got up and stood on her other side. He and Vincent shielded her. Giving Jonah a watery glance, she saw him turning almost purple.

"I never said I found Rosie a nuisance." Ted looked hurt. "But God, Ellie, you're pregnant, *again?* Shit."

"Pregnant?" Jonah said. "Pregnant again? How the hell?"

"I think you know how she gets pregnant, Jonah, or didn't you learn that the first time?" Greg gave Ellie a squeeze. He ought to move away, it would only inflame Jonah more.

"Shit, Ellie." That was Ted again.

Jonah's hue had turned to white. His nostrils flared. She felt hope pouring away.

"I know," she mouthed at him.

It feels like the end of the world. I don't want to leave you two. She patted Greg's hand; gave Vincent an apologetic smile. Then faced Ted squarely.

"I'm so sorry, Ted."

"Hell, Ellie. You don't need to apologise to me. But this might pose a problem. Damn. What're we going to do about it?"

Bonnie shot looks like daggers from the far end of the table.

"Kids aren't supposed to be around here," she emphasised. "So you won't be able to stay."

Greg's hand tightened on Ellie's shoulder.

"This is a different situation from yours, Bonnie," Ted pointed out. "We've been through this. Now, let me think. . ."

"I can't believe it," said Jonah. "Shit, man, I can't believe it."

She did feel sorry for him. Rosie had twisted around on his lap, was patting his face.

"Dadda." She took hold of his chin with both hands.

"How is it different?" Bonnie asked aggressively.

"We're not discussing your children right now, Bonnie. Ellie lives here, her child was born here, now the question is whether we can manage the household with another child in it, taking into account Ellie's role in our community. We're gonna have to take a vote on this, folks."

Bonnie exhaled a sibilant breath, intent on making her point.

"To be honest, Ted, I think that is extremely unfair. If Ellie can have her children here, why can't I have mine?"

You left your children behind, Bonnie, never mentioned them until you were settled in.

"For fuck's sake, Bonnie, can we not stick to the matter in hand?"

Ted didn't often get angry. Bonnie sat back in her chair, arms folded tightly.

Greg removed his fingers from Ellie's shoulder. There was a cold space in their wake. He went and sat back in his own chair, chin sunk on his chest, looking at Ellie from under his brows. *His lovely, light-brown brows.*

Everyone was discussing Ellie's latest stupidity.

Rosie let go of her father's chin. She struggled down and stumbled between the chairs to Ellie.

"Mamma?"

Ellie buried her nose in Rosie's hair. This was the only child she wanted.

"You've done good work for us here, Ellie," Ted said at last. "The Children's Musical Choir would never have happened without you. Hmm."

He was visibly at a loss.

"Can I say something?" asked Jen, putting her hand up. She waited patiently for her quiet voice to be heard.

"Go on," said Ted.

"If we're being asked to vote on whether Ellie should stay or not, what I'd like to know is, would Ellie prefer to be in the room or not when we vote. Ellie?"

"I'll stay," Ellie said. "I won't blame anyone whatever they vote. I can understand it if you don't want another baby here."

She plucked up courage to scan the blank faces, take in Jonah's gaze, now black.

She wrung her hands together miserably. *How could I have been so bloody stupid?* She was her mother all over again.

"Don't apologise, Ellie," Ted repeated. "What's done is done. Alright everyone, let's take a vote. All those in favour of Ellie continuing to live here with us and carrying on in her role as administrator and crèche supervisor whilst being the mother of two children," he took in a breath, "raise your hands now."

Spring 1984

Bonnie was the only one who voted negatively. John-Paul took a while to raise his hand but he must have realised that if he voted to have Ellie leave it would affect his relationship with Jonah.

Mike voted yes for Ellie to stay, but made it clear it was with the proviso that she kept her children under control; and in her own room at night. Ellie agreed and promised to make sure her children (*children*, telling the rest of the housemates had made it real), kept 'to a proper bedtime'. It would probably mean she spent every evening in her own room, but it was worth it to be able to stay.

"Now, are you sure you're going to have enough space for another baby, Ellie?" Ted spoke with her privately after the meeting. "I can't offer you an extra room, you know that really wouldn't be fair."

"No, no, of course not," Ellie said. "I – we'll – be absolutely fine in my room. Babies don't take up much space."

When the baby was born Rosie could move onto the mattress that slid underneath Ellie's bed during the day. She was trying not to think too far ahead. Jonah was always promising a record deal was around the next corner – maybe they'd be able to afford to rent a cottage in the village soon. She could continue to work on the project while Jonah took off to London or wherever he felt he needed to go. Relations were, unsurprisingly, strained between them again.

———————

Although it was a warm spring, Ellie often felt cold. She avoided watching the evening news and the hot, blue sky made her nervous. The world outside her own contained sphere also seemed to be in turmoil. She had dreams about falling planes.

She got herself booked in at the maternity hospital, an easy bus ride from Pottersea.

"Nice to see you again: and so soon," the booking-in midwife (it was Jane) said with sarcastic emphasis. "And just look at this little madam, isn't she growing up?"

What's a girl like you doing getting yourself into trouble again?

Ellie went to visit Maria at the house she shared with two other students. The best friends had grown apart now their lives had diverged.

Maria was dressed in neon colours. She wore a pink headband and legwarmers. Her dark hair was fluffed and teased beyond belief. Ellie felt middle-aged in comparison.

"I can't believe you're doing this again, Ellie." Maria went pale under what looked like stage make-up. "What are you, twenty? You know what they say, one mistake can be forgiven; two is utter carelessness!"

Who says that? But it didn't matter, it was true anyway.

"I don't know how it happened..."

But that was plain stupid. Having sex with Jonah was how. Maybe she should get sterilized after the second baby was born.

"That effing Jonah," Maria muttered, but not quietly enough. "Couldn't you have, you know, uhm, got rid of it this time? Rosie's lovely but, did you really want to tie yourself down so young?"

Maria was just finishing her third year as a university student. She had no idea how it felt to be a mother. Her initial enthusiasm for Rosie had lessened considerably as the months went by. "It's not like on the soap operas, when you hardly ever see the baby, is it?" she once complained to Ellie. Every time they got a conversation going, Rosie interrupted it.

Ellie was trying hard to believe the new baby was coming for a reason, but she couldn't work out what it was.

"It'll be nice for Rosie to have a little brother or sister though, won't it?"

"Well, I suppose there is that," Maria said after a long pause. "But it has to stop there, Ellie. You have your own life to lead."

———

Deb and Sam lived in a semi-detached house on a brand new estate in Bedford, paid for by both sets of parents. Ellie swallowed her resentment: who wanted to be a Stepford Wife anyway? Sam was training to be an engineer at a nearby factory and Deb was now the mother of a baby girl named Florence, born in April. Ellie'd been right that Deb was two months pregnant at the time of her wedding. But she was still confused as to how Vivian could have known when planning the wedding at least a month before.

"Do you think she looks alright?"

Ellie was visiting the new family. She'd travelled to Bedford by bus and train and had left Rosie behind with Jonah. Though it was several weeks after the birth, Deb reclined on a couch in her darkened bedroom, a quilt tucked around her. A black and white film played on a small TV in the corner, the light flickering over Deb's face.

"You know; normal and everything? The nurse said she was fine. But she hasn't had her six-week check-up yet."

She retrieved the baby from an excessively-flounced Moses basket and handed her to her heavily pregnant sister.

"You can give her a bottle if you want."

Ellie moved the curtain aside and stared into the baby's unfathomable eyes.

"She looks absolutely beautiful to me." She smiled at her sister. "Well done. Are you sure you're alright? Are you happy?"

"Yes of course." Deb had the familiar snap back in her voice, a fallen branch breaking underfoot. But her blue eyes had a flat look.

Sam came in from work. He made a show of smiling and exclaiming greetings, but there was something mechanical about it all. The sparkle switched off when he turned away. She felt sad for the heartbreakingly young couple thrust into a lifestyle more suited to a pair in their thirties. She was glad that she still thought of her own life as free.

18

May 1984

She was having regular bad dreams. In them, the perfection of a blue sky was scarred by a white rocket. Then a mushroom cloud would blossom into the atmosphere. The world was a scary place, and she was stupid enough to be bringing children into it.

Hayley's mum had always shown an interest in Rosie. She'd been a midwife 'back home'. She told Ellie she'd like to be involved in the delivery of her second baby.

"You could have him here, at Running Hare House," she suggested.

"Don't be ridiculous." Jonah almost choked when Ellie told him her plan. "It's probably not even legal."

"Of course it's legal." *Be patient with him, Ellie.* "But I'd have to change my booking to a home birth. Constantine would help the community midwives deliver the baby. Help me, really, she's my doula. It's what I want to do, I've decided."

"What the hell's a doula?"

"The person who is there for the woman giving birth." They exchanged a meaningful glance. "An experienced mother," Ellie clarified. She'd only just heard of the word herself.

"I've never been good enough for you, have I?"

"It isn't like that."

But Jonah said he'd have nothing to do with the birth if it took place at Running Hare House. "I'm washing my hands of it."

Like it mattered.

Three days after this outburst, Jonah appeared at her door looking all scrubbed up. He knocked first and then waited.

They'd barely spoken since she told him her birth plans.

When she invited him in, he said, "I think we should get married."

"What?"

She moved back into the room and switched the radio off. The talk about the miners' strike made for miserable listening anyway.

Panic blossomed in her chest, surely not the correct reaction when the father of your two kids asks you to marry him. Well, states that you should.

It was hot. She wore a voluminous sleeveless cotton dress and fanned herself with a knitting pattern.

"C'mon, Ellie, we've been circling around each other these past couple of years; we're going to have two children together now. Let's make it legal – make a proper commitment. Please, I want to."

Ellie just stared at him.

Why, suddenly?

She felt her way over to the bed, the baby's heel poking her right side so sharply that it might break through. You could see it through the thin cotton. She leaned back, bracing herself, her hands sinking into the mattress.

Jonah sat a distance from her, fingering the bedspread, his face twisted into a slideshow of expressions. She saw him as vulnerable for the first time in ages. If only John-Paul wasn't around, she found herself thinking. Maybe they could have made a go of it without him always there. He was a constant thorn in her side, like this baby's foot. She pushed at the miniature heel and it receded, she imagined the foetus tucking its limbs back against its body. Jonah was right. They were unavoidably committed to each other by shared parenthood, unplanned as it was. She shouldn't have slept with him if she hadn't meant to strengthen that commitment.

A shadow flitted at the corners of her mind, Greg-shaped... Another time, another place. Another life, more like.

She looked down to hide the brimming tears.

Since Bonnie was spending more time in Hull – there was even talk of her getting a small house so she could have her children back (she wanted Greg to move in with her but Vincent said he had no intention of doing so), Ellie and Greg were close again. The pregnancy made it safe; Ellie was now out of bounds sexually.

Not that they'd ever...

...If things had been different...

"Wow. Married... it's a big step, Jonah."

He smelt clean. He was wearing a crisp shirt; dark blue jeans. She touched his cheek, freshly washed and shaved. He'd fastened his hair neatly back.

Husband. She let her hand drop again.

He looked defeated.

He'd made an effort to do this thing; left John-Paul and his instruments behind, for her, but...

Would she have even been with him if not for the children? Definitely not. But there were the children to think of. *What do I do?*

Her back ached.

"Sorry, I need to walk around a bit."

She stretched and got up clumsily, went over to the line of open windows, hoped for some hint of a breeze, for inspiration. The scent of roses and the salty tang of the mudflats hung in the air. Stan sprawled in the shade by the barn wall across the yard, guarding Rosie who was asleep in her pushchair.

Ellie dug her toe into the whorls of red carpet.

The mattress creaked beneath Jonah as he pushed himself off it.

He came up behind her, his breath on her neck, and she felt a jolt of lust.

When I close my eyes, I remember the way he used to make me feel. It could be like that again, if I concentrate. Our bodies can still do the same things.

She wasn't sure about their minds.

But there was no escape, they were already irrevocably connected.

Turning slightly, she let her face move closer to his, allowed the magnetic pull of his eyes, utterly focussed on her, to draw her in. She didn't know where his newfound desire had come from but it felt erotic when he touched her like this. He fitted his hands around her belly, making her womb contract to the point of pain, leaving a lingering ache.

They kissed.

"A baby: that's what the big step is, Ellie, and we've already made it. It was you talking about the birth that made me realise. I don't know why it took me so long." He caught his breath. "I'm sorry I've been so distracted by the things *I* wanted to do."

All words, but they'll have to do. Then another electric jolt fired through her as he moved his hands lower down her huge belly.

"Rosie, well – she's the most amazing thing. . . I can't imagine life without her now."

His breath shortened. She was wet between her legs, was it this easy?

"And now we're going to have another baby. We need to be married, Ellie, I want to make that commitment to you. Rosie needs it too."

I wonder if his dad has offered him money. . .

The faintest tickle of his lips on her neck. . . Shit, no. Yes. She leaned onto his fingers, the solid mass of her straining against him. Her hands had found their way to his crotch. She had an orgasm, immediate and sudden. Almost at the same time, Jonah shuddered and let out a groan. They stood back from each other, red-faced. Her womb throbbed and the baby kicked.

Breathing heavily, Jonah pulled something out of his pocket, a small velvet box. He popped it open to reveal a ring and all she could think about was the smell of her on his fingers.

Ellie stared at the ring. An understated emerald sat between two diamonds on a gold band.

"Where did you. . . ?"

"I mentioned this to my dad on the phone." Jonah cleared his throat. *So it was to do with his dad.* "He insisted on sending me this ring. It was his sister's, you know, the one who practically brought him up. He said he'd always intended to give it to Rosie anyway but this way she can inherit it from you. I hope you don't mind that I haven't bought it myself."

Ellie allowed the ring to fall into her cupped hands.

"Put it on," said Jonah.

———

Ellie felt sorry for her mother.

"You could get married in a church," she kept saying. "If you waited until you've had the baby."

Unthinkable that you could walk down an aisle hugely pregnant. Ellie didn't think she could have made herself go through with a fancy church affair anyway, but it didn't seem so wrong, despite her emotional misgivings, to have a simple register office ceremony. It was just a legal thing for the sake of the children.

"I'm sorry, Mum, I can't. Jonah's already booked the register office."

Rosie, still aged under two, was a bridesmaid for the second time in her life. Ellie had to let out the dress her daughter had worn for Deb's wedding. Vivian bought a similar dress in a tiny size for baby Florence. Ellie wore a loose pale grey shift with a ruffle around the hem. Leopold took Jonah shopping for a new suit.

It was family only at the register office, then a party in a pub a short walk away, to which the Running Hare housemates were invited. Ray refused to attend, disgusted by Ellie's condition.

I like you so much better when Dad's not around. Ellie smiled as she watched her mother dancing to *Wham!* with Jonah's Uncle Gerald.

Deb and Sam left after half an hour.

"She's not been feeling well – baby wears her out," Sam apologised.

Deb allowed Ellie to brush her cheek with the briefest of kisses, but she didn't offer one in return.

"Welcome to the family, dear." Jonah's mum gave Ellie a hug before she and Leopold got into the car to drive back to Luton. "Please take this cheque, buy something for my new grandchild. I'll see you all after the birth, can't wait!"

19

June 1984

Rosie was sleeping in Jonah's room for the first time. He'd moved his recording equipment into Martin's room, necessitating a tidy-up for both of them. Ellie made him swear he'd got rid of all traces of smoking equipment, of any kind.

They spent days preparing Rosie for the imminent birth. Jonah stayed in his room with her on the actual night, only leaving when one of the midwives popped her head around his door to tell him if he wanted to catch the birth he'd better get a move on.

Immediately after the baby was born they heard a cry from Jonah's room. Rosie had woken up in sync with her brother's emergence. She insisted on seeing Ellie and the new baby straight away. Jonah carried her in and she stared at her new brother for a long time, then leant forward to give him a kiss.

Apart from all the other discomforts, Ellie had an ache in her chest: Rosie looked so big now. Soon the toddler requested to be taken back to bed.

"Dadda stay with me."

"You'd better," Ellie advised. "She might wake up frightened later, when it all sinks in."

She now had two children.

Two.

She was relieved the disaster dreams that had plagued her hadn't come true. Her son was out of her body, safe and well. *My son.*

A steady stream of visitors came in. Vincent and Greg arrived together.

"Would ya look at that?" Greg's hand shook when he touched the baby's head. He tried to laugh it off. "I gotta say I admire you, Ellie, putting yourself through that. I could hear your screams in my room even with Janis Joplin on top volume. It was horrible."

"I was screaming to try and drown out your bloody music," Ellie shot back. "That's all. It was distracting me."

"Ah, well sorry then." Greg looked chastened. "Didn't mean to distract you from your work there. . ."

"Only joking," said Ellie. "Hold the baby, please. Pass him on, Vincent."

Greg took the warm bundle that Ellie couldn't stop feasting her eyes on.

"But my, he's a bonny chap though, isn't he?" Greg seemed surprised. "I can't believe you've gone and had another one, Ellie."

Ellie winced at the word bonny. Then she and Vincent exchanged a look. She could tell he was struggling not to laugh. Ellie winced again as the massive pad she wore between her legs nudged the sore bits.

"Where is she, anyway, Bonnie?"

"Not here," Greg said shortly. "Let's not talk about her, eh?"

Ted came in with his girlfriend, Barbara. She'd turned out to be an interesting woman, a puzzling match for Ted, tall and Transylvanian-looking as he was. Barbara was short, middle-aged-seeming, hair in a perm. She wore matronly dresses. But Ellie liked her. She gave Ellie some indulgent bath products.

"Nobody ever thinks about the mother, it's always *baby, baby, baby,*" she commented.

"Good God, it's tiny," was Ted's reaction. "I feel like a grandfather all of a sudden." Ellie was touched.

"Why Kester?" asked Barbara. "Unusual name…"

"It's to do with *Bird World,*" Ellie explained. "We thought about Kestrel but it seemed a bit fey. Rosie's favourite bird is the vulture but that didn't seem appropriate either."

"Well, I think it's lovely."

"Placid little thing, isn't he?" Ted remarked. He made a funny face at the baby.

20

October 1984

Kester was *one of the family* from the very beginning. Nobody could compare having him in the house to Bonnie wanting her children there: Kester was a Running Hare baby. He was, as Ted had pointed out, a placid little chap, anyone could take him off to their room. Ellie's only rule was no smoking around him and it seemed that since his birth, people were taking their smokes outside more.

Whereas Rosie had been attached to Ellie all the time, Kester was apart from her for hours. He was returned to her to be fed and then somebody would whisk him away again.

"The Hot-House baby," Ted called him. Kester was present at various music, sculpture and painting workshops from a few days after birth. "I fully expect him to manifest as a child genius."

Visitors loved him.

Ellie got back to work straight away, anxious to reassure everyone they'd made the right decision in voting for her to stay.

There was a charity that offered funding to site-specific historical projects. Ellie decided to look into the history of Pottersea. She started by posting a request for information on the village noticeboard. Following that, several pensioners called at the house for tea and a chat, and a cuddle with the new baby. Word spread. There were families that had lived in Pottersea for generations, and Ellie was able to build up a folder of word-of-mouth accounts of the past.

The work was energising and rewarding; she was capturing history. The one year she'd completed of her degree was coming in useful after all.

A few weeks after the birth, Ellie was ready to attempt the mammoth task of research in a public library whilst in charge of a small baby again. At least she knew what to expect this time. And also, most of the bus drivers and regular passengers knew her by now, she got help to get the carrycot and transporter on and off the bus, and unfold it at the other end.

Ellie did this several days in a row.

"It's nice to get you to myself," she whispered to her son the first time she settled into the bus seat with him. She'd left Rosie in the Running Hare créche with Helena.

At the reference library, Kester dozed peacefully in the pram beside his mother (he wasn't the screamer Rosie sometimes had been).

Ellie sat with a tower of books at her elbow, investigating the lost Holderness villages, now fallen into the sea. The original Pottersea had been one of these.

At night she dreamt of a church tumbling over the cliff, bones from the graveyard exposed on the beach below, families running for safety as the walls of their houses crumbled. Somehow in her dreams the disorientated families she saw became confused with those she kept seeing on the news. The violence and disarray of the miners' strike was still going on.

After a brief honeymoon period following their wedding, she and Jonah were sleeping apart again.

Kipple built up again in Jonah's room. But Rosie still sometimes slept in there. It was now at least a smoke-free zone and the band's late evening sessions had moved permanently into Martin's room.

Ellie put together her most ambitious financial proposal yet. She was seeking funding for a year-long series of cross-media workshops involving children and pensioners from Holderness schools and residential homes. They would work together on a historical memory project, the children collecting stories from the older people and interpreting them with the help of a writer. The project would culminate in an exhibition and musical showcase at the end of the series.

Ellie was invited to talk about it on *Viking Radio*. A producer in an adjoining studio looked after the baby while she was fitted up with headphones and settled in front of a microphone. She had to answer listeners' questions live on air. When she got on the bus to go home she was treated like a celebrity by locals who knew her.

November 1984

Kester was five months old; plump and healthy. He hardly ever cried.

I'm so lucky, Ellie thought regularly. She couldn't get the images of those helpless mothers with starving babies on that Band Aid video out of her head. *If my children had been born in another part of the world. . .*

Things were falling into place; she'd worried so much about not being able to carry on working as the mother of two children but it helped living on site. In the mornings, after giving Kester his early feed, she watched the young woman across the road packing her children into her car.

Imagine having to drag your children out of bed at six-thirty, drop them off at a nursery; be apart from them all day. It was bad enough that her housemates were always taking Kester off for a walk. She missed him, but at least he was brought back to her for feeding. Rosie spent half of each day in the Running Hare créche, now staffed by Helena and another young woman named Catherine.

Ellie had been well since the birth.

"You've always got roses in your cheeks; must be the sea air," Mrs Everington, one of the regular contributors to the Project remarked as she sipped her tea in the annex lounge. "Not like some of these pasty-faced young girls you see today."

She gave Ellie's stomach a pat. (Ellie squirmed). Mrs Everington took another piece of Barbara's lemon drizzle cake. "Got plenty of healthy baby-weight left as well, haven't you, lass? We didn't waste time trying to lose it in my day either." Crumbs fell out of the corner of her mouth. "A woman's supposed to be rounded like that."

Ellie felt like crying. Mrs Everington wasn't known for her tact but her bluntness rang an alarm bell in Ellie's sharpened senses.

God, no.

"Excuse me." Perspiration prickled on her forehead. *I'm going to be sick.* "I'll be back in a minute, Mrs E. Would you watch the baby for me, please?" Kester was spending a rare afternoon with his mother instead of being kidnapped, as usual.

———

"You've been overdoing it, haven't you?" Vincent caught her en route to the toilets on another occasion. "You don't have to prove anything to anybody, you know. We all know your worth. Come on."

She'd come out sweating and trembling. "Come and have a sit down in the lounge. Where's that baby of yours, shall I go and fetch him for you?"

"Hayley's got him," Ellie said shakily. "Haven't seen him for ages, he must be ready for a feed by now." Her breasts tingled. Sometimes his birth felt like a dream and she was afraid she might wake up and find he didn't exist.

"I *would* like you to find Kester for me. I really miss him," she said when Vincent brought her a cup of tea. Unexpectedly, tears gushed out.

"I thought you were doing a bit too well. But you're not a superwoman after all," Vincent seemed relieved. "Wait there, don't move a muscle, take the opportunity to have a nap. I'll go and find the babba."

21

February 1985

In the new year, the results of the Site History Grant Awards were announced. Running Hare House was delighted to be told they'd received the full amount of Ellie's bid.

"I don't know what we'd have done without you, Ellie," Ted toasted her at the celebration party. Representatives from Holderness council and the local schools and residential homes were there.

"What an adorable baby," a blue-rinsed woman who'd come in lieu of the mayor praised Kester, struggling in Ellie's arms. He was under the false impression he could walk already. "And the little girl over there, she's yours as well, Ted tells me."

"She is." Rosie was two and a bit. She wasn't backward in coming forward, as Grandma Maud used to say. Ellie missed her grandma. She still hadn't got over the shock of her death in the nursing home, just before Christmas.

Rosie walked around the annex lounge holding precocious conversations with anybody who'd listen, offering crisps from a wooden bowl.

"Well, congratulations on your lovely children and your fantastic work on the Project, my dear." The woman's eyes flickered over Ellie's body. Ellie instinctively hunched over herself, repositioning Kester like a shield. She hadn't managed to lose the baby-weight at all.

"I don't know how you manage it all."

Before the end of the party, Ellie was so exhausted she took Kester into her room and lay down with him. He was fair, his hair much thicker than Rosie's had been. He had blue eyes and fat cheeks and was cheerful all the time. She gave him a quick feed and then asked him to lie quietly with her. She watched his eyelids dropping, fluttering open; dropping again over his glazed eyes until he couldn't resist the pull of sleep. She tightened her arms around him, fearing he would slip away.

Early April 1985

No. No, no, no. No, no. Please, no.

Iamsuchastupidbitch. . .

It can't be true.

It is.

Face it, Ellie.

The first few times, she managed to convince herself it was wind, or her insides continuing to reorganise themselves after Kester's birth. It's bound to take longer to feel normal the second time.

The lack of menstruation she'd put down to breastfeeding, it was supposed to be contraceptive as well. But she couldn't deny the reality of the heaving movement that pushed up under her hand; the small knobbly shape skittering from one side of her belly to the other. It returned the pressure when she pushed on it. She prayed for it to go away. She checked the toilet every time for blood, but there was none.

The increasingly strong practice contractions of her womb: she couldn't deny them either.

She refused to think about what was living inside her, that squatter: that parasite.

Bad dreams of riots in the cities; starving millions; nuclear disasters, everything awful plagued her sleep. Kester slept in bed with her. She woke sobbing in the night, cuddled him so tightly he struggled and cried to be released. My baby. She wanted no other.

Everybody noticed her changing shape, even Rosie.

"Mamma fatty," Rosie giggled. "Fat belly, Mamma?"

Jonah glanced at her, "What the hell have you been eating, Ellie? Don't mean to be rude, but maybe you need more exercise. I can look after the kids for a bit if you want to start running or something?"

Vincent took her aside. "Are you sure everything's alright, Ellie? You look different."

Ellie spent less and less time in the communal lounge, and she stopped eating her meals with Vincent.

If she ever passed Greg in the hall there was just a look, nothing more.

Bonnie had moved out at the end of February, to a small terraced house on a large estate on the outskirts of Hull. A social worker was helping her regain custody of her children.

"I could have wept when I saw the house she's got, Ellie," Greg was insensitive enough to tell her. He'd managed to catch her in the kitchen one evening when she thought no-one was around. "You should have seen the house she used to live in with her husband."

She shouldn't have left it then.

Ellie had her own problems. She was being subsumed by a thick depression. She dug around until she found a voice.

"What about you, are you moving in with her then?"

Greg looked downcast.

"No, I've broken it off with her. But I do feel bad though. She only left her husband because of me."

"Sorry." Ellie made herself look him in the face. "It must be a sad time for you."

But why should I care?

Greg put on the expression he was always giving her lately – I know something's wrong, I can even guess what it is, but I need you to be the one to say it.

It was amazing that Jonah hadn't understood what was going on. Maybe like her, he was blocking the reality out, or maybe it was because he never really looked at her anymore. The Travelling Man now had a new (female, long blonde hair and figure like a whippet; Stevie Nicks style of dress) singer named Kristy. They had a busy schedule of gigs lined up in Hull, Beverley, Driffield and York. They'd also got a regular slot at a pub in a nearby village so Jonah wasn't around much in the evenings, and in the daytime the band was busy practising. Ellie was lucky if she even got a sideways glance from her husband.

"I'm doing it for you and the children, it won't be long until we get a record deal now," he'd be bound to say if she bothered to challenge him about his lack of involvement with his family.

She tried not to let her depression affect the children, but Rosie was careful around her, which was heartbreaking.

———

The Site History project was underway. The name 'Pottersea under the Sea' was voted in by participants. Minibuses brought schoolchildren and elderly adults to the house three days a week for workshops.

One morning each week Ellie oversaw a meeting with the Running Hare practitioners to make sure they were maintaining the links between all the different workshops.

She felt exhausted, and totally lost, but was afraid of letting anybody know.

Anyway, years of living with her father had taught her to keep her feelings hidden.

The Hull Daily Mail printed a feature about Pottersea under the Sea. Ellie was able to negotiate a deal with the City Council for some extra workshops to take place in five local libraries. Jen led them. She took groups of children exploring in the libraries' local environments and together they produced land art on the edges of car parks and street corners.

A reporter set up a temporary office in Ted's dining room. In there he interviewed Holderness residents whose families had lived in the area for generations. Ellie sat in on the interviews, fascinated by their handed-down stories of villages collapsing into the sea. Some brought photographs from the Victorian era; or artefacts known to have been rescued from fallen homes. Ellie arranged for a selection to be put on display in the library van that travelled round the villages.

"When you young people first moved in here, I've got to admit my husband and me were concerned," a close neighbour confided to Ellie. "You know, what with you all having long hair and them dreadlock things." She cackled as Ellie helped her on with her coat, despite the warm weather and the short walk back to her own house. "Not to mention half of you being unmarried mothers. But you've done a good thing, really brought life to the area."

She paused to light a battered cigarette that she pulled from her pocket. Ellie moved her face to avoid the billow of smoke. "Well done, love," the old dear continued. "It's been great, reliving them stories that my great-aunt Ida used to tell me when I was a young girl."

22

Greg

Late April 1985

Greg was in the workshop when he saw Ellie coming back from a walk with the kids. Her gait was lumbering and she hardly seemed to notice little Rosie, trotting beside her, tugging at her skirt. Ellie was pushing Kester in the pushchair. The little lad was waving his arms around, looked like he might be singing.

If he was going to be honest with himself, Ellie'd let herself go a bit lately. She always seemed to be dressed in too many layers for the time of year, wore her hair scraped back from her face when it used to look so pretty hanging down.

He had a horrible feeling he knew what was wrong with her, (he did know what was wrong) but he didn't want to let the thought form properly, even in the privacy of his own head. Once it was out, it'd never go back.

When Ellie closed the yard gate behind her, Barbara came out of the main house. Greg saw the inspection she gave Ellie, a sweeping glance from top to toe. Ellie seemed to be facing her out, she had that brazen expression on her face that reminded him of a kid. It tugged at his heart to see it, poor love. Greg leaned closer to the open window. He saw Barbara step back and heard her ask if the younger woman was all right. She wasn't getting much response from Ellie. He heard Barbara offer to look after Ellie's children so she could take full part in the spring meeting.

He was a bit late getting in to the meeting because of that teacher from the primary school, Miss Fairfax, (call me Donna!). She always wanted to stay behind and chat after a workshop, even though the group of ten-year-olds she brought with her were desperate to go for their promised playtime on the beach.

When he reached the dining room his eyes searched for Ellie straight away. She sat between Hayley and Martin, hunched forward, arms crossed over her front.

She'd taken the bands out of her reddish hair (hennaed, he'd seen the packets in the bathroom bin), and it lay on her shoulders and her fringe was almost in her eyes. She wore a different loose cotton dress than the one she'd been wearing on her walk, with a thick cardigan, she must have been hot. When she moved her arms to shift her chair for Mike to get past, Greg had to admit her belly was undeniably large. He was amazed no-one had mentioned it. Maybe, like him, the others didn't want to bring things as they were to an end.

Ah, fuck, she'll never be able to stay on at the house now, not with yet another kid.

Why do you keep doing it, Ellie?

Before the meeting officially started, bits of conversations conjoined to make a buzz like a swarm of bees.

"What about that little blonde girl who wrote the story down for that lady – what was her name? Oh, you know, the one with the. . ."

"Elsie. You mean the one with the crazy walking stick, carved like a totem pole. . ."

"Yeah, that little girl who wrote her story. . ."

"Melanie. The girl's name is Melanie."

"Oh yeah, that's right. She's the funniest little thing, isn't she?"

"Greg," said Jen, giving him a poke in the ribs. "Did you know that great big boy from School's Out broke the circular saw this morning?"

Greg tried to blink off a feeling of unreality.

"Which boy?"

"You know, the big-built one, okay, the fat one. He's really fat."

"Oh yeah," Hayley piped in. "I know which one you mean. . . He is big.

I'm a bit scared of him."

"Me too," said Jen. "Quite aggressive if he doesn't get what he wants."

"Paul, his name is," said Greg. "Arsing around as usual, I expect."

Greg didn't want to be distracted from Ellie.

"I'm going to have to re-think tomorrow's workshop now," Jen tutted. "Well, every workshop until we can get it fixed."

There was laughter, the crumpling of crisp packets, the popping sound of a plastic bottle withdrawn from sucking lips.

Ted came in and sat down.

"Order."

When quiet finally settled over the group, Ted asked who was taking the minutes.

"I will," Jen offered.

"Thanks, Jen." Ted gave her a rare warm smile. He shuffled his papers on the table; seemed out of sorts. "OK, well. . . "

Ellie put her hand up.

No. Greg felt a tightening in his guts. He glanced at Ted.

"What is it?" Ted asked slowly. Greg knew that expression, the meaning of Ted's knitted-together eyebrows. The boss was finally picking up on the sense of doom in the air. Ted peered at Ellie over his reading glasses. When Ellie still didn't speak, he removed the spectacles and laid his pen on the pile of papers.

"I'm so sorry about this." Ellie's voice shook. She grasped one of her hands with the other on the table in front of her.

Greg's stomach tightened even more. "I just need a moment with Jonah outside," Ellie continued. "It'll just take a minute."

Greg dug his (admittedly blunt) fingernails into his palms. Don't let her go.

"Please," Ellie glanced miserably round the table. "Just do the first item on the list without us; I don't want to hold things up."

"Thank God for that," someone muttered, probably that selfish fuck John-Paul.

He watched her get awkwardly out from behind the table. As she moved, she overbalanced slightly. Hayley put a hand out to steady her, and Greg heard Hayley's gasp. She was looking directly at the expanding mound of Ellie's front. He saw Ellie's tear-filled eyes meet Hayley's. The moment hung, unresolved, until Ellie nodded dejectedly. Greg could've wept.

"Ellie?"

Jonah was in the act of pouring himself a glass of water from the jug in the centre of the table. He looked disgruntled at being disturbed from his cosy chat with John-Paul. Pity his love-affair with his best mate hadn't stopped him from fucking up Ellie's life, from fucking Ellie, in fact.

"Couldn't this wait?" the pig whined.

"No," Ellie snapped.

You tell him, girl. He wished she'd told him to lay off her before this happened again. Jonah's dick shouldn't be let out of his trousers.

Greg's hands itched to strangle him.

Muttering, Jonah followed Ellie out through Ted's back door into the yard where Greg could just see them at the picnic table. Ellie was standing, hands in the hollow of her back. It broke his heart, the undeniable bump of her latest pregnancy thrust forward like that. All of them who'd previously purported not to have cottoned on, including him, could no longer kid themselves, it was bloody obvious.

Out there, Jonah looked at the ground, perched on the edge of the table. His knee was jiggling.

"Right you are," Ted said to the room. He sounded subdued and he kept his chin down. "Look to it, everybody... Item one on the agenda: Housekeeping Matters. I know several of you have got a point you wish to make; who wants to start?"

Greg wasn't listening to the diatribe about unravelled toilet rolls from Mike. Instead he heard an imaginary conversation in his head, the one Ellie and Jonah would be having...

I'm pregnant, Jonah.

You can't be; how did that happen?

How the fuck do you think, you prat? (She might not have said that, but he would, or worse).

Well, it's not my fault, (that was typical Jonah dialogue). You never have any sympathy for what I want. (Well whose fault is it, then?)

"Look, I'll get you a drink of water. I'll come straight back out, I promise. Stay right where you are."

That was Jonah in actuality, coming back into the house. Greg fought the urge to go in the kitchen and thump him. He obviously hadn't allowed Ellie to speak.

Hair stuck to the back of Greg's neck. He met Hayley's eyes over Jen's soft, fair head, bent forward over a list she was reading out. He couldn't concentrate on what was being said. Hayley knew that he knew about Ellie's pregnancy, it was clear from her panicked look. She shook her head sadly. There was a deep ache in Greg's chest and he thought he might pass out, kind of wished he could.

Why did Ellie have sex with Jonah? It was lethal for her. Surely her poor body couldn't cope with the constant reproduction?

She was getting more and more trapped in Jonah's web.

Maybe he'd still hoped... especially since he'd broken it off with Bonnie. But now Ellie would have almost the same amount of children as Bonnie. And she was married to Jonah. Married. Dear God.

He turned his head back to the open window. Ellie was sitting on the bench now, sipping from the glass of water Jonah had carried out. Jonah stood above her, in front of the opposite bench. Greg saw Ellie look up and speak. Jonah sprang back, scrambling to get his legs over the bench backwards, his long shadow snaking forward over the table.

"What the. . . ?" he yelled, loud enough for everyone to hear.

How couldn't he have seen it?

The meeting suspended itself and everybody craned their necks to listen. Ted didn't call for order; nobody protested that they had to get on. An ending was happening and they needed to bear witness to Ellie's shame.

"How the. . . ? Why didn't you tell me?" Jonah plunged his head into his hands. "Not again, this can't be happening."

"Why didn't you tell me?" Ellie screamed back. "I want nothing to do with this."

If she'd been a man she would've had that choice, wouldn't she? Stan scrambled out from under the table. The dog pushed between the chairs and moved to the window, shoved his nose out into the warm air.

"I didn't want it; I didn't choose to put it there." Ellie'd gone crazy and no wonder. Dealing with that idiot.

"This is so typical of you, you blame me for everything," she screamed. "I'm going to be the one to be punished, not you."

She started crying, hard enough to die. Greg's heart palpitated. He wished he could go to her, but what good would it do?

Jonah's hands came away from his head and the right one curled into a fist and banged the table. Ellie stumbled back, sobs almost choking her.

The room was deathly quiet. Then chairs started scraping on the wooden floor and one by one the residents joined the dog at the window. Greg was the first.

"What do you mean, you'll be punished?"

Greg strained to hear as Jonah's voice dropped several decibels.

From the marshes a flock of silver-backed seabirds rose in a grey cloud. Boris the vulture made a raspy, grunting noise beyond the fence.

They were all pouring outside now, drifting towards Ellie and Jonah in a steady stream. She must have felt like she was going to be escorted to the scaffold. Greg held back, watching the others go down.

Vincent was the first to reach her.

"We couldn't help overhearing," Greg heard him say. "Not as if I hadn't already guessed, and a few other people too, I expect."

Greg noticed Ted recoil. The dope had only just realised. The big man hopped about like a giant crow, wings of silver-and-black hair flapping, his shoulders hunched in a black t-shirt. The folder he was holding slipped to the ground.

"Ellie... you mean?"

His long hands gestured in the air.

"It was bound to come out in the wash, honey." Vincent pulled Ellie gently towards him, ignoring Jonah.

"Why is this happening to me? I don't want it, Vincent... but it's too late. I wouldn't let myself believe it until recently. What am I going to do?" Ellie was sobbing and choking in Vincent's arms.

Jonah stood apart. Greg almost felt sorry for the bugger, he looked utterly defeated. After a minute John-Paul came out the door of the other house. He went over to Jonah and handed him a smoke.

"I don't know, babe." Vincent patted Ellie's back. "I don't know."

A Genesis lyric about chances slipping away, that he'd often heard Ellie playing, went through Greg's head.

He strode over to Vincent and Ellie, patted Ellie's arm. She gave him a miserable nod and drew apart from Vincent. Snot-faced and tear-streaked, she fumbled in the pockets of her voluminous cardigan.

"Hang on there, Ellie, I'll fetch you some. . ."

But he didn't have to. Hayley had brought out a length of toilet paper.

"Thanks," Ellie mumbled. Her voice was hoarse.

She faced Ted at last.

"We need to discuss this, now, Ellie." Ted had folded his wings, so to speak. "I'm sorry if this is a bad time but we've got a busy week ahead and I might not be able to get everyone together again. May as well get it over with."

You know how fond I am of you, Ted's expression said, but we have to draw the line somewhere. This is the end of your career here; you do realise that, don't you?

Of course she did, poor Ellie. They all did.

23

Iceland

February 2013

"Do we have to go?"

"Ellie, you know we promised to follow Eliza's itinerary. We'd feel bad if we let her down now."

Where has this steady, reliable Jonah come from? Ellie's got used to having him around over the past week. He's the one keeping her going.

They're sitting in the lounge of their hostel (it's not the one Eliza works in), finishing breakfast. English pop music is playing on an Icelandic radio station. The music finishes and what Ellie assumes is the news comes on, in Icelandic, of course. But she recognises the name the announcer has just spoken: that of a well loved paralympic athlete. Terrible, terrible. Why do bad things happen?

"Ellie?"

Jonah's haunted eyes are searching hers. His face seems to be sinking in on itself. He's trying so hard for me, to do the right thing. They've almost covered everything on Eliza's list.

And Jonah's right that they should complete it. Eliza needs to be in control of her world. Give her this.

Towards the end of the week you should go to the Blue Lagoon, when you're starting to feel exhausted from all your trips. Honestly, Mum, you'll love it. I went for the fourth time last week with my co-workers from the hostel. You can't imagine how relaxing an experience it is. By the time you see me at the end of your holiday with Dad, you'll be like a different person!

"You're right, I don't want to let her down."

"Good girl," Jonah says. She lets the condescending term of endearment go because the efforts he's making are holding her up.

They take their breakfast plates to the dishwasher and climb the three flights of stairs to the dorm room to fetch their boots and coats. Ellie's knees complain. Again, it was Eliza who insisted they stay in a hostel rather than in the hotel Jonah wanted to pay for.

I want you to experience the way of life I've been living since I was sixteen. Please do it, Mum and Dad. Maybe you can finally learn to understand me after all these years.

I kept telling her what an intelligent girl she was. Insisting that she should 'do something' with her talent, thinks Ellie. It was me who was stupid, not to appreciate her enough. The two girls sharing their room are still asleep in their bunks, one of them snoring loudly. The sky is fully light now and Ellie's surprised the sun hasn't woken the girls up. Still, she and Jonah are careful not to make any noise. He goes into the bathroom to put his trunks on and change into his thermals. Ellie changes quickly in the room. One of the girls turns over in her bed in a rustle of quilt. She opens her eyes, focussing briefly on Ellie, then lets the lids drop. She has all the time in the world.

Ellie sits on the edge of her bunk and imagines she and Jonah are young again, travelling like this before they've had any children.

With their towels in rucksacks, they clatter back down all the stairs to wait for their bus. Four other people are also waiting to be picked up; a Dutch man Jonah was speaking to earlier, and a bunch of Irish boys. Their accents make Ellie think of Greg Mulligan from Running Hare House. She wonders what he ever did with his life, if he made it big in the art world like he dreamed of. She suspects he didn't (she's googled him more than once and come up with nothing).

Nerves make her visit the toilet one last time and when she comes out Jonah is the only person left in reception.

"It's here," he says. "I asked them to wait."

The bus is crowded and she has to sit apart from Jonah. He ends up next to Harry, the Dutch guy, and immediately resumes an earlier conversation they were having. Ellie's seat companion, a well-travelled woman in her sixties, maybe, attempts to make conversation as well but Ellie keeps her responses clipped. I must be coming across as a stuck-up cow. But she can't help it. She doesn't want to answer any questions. The woman gives up and converses over her shoulder to a person in the seat behind.

Jonah casts Ellie a sympathetic glance across the aisle, and she's suddenly afraid of when their trip is over, and she'll be in the house alone again. Seth still lives at home, but he's hardly ever there. Funny how much I longed for solitude in the past. But everything's changed now, she's frightened of the company of her own mind.

———

It's freezing when she moves outside from the changing room to the pool. It's February. In Iceland. And she's in the open air, wearing next to nothing. Ellie pulls the skirt of her swimming costume down, shivering. Worse, she's shaking, hard. She can barely see because of having no glasses on. For a moment she searches frantically through the many blurry human shapes for Jonah. And there he is, waiting for her right by the door. He looks skinny in his long shorts.

She grips the freezing metal rail carefully as she progresses into the water behind Jonah. When she's far enough in she slips under warm covers. Ah. I could keep on going under. Go to sleep. But she brings her head out of the water again, feeling her hair cooling. When she opens her eyes, white mist softens everything. She's glad she left her glasses behind. Nobody can see anything clearly out here anyway. And you can cry as much as you want without anyone noticing. Except Jonah. But who's to say whether the moisture on his face is from the lagoon water or his eyes?

Soft grit is under her feet, sucky silicone mud. She curls her toes. Everything feels in slow motion. They both move in slow motion, out into the centre of the largest area of interlinked pools in a series connected by watery passageways and arched wooden bridges. It goes on forever. They explore the misty, otherworldly environment through the white steam, not talking. Out in the middle of the water she moves sluggishly away from Jonah until she's alone, sound and vision muted. The sky above the steam is dimming. Lights are coming on in the distance.

"Ellie."

She hears Jonah's voice.

"Over here," she calls back with some reluctance.

That craving for solitude she's always had. Ellie's warmed through now, lulled, exactly as Eliza suggested, into a deep sense of relaxation. The panic is behind a stretchy wall, like an umbilical sac, she thinks, for now. When she stands up she feels icy air on her shoulders and it makes her take a deep breath before she sinks back into the warmth.

"Look what I found over here."

She follows Jonah through a tunnel. It leads into a womb-like cave. They both float on their backs in silence for about five minutes, turned in slow circles by the gentle motion of water. Then a group of middle-aged Asian women chatters into the space with them, crowding between Ellie and Jonah.

They move to opposite edges of the enclosed pool, glancing across at each other. Time to leave the cave.

24

Ellie

Hull, Summer 1986

Ellie felt like the doomed space shuttle, Challenger. It promised hopeful explorers the universe, only to disintegrate on the way up. That was the kind of mother she was. As each day progressed from morning to afternoon, she sensed herself disintegrating into a million scattered molecules.

Jonah was getting ready to leave the house.

"Don't go out again. I can't cope."

Earlier, Rosie had cut her finger on a cat-food tin and the din of her resulting trauma had only just died down.

"Ellie, you have to learn to cope at some point," Jonah-the-martyr declared.

Pompous bastard. "I'll get set up at the venue, then come back and read to Rosie and Kester before the gig starts. It's only up Cottingham Road."

He'd probably spend the afternoon playing Arkanoid.

While she wiped snotty noses and cleaned out the cat litter tray.

"Mamma," shouted Kester, pulling despairingly at his nappy. She couldn't get him potty-trained, yet he hated wearing a soiled nappy. More molecules split away from her and floated around the room. She put her arms around herself, ignoring the boy-child tugging at her skirt.

"Mamma!"

Jonah studied his reflection in the living room mirror; checking his teeth (they'd had overcooked broccoli at lunch: yesterday's leftover pasta). He spoke around the elastic fastener gripped between them, muttering about being lucky to be earning at all, however small the amount, what with the unemployment figures now being over three million.

As if he was making sacrifices. As if he would ever consider an ordinary job. She hated him.

He swept back his hair, removed the fastener from his teeth and secured his ponytail. Ellie wished he'd look at her when he was speaking. She was invisible, buried beneath a tower of nappies and children.

She mourned the old Ellie. That girl was strong, vivacious; empowered. Now she found it hard to make decisions, she was tired all the time. She'd disappointed herself as a mother, (the mother she never meant to be anyway).

Ellie missed Running Hare House so badly that she hadn't been able to bring herself to take the children to visit as she'd promised she would.

I've let them all down: Vincent, Ted. Greg. . .

She now spent her life feeding, washing baby clothes and watching television. If only she could be like Bobby Ewing in Dallas and wake up to find the past year had been nothing but a horrible dream.

"Ellie. . ." Jonah glanced at her. With a sigh he moved to put his arms around her, tucking hers in tightly against his chest. But she felt no warmth in the gesture.

He was moving on, he'd left The Travelling Man behind and was in a new band, but she was stuck in this pit of domestic drudgery.

He tilted his face back to speak and she smelt cannabis on his breath and clothes.

"Things are going well for Tempest; a record deal is just around the corner now, and when it comes it'll solve all our problems. We'll buy a house of our own. On The Avenues maybe, you've always liked that area, haven't you? A real family house with a proper garden. We won't always have to struggle to pay the bills and one day you can start doing something you love again. I'm sorry it's not much fun for you at the moment but it'll be worth it in the end."

A record deal just around the corner, same old story, different band. She'd dared to hope when he and John-Paul fell out that he'd have more time for her but he was busier than ever with his new band.

He gave her shoulder a perfunctory pat, let go of her and gathered a tangle of microphone leads from the table. But at the door he hesitated, letting his breath out in controlled exasperation.

She is such a nuisance, he'd be thinking.

He tapped his free hand against his thigh. Tick-tock. Then he swivelled towards the archway that led to the dining room.

"Rosie, do you want to come with Dadda and see a nice lady at the pub?"

Their almost-four-year-old let out a shuddering breath, inspecting her sore finger as if it would give her the answer. It didn't take her long to decide. Rosie went to fetch her shoes from the shelves under the stairs and came running towards Dadda, eyes shining, hair that had darkened as she grew, swinging against her cheeks. It was clear Rosie would choose Jonah over her, any time.

"Ann, the landlady there, has a little girl about Rosie's age," Jonah explained. "I can put Rosie upstairs with her until I come back here later."

So how well does he know this Ann?

He could be getting up to anything away from his family; after all, his wife wasn't much of a temptation. She was also shocked that he would take Rosie into the smoky environment of a pub, but he'd said upstairs so it should be okay. She wanted to believe it, anyway.

Ellie's whole body loosened at the thought of the break she'd get. More than anything she wanted to escape into years of sleep, only waking up when the children were more manageable.

"Take Kester with you as well?" She hated hearing herself plead, but that's what she did all the time. Their son was still whining.

A clean nappy should last him the afternoon. She didn't dare risk suggesting Jonah took Eliza. He'd only use it as ammunition against her when he next chose to criticise her mothering abilities.

She's looking at me again. Ellie fought the creeping numbness gripping her arms and stomach. Eliza was what people called 'an old soul'. Only a year old, undersized, the health visitor had booked her in for extra checks. It was hard to think of her as a baby. She was a changeling; hair the colour of water and grey eyes like stones, an underdeveloped photograph of the child Ellie would have had if she'd incubated her with love and acceptance.

Eliza, mouth hanging open, dropped her gaze: stones plopping into water. She continued playing quietly by herself in the darkest corner of the room.

Casting spells.

"Don't ever say anything like that about her again," Jonah had warned when she once mentioned that Eliza was the result of some sort of witchcraft.

She was the wicked one, for thinking things like that about an innocent baby.

Jonah had the uncanny ability of reading her thoughts. "OK, I'll take Kester off your hands for a few hours as well."

What a superhero you are.

"It'll be good for you and Eliza to spend some time together."

25

Summer 1988

Once Rosie had started school the health visitor, (more forcefully than ever) encouraged Ellie to take Kester and Eliza to a mother-and-toddler group in the church hall on a Tuesday. Ellie eventually ran out of excuses to refuse. Sometimes the woman popped in to check she was there, an unspoken warning. Be a better mother. . .

From Eliza's birth Gloria Channing had been monitoring 'the situation', weighing and poking at Eliza; pestering Ellie to take her anti-depressants, but Ellie was signed off from those now.

It's a pity I didn't take Gloria's advice to go on the Pill, though.

Kester was outgoing and sociable; he couldn't wait to start school the following year. He led a troop of energetic four-year-olds on an assault course around the centre's play equipment. Ellie smiled; her golden boy. She looked up a moment later to see the health visitor watching her.

Eliza behaved the same as she did at home, tucking herself into the farthest corner to play on her own. The health visitor's beady eyes tracked Ellie's interactions with her daughter. I'm on a list somewhere, Ellie thought. Inadequate parenting skills.

Eliza had been flagged up as failure to thrive, but she was putting on weight now. No item of food was allowed to touch any other on her plate, and no-one was allowed to look at her when she ate.

"Excuse me." A sudden wave of nausea caused Ellie to get up in a hurry, startling the woman next to her. She put her teacup hurriedly down on the chair behind her, brown liquid sloshing into the saucer. From the corner of her eye, she saw the health visitor write something in her notebook. Health and safety hazard. She slid the cup and saucer off the chair again in a panic.

"Would you mind. . . " She paused, pressing a hand over her mouth, already backing away. "Watching my daughter, over there in the corner, and my son," she looked around wildly, "on the slide at the moment, the fair-haired one? I just need to. . . " The woman looked flustered, but nodded.

Still carrying a rattling cup and saucer, Ellie made it to the toilet just in time to be sick.

There must be a reason this had happened again. What am I meant for? Maybe Ellie was destined to be the mother of a child the world was waiting for, someone very special, and she hadn't got it right yet. More likely she was being tested. She'd failed so miserably with Eliza, Fate was making her do it all over again.

"Don't cry dear, I'm thrilled," was Sarah's reaction when she visited on Kester's birthday and learnt the news. "We could only have the one, you see. Women's problems, you know. Still, I'm lucky enough to be granny to a proper horde now. I wonder what you'll have this time. . . boy or girl?"

They were still living on Gee Street, in a flat-fronted terraced house with the front door leading straight out onto the street. Jonah sometimes managed to get work in a local recording studio and there were regular Tempest gigs, but they still relied heavily on benefits. Their situation no longer seemed to bother Jonah's parents, though Vivian visited less and less often; Ellie was sure because of Ray.

"I could let you have the money, now," Leopold offered his son. "To put a deposit on a larger house: you know, the money I was going to give you when you finished university?"

Ellie was sure they must have had it already, Leopold had bought them a second-hand car the year before.

Anyway, she found it hard to contemplate moving. She was constantly being tossed about on a sea of change, mostly pregnancy.

18 September 1988

It was Rosie's sixth birthday and Ellie's twenty-fifth.

They'd got Rosie a pair of kittens, following the death of poor old Netty from cat flu the previous month. Grey Cat had disappeared the second year they lived in Pottersea.

Rosie's tea party was in the afternoon. She was a popular girl at school and Ellie had to help her edit down her guest list, with frequent revisions. It didn't help that Ellie's temper was short and her energy low due to pregnancy.

The invitations were handed out the week before at school. On the day of the party, Rosie changed her mind and wanted to swap invited guests with non-invited ones. She screamed until she made herself sick. Ellie was on the point of cancelling the whole thing when the first child arrived early, (one whom Rosie had declared she no longer liked).

The moment the doorbell rang, Rosie immediately turned the tears off and the charm on and later the party appeared to have been a success despite Ellie's ragged nerves.

She knew the other mothers thought her stuck-up. She hadn't really made any friends of her own. Terry at the corner shop was always friendly and the woman next door asked after the children, and she exchanged telephone numbers with the mothers of Rosie's closest friends so they could visit each other's houses, but that was all. When it came down to it, Ellie hardly ever had other children back to hers. She already felt like the old (young) woman who lived in a shoe.

"You're just mean, Mummy," Rosie stated. "You should try to make friends with people. Emily said her mummy said you were stand-uppish."

<hr>

Ellie lay in bed, unable to sleep. The slippery aftermath of sex made for discomfort but inertness prevented her getting out of bed to go to the bathroom.

She clamped her legs together with a sudden bolt of lust as memories of their evening resurfaced.

She'd left her hair loose that night, something she hardly ever did now because of sticky hands grabbing it, and she'd also re-hennaed it. She wore a green linen dress that fitted loosely over her bump

After Rosie's party, Sarah and Leopold remained at their house to babysit. They were staying in their usual B&B on Spring Bank West.

Ellie and Jonah went to the pub on Cottingham Road (where Tempest had a regular gig) to celebrate her birthday. Ellie was now acquainted with the landlady, Ann, who lived there with her lesbian partner and their two children. Silly me; worrying that Jonah was having an affair with Ann.

Martin was at the gathering with his girlfriend. Maria also turned up, but she was late. She'd brought her Spanish cousin with her, a dark-haired guy with amber eyes who kept telling Ellie how sexy he found her. Ellie thought maybe Maria had paid him to do it but she still found it erotic, and could forget for a while that she was a mother of almost-four.

"You're unbelievable, Ellie," Maria remarked. "Every time I see you you're pregnant. Whatever happened to the two girls we used to be?"

Maria had come straight from work, which was in an important office, apparently. Something to do with being a civilian attached to the police force, Ellie could never make it out. Maria wore a blue suit with a tight skirt and huge shoulder pads.

The Thompson Twins were singing 'Hold Me Now' on the jukebox and it reminded Ellie of the meeting at Running Hare House when she had told them all she was pregnant with Kester. Straight afterwards the radio had been switched on and it was that song playing.

Ellie couldn't even remember the university girls Maria was talking about. I'm twenty-five years old and I didn't see what happened to my youth.

Stroking her belly now while she lay sleepless, she felt the baby stretching as it woke up, someone to keep her company. It kicked against Jonah's back. It must have felt secure, sandwiched between its parents. She wondered about the person inside her in a detached way, mildly curious. All would be revealed in time. She remembered how she'd denied Eliza and felt sick with a recurrent awareness of the damage she might have done to her second daughter.

Sometime later she half-awoke to soft footsteps on the bedroom carpet. The mattress on Ellie's side of the bed dipped as a small figure snuck under the quilt and pressed itself against Ellie's back. She wasn't even sure whether Eliza was truly awake when she paid her mother these occasional night-time visits. She daren't move for startling her. If Ellie acknowledged her, she would leave. Jonah slept on and the baby inside Ellie had gone back to sleep as well.

She measured her breathing to match that of her daughter's in the darkness, and hoped the sorrow she felt was atonement enough.

26

East Yorkshire

May 2013

Ellie's hands shake on the wheel. Panic freezes her brain. Breathe, just breathe. She checks both wing mirrors, signals and pulls into a layby. She can't stay on the road a moment longer. When she's rendered the van motionless she heaves the handbrake into position, checks it twice and wriggles the gear stick. It's long and completely different from any car she's ever driven. She gives a final pull on the handbrake to be sure. Safe. Trembling, she reaches across Jack and clicks open the passenger door. She opens her own door and steps shakily down to the ground.

Jack jumps down. He runs into the long grass at the edge of a field and cocks his leg, sniffing the breeze before returning to Ellie's side.

She gnaws at her knuckles.

"Jack, what am I doing?"

The dog pushes his nose into her crotch, wagging his tail.

"Get off." Her hands are still shaking. *I can't get back in that thing.* She buries her fingers in Jack's fur. He tilts his head on one side.

"What do you think of our new home?" she forces herself to say. *It's the only one I've got now.*

They both stare at the bright yellow van.

"I'm sure I'll get to love it eventually."

If I say it enough times I might come to believe it. She's terrified of the prospect of her first night in a bed she hasn't even put together yet. She's free-fallen into a new life without boundaries or comforting rules, no-one to make demands on her. *Where will I spend the night?*

She realises how poorly she's planned this out, or not planned it out. *I'm running away.* And yet hasn't she spent her whole adult life wishing she'd been allowed to follow her own dreams?

She has to go back to her house one final time and collect the pitiful few possessions left in there that she's able to carry in the van, and then push the keys through the letterbox. This means conquering her panic at the thought of climbing back into that huge motorised canary that now feels like an articulated lorry.

It looms before her in the layby. She tries to steady her shaking hands.

"Oh my God, Jack, what have I done?"

The dog sits in the grass at her side, panting slightly.

Everything belonging to her children has already been removed from the house; stored away in the children's own homes or backpacks or memories. Jonah will keep some of their shared past in the house on the Boulevard that he bought when they split up in 2000. He's also rehoming the two cats, daughters of one of Rosie's childhood kittens.

But at least you're coming with me, Jack.

Jonah's house is often occupied by different people, sometimes his children, sometimes others. He rarely stays there himself. When he's in Hull he sometimes stays with Ellie in their old home, in a separate bedroom. It doesn't feel much different from living together and apart all those years ago in Running Hare House.

They could've carried on being married. If he hadn't put his cock into someone else.

Bryony, the sister of Ann at the pub on Cottingham Road. Ellie felt so betrayed: stupid for not realising. Was it worth it, Jonah? The affair was over even before their marriage properly peeled apart but she refused to have him back.

She must get into the van again, it won't drive itself.

She manages the drive through town and the busy right turn onto Anlaby Road from Ferensway. Over the flyover. Nearly home.

Only for another hour or so.

The engine sounds louder than ever as she hauls the steering wheel to the left. Down St George's Road she drives. Keep going, she says to herself; over the railway track.

The dog gives her an affronted look. "Sorry, Jack, did that rattle your bones?" Her jaw is all tensed up.

Waiting for a gap in the traffic she takes her chance and turns right, down Woodcock Street, ignoring the horn blaring behind her. Is the indicator working? The tick is too quiet. The van feels too big for this road, but at least it's less busy down here. She takes the right onto the street of her former home a bit wide, almost knocking a flat-bed truck sitting on the corner by the park.

"Oh my God." Sweat prickles on her forehead and in her armpits. "I don't think I can do this."

But she has no choice now, the house isn't hers anymore so she can't stay there. She has no other home than this van. She brings the vehicle to a stop with a final roar of the motor. Jumping down she checks the distance between van and curb, hopes other drivers will have room to clear her wide attempt at parking. How am I going to get it turned round in this road? Don't think about that yet.

Keep on keeping on.

Jack thinks they're just going home. But nothing will ever be the same again.

Ellie opens the door and they both enter the empty hallway. Soon it will be someone else's home and the Whitefern family's two decades of history here will be erased. Two of her babies were born in this house, her fourth when they'd only been in it two weeks.

She runs a hand over the cream panelled walls in the hallway. When they first moved in they tolerated the ubiquitous wood-chip wallpaper so common at the time. Later they stripped the walls and had them re-plastered and eventually put up the panelling. The multi-fuel stove wasn't a fashionable choice in those days but it helped influence the rapid sale of the house to the young couple who fell in love with it just a few weeks ago. The sale went through quickly.

Might I have changed my mind if it hadn't? Too late now.

The old floorboards were covered with brown cord carpeting when the children were small but later they had them stripped and varnished back to their original finish.

Now all traces of their family have been removed from the property, the last of the furniture went just this morning. Ellie realises the true extent of her loss. It's over.

She feels as she did thirty years ago when she witnessed the launching of Jonah's career while she stood in place, weighed down by a baby.

Genesis lyrics flooded her head; she missed Jonah now. She would give anything to go back and start again.

Before she leaves town she's taking the van to a joiner friend to have a fold-away table fitted for the sewing machine. It will swing out from the end of the bed, over the tiny wood-burning stove. Her sewing machine is hand-operated but can also run on electricity. It once belonged to her grandma. It had sat unused in Vivian's attic for twenty years and when Ellie asked if she could have it, Deb happened to be there. She expressed a sudden interest of her own; Florence was doing a vintage project and would need the old Singer for authenticity.

Vivian listened to both sides.

"I'm sick to death of you two girls arguing," she finally pronounced. "Eleanor, I'm going to ring Florence now and ask her thoughts on the matter."

She came back into the room.

"Florence is perfectly happy for you to take the machine, Eleanor. She says she has plenty of opportunity to use old-fashioned machines at the studio."

Ellie warmed towards Florence, despite her parentage.

She often feels that she and Deb must have each other's daughters. Rosie is more like Deb in both looks and temperament than her mother, and Florence is more like Ellie than Deb.

She stows everything away in its allotted place in the bus. The sewing machine is tucked into a cupboard under the foot-end of the bed, the large box of fabric and accessories at the head-end. Florence, on hearing her auntie's plans, gave her a good deal of discarded stuff from the designer's studio where she works. Ellie's dolls will be well-dressed. She'll also make attractive cushions and quilts with these materials.

"If you need anything else," Florence had offered, "Just let me know. I'm so sorry about everything, Ellie, so sad. Edward is too. He really liked. . . "

She had stopped speaking to blow her nose. Edward looked up from his computer in the corner of their dining room and gave Ellie a sympathetic smile. Florence gave her nose a final wipe and folded the tissue over; tucked it in the pocket of the man's shirt she wore with a wide belt.

She dipped her close-cropped head, red earrings swinging.

"And don't worry about Seth and my sister, either," she said. "I'll be going over to visit them next month. I think it's sweet, I don't care what Mum says."

Florence was closer to her youngest sister, Catherine, than to Imogen, exactly between them in age. Ellie was fond of 'little Catherine' as well. Never mind that Catherine's own mother was blanking her, as she was Ellie. Catherine would still have plenty of support.

The first night in the van.

"Oh God, Jack."

It's getting dark. Ellie hopes she's safe in this layby. From burglars, rapists and wild animals. There's a slight bank with a hedge on the ridge between her and the road. She parked as close to the grass verge as she could, in case another vehicle drives through in the night, and doesn't notice her van.

Once she's taken Jack for a short walk on the lead, she places his food on the verge and peers anxiously out at him between bouts of making the bed. Earlier, she had to slot a board between the benches on either side of the van and lay out the three sections of mattress. Now the bed's in place she'll leave it there permanently. There's just enough floor-space left to go about her normal business, but she and Jack will have to learn to move carefully around each other.

She finishes tucking in the bottom sheet and smooths out the quilt, then calls Jack inside and locks the door. Tea, she thinks. But nothing happens when she tries to light the gas ring. Ah. She has to open the door again so she can go round the back of the van, open the back doors and turn the gas on. Evening dew wets her feet as she stands, breathing in the night air. An owl hoots. Apart from that it's quiet; no traffic on the road.

She slams the back doors shut. Before she comes back inside and locks the side door for the night she checks that the driver and passenger doors are locked too.

It's hard to light a fire with shaking hands, she keeps knocking her knuckles against the inside edges of the stove. Eventually the firelighter and then the twigs take light and she piles some kindling and a small chunk of wood on top.

Her phone rings. She nearly jumps out of her skin.

It's Jonah. Her hand trembles against her cheek as she presses the mobile to her ear. He asks if she's alright – if she wants him to come and fetch her. We can easily kick those dossers out of the Boulevard house and claim it for ourselves.

"Ellie, babe. My offer for you to come back and live with me still stands."

"Oh, don't be so stupid." Ellie speaks more sharply than she meant. "Give me a chance to try this, at least."

"Why are you crying, then, girl?" Jonah asks. "Let me try and make you feel better."

She thinks how he would once have demanded sympathy for himself, but he doesn't now. He's changed a lot over the years. And it hurts. Everything hurts.

"I don't want to feel better. I don't deserve to."

There's a long silence, punctuated by the snapping of the fire in the van, and their gut-wrenching sobs on both ends of the phone connection.

<hr>

Ellie's come up-country to start her new life. She's in North Yorkshire, not far from Pickering. Jonah and she used to take the children camping around here when they were young.

She has a short sleep after her painful conversation with Jonah, then sits upright on the bed, ticking things off in her head. The old gas bottle has been replaced by a new one, (tick). She filled the water tank at a garage and emptied the waste-water even though there was hardly anything in it, (tick).

The portable toilet is brand-new; the man at the caravan shop showed her how she must empty it when it becomes full. He sold her the bio-fluid to put in the holding cartridge,

"It won't smell," he promised, (tick). She opens the fridge and checks it still contains the food she bought earlier; (tick). She flicks the switch to heat water for her bedtime wash, (tick).

She has everything she needs but she still wants to go home.

Jack gives her a scolding look.

"Yeah, I know." She strokes his back, overcome with weariness despite the sleep she's had. "I am home. This is it now."

Thank God for the dog.

When she's eaten, (beans on toast, it seems the easiest thing) and washed the pots, she washes her hands and face and uses the toilet. Then she cleans her teeth at the tiny bathroom sink.

There's no reason now not to climb into the freshly made bed, warmed by the hot water bottle she's prepared. But she reads for a while before she can persuade herself to turn out the light. Then it's a surprise to find that she is falling asleep easily, lulled by the sounds of passing traffic and sheep bleating on the moors throughout the night, and Jack's snores at the end of the bed.

27

October 1988

The house on Somerset Street needed minor renovation and Jonah had to help with the work in return for the deposit his father was giving them. They managed to get an interest-only mortgage, covered by their Housing Benefit, so as far as Ellie was concerned they didn't really own the property. But they had a bigger kitchen than before and four bedrooms (one tiny). There was a small park opposite and if Ellie sat in the bay-windowed front room where she had a table set up for her sewing machine she could watch Rosie and Kester playing there with the children from down the road.

She was making a soft toy for the new baby and one each to give her existing children when the baby was born.

Eliza had adopted a corner of the dining room in the middle of the new house. She was distressed by the move and wanted somewhere to hide, so Ellie gave her a pile of old curtains to construct a den.

Ellie didn't want to go back to the hospital to give birth; too many unhappy memories. It had to be different. None of her pregnancies had been complicated, so her GP finally agreed to a home birth but it didn't matter anyway because she had already made an arrangement with the community midwives.

March 1989

Kester had started school and Eliza was at nursery in the afternoons. She didn't speak much while she was there and played mainly by herself. There were a few things she refused to do, such as go in the quiet room with the other children. She told Ellie that it echoed in there, it hurt her ears. But the teacher was kind and Eliza hadn't yet had a meltdown at nursery. This meant Ellie got two precious hours at home, five days a week, with only the baby for company. Lily had just turned four months old. She reminded Ellie of Kester at the same age and Ellie felt the same contentment when she sank into the armchair to nurse her.

"It's for three weeks," said Jonah.

When he was excited, every muscle in his face was active. There was also a scent, she couldn't explain it but she sensed it whenever he showed any kind of passion. Ellie felt her first erotic twinges since Lily was born. She turned slightly away and continued pressing pastry into a pie dish.

"I'm pleased for you," she said. "It's great news, well done."

The 'how to talk to children so children will listen' course the health visitor had sent her on when Eliza's well-being was in question had had a lasting effect on Ellie. She was learning to pay more attention to Jonah's feelings as well. Their relationship had improved.

"But are you sure you can manage on your own for that amount of time?" Jonah asked courteously. Evening light streamed through the kitchen window, showing up smears on the glass.

"You've worked hard for an opportunity like this," Ellie acknowledged.

She reached for the saucepan containing the filling, a mess of tomatoes and vegetables with chopped-up sausages from last night's dinner, and poured it in. She pinched the edges of the pastry lid to the sides of the base, then stabbed the centre of the lid with a knife.

Lily was starting to grizzle in the other room and she hoped Rosie would pick her up and cuddle her.

"I'm proud your talents have been recognised, Jonah. Getting session work as a drummer is a great way to ensure exposure for the band." *He still hopes so desperately for that record deal.* "And the money's good, too." *I've never had enough faith in him before.*

She opened the oven door and lowered the pie onto the shelf. Straightening again she blew hair out of her eyes and turned to look at him.

"Thanks," he said. "I know it'll be hard for you when I'm away."

He was leaning against the work surface, his arms folded. He looked young, and of course, he was.

A bolt of tenderness shot through her. *It hasn't been easy for either of us.*

Lily squealed from the other room.

"Mummy," shouted Rosie. Her parents flinched. Thudding footsteps sounded in the hall. "Come and get the baby, she's annoying us."

"Don't worry, we'll manage," Ellie said, laying a hand on Jonah's arm. "Coming," she called back before Rosie could burst in and ruin the evening with a tantrum.

May 1989

She picked Rosie and Kester up from school and Eliza from nursery, an excited feeling rolling in her stomach.

"Put your book-bags in the tray under the buggy."

"Where are we going, Mammy?" Kester hopped from foot to foot. He could never keep still.

"To Queens Gardens. And then Mammy's got to go and talk to a woman at the college, so you'll all have to be good."

She lifted Lily from the buggy and inserted her into the sling. "And quiet," she added to Kester, specifically.

"You get in the buggy, Eliza." It was easier than trying to make her walk all the way into town. Ellie felt light, despite the weight of the baby on her front.

"When's Daddy coming back, Mum?" Rosie asked once they'd set off. She'd just graduated to the shorter title from 'Mummy'. *She has to be different.*

"Look both ways," Ellie instructed. They crossed the road by the old fountain at the Boulevard. "He's away for two weeks this time, you know that, Rosie. So that means he'll be back at the beginning of next week."

They continued along Cholmley Street. A cat leapt over a wall in front of them, and Eliza made an uncannily accurate mewling noise from the buggy. Sitting on a dustbin, the cat followed them with its eyes as they passed.

"But where does he go?"

Rosie always got whiny when Jonah was away. Ellie took a deep breath. *Don't let her ruin your good mood.*

"He's in Birmingham this time. You know that, as well. He's at a recording studio."

"But why?"

Rosie kicked out at the buggy wheel, scuffing her sandal toe. Ellie wondered if she could cover the mark with polish. If they had any in that colour. *Don't respond with anger,* the how to talk lessons reminded her, *just answer her question.* Rosie was going through a phase. *And take another deep breath.*

"Because the people there heard what a good drummer he is and they asked for him especially. He's going to be on a record; that's exciting, isn't it?"

Rosie looked up at her mother and made a twisted face. She parroted Ellie's tone when she asked, "Why are you talking in that stupid voice?"

"They've found a mummy, Mammy," Kester chanted repeatedly to a tune Rosie hummed for his benefit. He was into dinosaurs and anything that'd been dug-up.

"It's four thousand years old. Older than you, even."

He must have heard about the ancient Egyptian on Newsround the evening before.

"Cheeky." Ellie smiled down at the cowlick on his forehead. He had dimples in his cheeks.

They trailed through Queens Gardens, admiring the carp in the three rectangular ponds. She let them throw the remains of their sandwiches in for the greedy fish.

Spring was just beginning and buds were opening on the trees. Flocks of sparrows landed and took off in the overhead branches.

Rosie squealed and put her spare hand over her ear (the other was holding Kester's, as instructed).

"I don't like the noise."

Rosie was easily overstimulated. And a show-off.

The baby wriggled, starting to cry. Ellie dragged up layers of woollen jumper and Lily latched on, still in the sling. She was easy to please.

"There is eels in the water as well, Mammy," said Eliza in her precise manner. She needed to say it three times before Ellie heard her.

"How do you know that?"

Eliza was out of the buggy, standing at the edge of the water, hands behind her back. She'd taken her shoes and socks off and placed them neatly on the ground beside the pushchair. Ellie might have been worried if it was one of the others but since she could walk Eliza had been as sure-footed as a bird on a cliff. It wasn't impossible to believe she might sprout wings and fly if a breeze took her.

Lily's mouth came away from the nipple. The sling hurt Ellie's shoulder so she loosened the ring-fastener and pulled it over her head, supporting the baby in her arm. She folded the layers of fabric around Lily and deposited the whole bundle in the buggy, fastening the strap. Lily fell quickly back to sleep.

Ellie engaged the brake and squatted at the edge of the pond. Eliza had on her blue corduroy pinafore dress and colourful winter coat. She wanted to wear the homemade dress all the time and cried when Ellie took it away to wash, consequently it was grubby and stained. Thank God they were understanding at nursery. The child's long hair, which she refused to have cut, straggled down her back.

The other week, Eliza had been sent home with a letter about head lice.

"Why are you trying to poison us, Mum?" Rosie demanded when she lathered their heads with the stuff from the chemists.

Eliza wiped her nose on her wrist, refusing the tissue Ellie wrestled from her pocket.

"Dadda told me," she said.

She had a good memory. Jonah used to take her out alone when she was a baby. He must have told her about eels then.

"What else do you know about the gardens?"

But Eliza rubbed her eyes.

"I don't know. I'm hungry; can we have an ice cream please?"

"It's a bit cold for that. How about a toasted teacake instead?" She checked to see that the café was still open. "That'll warm your tummy." Jingling her hand in her pocket, she assessed the number of coins she could feel.

Rosie and Kester lifted their heads from the patch of earth they'd been excavating for mummies.

"Toasted teacake!" Kester shouted.

Rosie joined in. "Toasted teacake, toasted teacake!" She danced on spider-legs and punched the air.

But Eliza was adamant. She shook her head, lips pursed. "I want an ice cream."

—————

The Head of Textiles at the college told Ellie she would be able to start in September. Ellie nodded; Lily would be old enough to leave in a créche by then. The woman, Julie Styles, looked dubiously at Ellie's brood. Rosy-cheeked from outdoors, they sat in a line on a two-seater sofa in the office, nibbling stale biscuits Ellie discovered in the bag under the buggy. The baby was still asleep, parked by the door.

Julie Styles gave Ellie an assessing look.

"How old are you, if you don't mind me asking?"

Ellie held her head up. "Not at all; I'm twenty-five."

There was a short silence. Julie smirked and looked around the room. Her gaze fell back on the children, Eliza in particular.

"Did you make that little girl's coat yourself?"

While Ellie nodded, Eliza glared at Julie, who looked away.

The coat was put together from patches of coloured velvet and corduroy. Ellie lifted her chin higher, pushed hair behind one shoulder.

"I did." She couldn't help the pride in her voice. "That's what I want to do, learn to make things properly, clothes and furnishings, stuff like that."

Julie closed the folder on her desk.

"The textiles course is more about developing your practice with a range of media and techniques. I mean, you'll develop your creative capacities overall."

Her gaze wandered nervously back to the children. Rosie and Kester squabbled quietly over the last crumbs of biscuit, Eliza was winding her hair into elaborate twists, still glaring. Julie's lips formed a disapproving shape.

Ellie felt her colour rising, tugged at the neck of her jumper. She hadn't really realized about the context of textiles as a subject. She'd been obsessed with the idea of sewing, just as she had been years ago, at Running Hare House. Now she felt stupid.

"You can go on to sewing things eventually." Julie must have noticed her confusion. "But you need a general understanding of the theoretical and conceptual issues which are central to the practice of textile art. That's what this course is about. Still interested?"

Well, I'm here now, Ellie thought, I may as well go for it. She smiled and nodded with what she hoped passed for intelligent consideration of the matter.

"Yes, I am."

Julie came round the desk and handed Ellie the college prospectus and application form she'd been waving about as she spoke.

"Get this in early," she advised. "Interviews are in a few weeks." She folded her arms and dared to look at each of the children in turn, even Eliza.

"They're quite good, aren't they?"

Now we're about to leave, she can afford to be kind. Ellie laughed. She moved over to Eliza, touching the top of her head.

"Get off me," said Eliza.

Ellie took her hand away.

"They are mostly," she said. "Come on then, you lot. Let's get back on the road."

"You can't walk on the road, Mammy, that's very dangerous."

Slipping off the sofa, Eliza moved over to Julie Styles. After some hesitation, she patted her leg. Ellie held her breath.

"Your trousers are really nice," Eliza murmured, eyes half-closed. Rosie and Kester burst into giggles.

"Don't do that." Ellie propelled her daughter towards the door, hands on her back. "You're invading Ms Styles' personal space. What have I told you about that?"

Julie stepped back to safety behind her desk.

"Children make me nervous." She brushed the side of her leg with her other hand. "They're such odd creatures."

Ellie struggled to get the buggy through the door. She pushed Rosie, Kester and Eliza in front of her.

"You can say that again."

28

September 1989

Lily was settling in well at the college créche and Ellie felt like herself again for the first time in years. She had a purpose and determination to succeed. She was learning to take one step at a time and enjoy moments as they happened.

Once the children were in bed, Ellie spent her evenings occupied with sketchbook, coloured pens and a pile of magazines, Prefab Sprout was currently her favourite record, a whispery voice singing about cars and girls. A bucket of tie-dyed fabric soaked in a corner of the kitchen, in preparation for the new curtains she intended to make. Home now felt like a place to set off from instead of a place to be trapped in.

As well as his semi-regular session work, Jonah had a part-time job in a record shop on Beverley Road.

Every week he had to declare his income so the DHSS could adjust his dole money. He was allowed to keep a small portion of what he earned.

"It won't be long," Jonah promised, "until we can get off the dole completely. The A&R man at Chrysalis Records said he'd listen to Tempest's latest tape, he liked the other one, he just thought we needed a bit more time to develop our style."

It would be a long time before they could stop claiming Housing Benefit, though.

"I wish I could persuade Rosie to eat free dinners," Ellie complained. "It would save on the cost of her lunches."

Every little helped. Kester loved dinner time at school but she knew Eliza would never consent to sitting in the crowded and noisy dining hall when her time came to start full-time after Christmas. It was a good job Ellie still got milk tokens because of Lily.

Jonah was usually out in the evenings, practising or at a gig. Their lifestyle reminded Ellie of the years at Running Hare House, only now they had a lot more children.

By the time Jonah came in on the nights he was home, Ellie had packed away her creative tools and given Lily her final feed. She might read for a while and then go to sleep. But sometimes she woke up when he got into bed and they had sex. She blamed her lust on the lingering post-baby hormones and the rush of creativity she was feeling.

18 September

Rosie's seventh birthday party was held in the local community centre. It was attended by most of her class. Taking a break after Pass the Parcel, Ellie got herself a cup of tea and sat back to watch the children play.

"She's going to end up as Prime Minister or something, your daughter," commented Sabina, Emily's mother. "She certainly knows how to get all the other children doing what she wants, doesn't she?"

As long as she doesn't turn out like Margaret Thatcher.

Ellie suspected Sabina secretly admired Rosie's strong-mindedness. She was the chairperson of the parent-teacher committee herself.

"Maybe it's down to her being the oldest of four," Ellie said. "Rosie has a lot of responsibilities at home. I'm just glad she's having fun."

Rosie wore the shimmering silver mini-dress Ellie had made out of a piece of fabric from the college scraps box. The girl had such long legs, and cheekbones like Nan-nan's. She looked older than seven. She's had to grow up so quickly. I can't believe it was seven years ago that she was born and we moved out to Running Hare House. However did the years go by so fast?

Ellie's body was thicker now and she felt her brain had slowed. Her hands were raw from washing-up. What would she be doing if she'd never met Jonah?

Maria and I would be travelling the world together, or I'd be working at the British Museum. Or anywhere.

Jonah and Ellie were having a meal together at home to celebrate her birthday; a rare night in for Jonah. After nibbling the sweet food at Rosie's party, Ellie didn't feel like going out.

"We can, if you want?" Jonah persisted. "It's your birthday as well as Rosie's. Mum and Dad have offered to stay over and babysit."

"No, it's alright. I know they'd prefer to get back to Luton tonight."

"Well, if you're sure," said Jonah. "I'll pop out to Marks & Spencer for a meal-for-two."

"Get Jonah to help you a bit more," Sarah suggested when she was helping Ellie put the children to bed. "You're looking pale and tired, sorry to be rude."

She attempted to tease a comb through Eliza's hair, while Eliza wriggled on the stool but didn't protest.

"She never lets me do that." Ellie met her daughter's grey-water eyes in the mirror. Eliza stared back unflinchingly.

Ellie tried to ignore the queasy feeling in her stomach. She picked up the brush and started on her own hair, which felt drab and limp between her fingers.

"Anyway, Jonah's working a lot. He needs time to practise with the band as well."

"I think you're very understanding, dear," Sarah said mildly.

When the children were in bed and Sarah and Leopold had set off on their long drive home, Ellie and Jonah sat down to their salmon wellington with lemon-and-pepper potatoes. Afterwards, Ellie felt a lot better.

"How much better?" asked Jonah, in that throaty voice he got sometimes.

She fingered the new silver heart at her throat; it ticked like a second heartbeat. Jonah maintained his steady gaze. When his eyes looked at her like that it felt like there was nothing else in the world for her to bother about.

That was what got me into trouble in the first place.

A second pulse started up between her legs. I'm twenty-six years old, she reminded herself. This is my husband. Everything slotted into perspective. I'm lucky we're still together.

"Ellie?" Jonah tried. "You know how much I still fancy you?"

He shifted on his chair and she imagined the hardening that was causing him discomfort. It sent another flush into her crotch.

Why not?

They hardly ever did anything spontaneous anymore.

She looked at the plates and cutlery on the table, the wine bottle with only an inch left in the bottom; the empty disposable containers from the food. Next to the sink was a bulging bin-bag full of paper plates and half-eaten sandwiches from Rosie's party. One of the yearling kittens was trying to claw its way into it. Jonah saw the direction of her gaze and knew what she was thinking.

"Leave it," he suggested. "I'll sort it out later." He probably wouldn't but the promise was comforting. Jonah reached over the table, his thumb running up and down the inside of her wrist. It was the most erotic thing he could have done.

Why not? thought Ellie again. Why not have some fun?

Jonah stood up, the bulge clearly visible. The dark blue shirt he was wearing had always been her favourite: it fitted his slim frame in a way that made her remember the first time she saw him, drumming in the band at her university lecturer's birthday party. Without even knowing him, she'd wanted to put her arms around his vulnerable-seeming torso then.

If I'd looked away that night, if I hadn't seen him again at the rock disco the following week and gone over to talk to him... we wouldn't be here now.

The thought brought a stinging to her eyes. Soppy cow. Jonah was still watching her.

"Come on, then," she said.

She got up and went to the door, checking for children-noises. Lily would probably be awake in about an hour. "No, not this way." She caught his hand as he followed her.

She felt the drumstick-callouses on his hand as she wound her fingers around his, pulling him into the new extension behind the kitchen.

"In here, standing up."

He unzipped the dress she'd had to squeeze into, pulled it down to the floor and she stepped out of it. He ran his hand down her back. Ellie stood in her bra, mindful of the loose stomach fat over the top of her pants. She closed her eyes. It was hot in here from the late evening sun and she felt slightly woozy but at the same time relaxed.

Jonah turned the tap on in the brand-new sink. He cupped water in his hands and held up her hair so he could dribble the water down her bare skin from the base of her neck to the hollow at the bottom of her spine. Ellie shivered.

"Dad-dah," said Jonah. She opened her eyes to see that he'd pulled a condom from his jeans' pocket. "I remembered."

He looked like a small boy waiting to be congratulated. We should have remembered one of those more often.

Ellie helped him unbutton his jeans and pull the condom on. The look in his eyes aroused her fully. Once they'd managed to negotiate the difficult positioning, they had sex quickly, listening out for the children, standing up against the door between the kitchen and the empty shell of the new utility room. It smelled of freshly-planed wood.

"I should hate you," Ellie whispered, haltingly. "You keep making me have children."

The pressure in her built. She was aware of a full feeling in her breasts and lower belly. During their eight years together, she'd spent most of the time pregnant or fearing she was, but God, she felt so horny now. It must be because my hormones haven't settled down after Lily. There was that one time we forgot to use a condom... but don't think about that now...

With a restrained cry, Jonah shrank out of her, his chin digging into her shoulder. But Ellie wasn't finished. She pulled him back, pressing the bones of his spine with the palm of one hand. She grabbed his hand with her other and pushed it between her legs.

"Come on," manipulating his fingers with hers until she came, her weight hanging on his hand, feeling as though Hurricane Hugo had just ripped through her.

November 1989

Ellie stared at the white plastic stick in her hand. Can these be wrong? These new tests? Her other pregnancies had been confirmed by the test tube and mirror variety that you had to wait an hour for. This gave a result in five minutes, it said on the box that a 'positive' was hardly ever wrong. Hardly ever.

Oh fuck, fuck, fuck.

U2 sang about an angel of Harlem on the bathroom radio. Vaguely, Ellie was aware of a news report about checkpoints being opened in the Berlin Wall. What? It was really happening, then. It felt like a year of hope.

But her mind was pulled back to her current situation. She was sitting on the edge of the bath. She'd meant to do the test before the children were awake, but she could hear Kester and Eliza downstairs already. Rosie slept as late as she could, especially at weekends. She was like a teenager, moods included. Eleven-month-old Lily was fast asleep in the parental bed with Jonah.

Oh, God.

She must be the most fertile woman on the planet.

She placed the stick carefully on the edge of the sink and stood up, looking in the smeary surface of the mirror.

She ought to clean it, it was filthy.

Glancing around the bathroom she took in the dirty clothes, damp towels, nit combs and bath toys on the floor. The bin overflowed, the toilet roll was unravelled. All this was normal in the Whitefern household. Dust and human hair gathered on the skirting boards; toothpaste and cat hair and Rosie's hair gel amassed in the grout between the tiles. Spilled shampoo was a safety hazard. Empty bottles piled up in the corners, ready to be washed and recycled. Sometime, never.

Cobwebs dangled from the ceiling. It was all too much. Whatever you cleared away always reappeared by the time you walked in the room again. How was she supposed to keep up with it all?

I thought I was accomplishing so much more these past couple of months but now I realise I've just been too excited to notice that everything has become even more overwhelming than before.

Downstairs in the new room off the kitchen she'd set up her sewing machine on a sturdy table.

The wall cabinets that Jonah had rescued from a skip were filled with fabrics and reels of cotton, patterns, scissors and buttons. The floor cabinets contained Play Doh and poster paints, newspaper and magazines and glue for the children to mess about with.

She'd planned a new, organised life, felt she was finally getting things under control: thought she was going to be producing something other than children.

She couldn't even cope with doing housework and looking after four children as well as manage her work for college. Not to mention the small sewing business she was hoping to set up.

But I've been much happier since I started college, we all have. Their house was a mess, dinner was haphazard, but she'd been more relaxed, feeling fulfilled.

Can I really bring another baby into this chaos?

Footsteps thumped up the stairs and someone banged on the bathroom door.

"Mammy,"

Just give me another minute.

"Mammy, I'm getting cross with you."

"Just a minute, Eliza, use the downstairs toilet, Mammy's busy in here."

She put the white plastic stick in the pocket of her dressing gown and gazed at her pale reflection in the grubby mirror. She had dark shadows under her eyes, but didn't every mother of four (five) under-eights? Her breasts felt heavy and painful to touch. The recent spate of renewed sexual activity between her and Jonah was dying down already, its job apparently done. It was always the way.

Was there a reason she was being sent so many babies?

Twenty-six years old and a mother of five. She was the butt of jokes among the younger students on her course already. But at the same time she could be a role model to the young girls. Surprisingly, she felt none of the panic and horror that had engulfed her when she learned of her third pregnancy. Lily had numbed her at first and then she'd only felt mild resignation. This time she seemed to feel nothing at all, apart from a desire to work out how she was going to manage. That had to be a good thing.

"I'm still waiting," came the cross voice on the other side of the door. "Me and Kester made you some breakfast."

"Eliza, sweetie," Ellie called through the door. "That's very kind of you. I'll be down in a minute."

After a pause she heard Eliza's footsteps recede down the stairs. Muffled voices came up through the floor from the kitchen; something crashed into the sink.

She gazed at her reflection a moment longer, tried to recall the eighteen-year-old who hadn't yet had any children; sure such a person must once have existed. Grant me the serenity, she reminded herself, an old refrain of her mother's (and St Francis), to accept the things I cannot change.

She wasn't going to let herself sink into a deep depression over another baby, and she couldn't contemplate doing anything about the pregnancy other than go through with it. But she was determined not to give up college. Maybe if she'd continued university after having Rosie, she wouldn't have ended up where she was now.

Do I still look young? She turned in front of the mirror. I still have freckles on my nose and cheeks, and I haven't found any grey hairs yet. She checked for wrinkles. Then she washed her face and smoothed moisturiser into her skin. She brushed her hair into a high ponytail, wondering whether she ought to get it cut.

29

Hull, 13 March 2013

"I'm so sorry about this," Seth says. His face is white and pinched. "Today of all days. It's awful for you."

Ellie's mind keeps wandering away, she tries to snatch it back. Inexplicably, she smells fish, a sick, dry smell. The fish were all dead, skeletons with flesh on their heads; hanging in their thousands from tall wooden racks in an isolated mountain location in Iceland, such an odd phenomenon. Why has it come back to me now? She forces her attention back to Seth.

Catherine is sobbing against her son's chest. He kisses the top of her head. They make a sweet couple. Cousins. It ought to be a shock but it doesn't seem to matter.

"Sit down, both of you," she makes herself say.

She places a hand on each of their shoulders and presses. They sit down together on the bed. She stands hugging herself, watching them.

I'm not really here, I'm back in Iceland. Those dead, dried fish, out there in the middle of nowhere. And the lake with the black beaches, high up in the mountains. Air blows through her.

She remembers Eliza's face when she and Jonah finally reached her. The last time I saw you.

Their news is a distraction. It's as good a day as any for it to come out.

One hour earlier

She catches Jonah's eye over the heads of Rosie's children, playing on the floor with their mamma's old dolls' house. Freya bosses her little brother around, just like Rosie did at that age. The tiny plaits all over Freya's head bob and dip like springs, bright beads on their ends hypnotising Ellie as they reflect light from the window.

It doesn't seem long ago that Rosie and Kester played with the same toys. . . While Eliza lay unattended in the carrycot.

The cherry-toned floorboards are obscured by feet. So many of them. Each set of feet leads up to a pair of legs with a person on top.

What are all these people doing in my house?

Jonah's in his old armchair in the corner by the back window. He's strumming a child's guitar: Kester's old one. In the thirty years she's known him, Jonah hasn't seemed to age until now. He's kept his hair long, habitually pulled back from his face. But now his cheeks are sunken, there are dark hollows beneath his eyes. He's got deep lines on his skin and his hair is all grey.

It happened overnight.

God knows what's happened to me. She doesn't care.

Everything stills, goes quiet. Jonah's eyes lift eternally to hers and she sees directly through his skin and muscles to the skeleton beneath. Her womb, which last bore his child twenty-two years ago, contracts painfully. The sensation is followed by an atrocious rush of desire, a terrible transgression. But she feels faint with it, and Jonah notices.

How can this be?

She bends forward, hands dug in to her stomach.

Maybe I can transport myself back to being pregnant with Eliza.

In slow motion, Jonah lays the guitar on the arm of his chair and starts to push himself up. He will come towards her. They will end up in her bedroom together; they will fuck themselves stupid. They must.

But. A noise like a squawking bird erupts from the other end of the room and stops them.

Deb.

At twenty-one, Catherine is the baby of the extended family. Seth's the next one up. At family gatherings the two youngest always gravitated together and they became close friends.

This must be why Ellie didn't notice something deeper was developing.

Out of all her children, Seth looks the most like his father, he more or less exactly resembles Jonah at the time she met him. Seth has the same deep-set green eyes and strong nose; the same scattering of freckles. But he wears his hair short, cropped close at the sides and gelled upright on top of his head, like Kester.

"We didn't mean this to happen, it just did. We couldn't help it." Seth pauses, his eyes examining her face. "It's not just a thing, Mum, I love her."

"It's not illegal," Catherine pipes up. The way she says it reminds Ellie of Deb. "We looked it up."

Ellie pulls herself back. "No, it's not." She thinks for a minute. "But it's uncomfortable, especially to someone like your mother."

Catherine shoots her a glance. She adores Deb, this will be the first time anything has come between them.

Ellie takes a breath.

"I didn't mean. . . " she speaks gently. "I just meant she has strongly-held views. It's difficult for her to adapt them."

Why should I be having to make excuses for Deb, today of all days?

Catherine buries her face in a handkerchief.

Ellie breathes deeply. She hears the murmur of voices, a wave of mingled conversations forcing their way up through plaster and ceiling joists and floorboards. What are they all saying? Talking about me, how I was never the best mother.

She wants Jonah. Her body wants him. It's not right.

Catherine's hand sneaks out and finds Seth's again. She lifts her huge eyes to him. Then she does the same to Ellie.

"I'm sorry. It wasn't meant to come out today. It's just that Mum was... she made an unkind remark about Imogen and Sadie. Imogen was just trying to protect Sadie. She said if Mum thought being gay was bad she should see what... She let it slip about me and Seth. She didn't mean to, it was in the heat of the moment."

"Imogen knew?" Ellie's surprised Catherine confided in Imogen rather than Florence.

"She found out a while ago," says Seth. He presses Catherine's hand to his lips.

God, he is so like Jonah.

Oh, the look that passed between me and Jonah downstairs. We could lose ourselves in each other. Escape.

"I was looking after their cats when she and Sadie were on holiday," Catherine explains. "They came back earlier than we thought and found us... together."

"They've been brilliant about it," Seth says. "I never knew Imogen was that kind."

Afternoon sun slants across the bed. The white curtain billows gently in a breeze from the cracked-open window. A branch of the tree in the back garden taps against the glass. I must get that trimmed. She thinks of the branch cut down, sawed into logs for the wood stove. Licking tongues of flame devouring it.

Ellie wants to bury herself in the quilt. Or under the ground. Sleep forever. Or fuck Jonah forever, make more babies. Not have to think about today.

"Are you alright, Mum?" Seth's face swims in the air. Catherine's comes close to hers, brown curls falling across her white forehead. A hand around Ellie's shoulders.

"Here, Auntie, lie down."

They both scramble off the bed, trying to arrange pillows under her head.

"Put that throw over her," she hears Seth say.

"Fetch a glass of water, Seth," Catherine murmurs. "I'll stay with her."

"Has your mum gone yet?" Seth from the hallway.

"Shhh, Auntie Ellie. It's alright."

The odd sound must be coming from her. She looks down on herself from a great height, a woman who used to be young, full of dreams. A woman who had so many children, she didn't know what to do.

I should have looked after them better.

Cushions are plumped around her, the violet-coloured throw tucked in place; Catherine leans forward, smooths hair away from Ellie's face.

"Yes," she whispers over her shoulder to Seth. "Mum and Dad stormed out just as we came upstairs. They took Nana and Granddad with them."

When Ellie wakes up Jonah is there.

"What happened to Catherine and Seth?"

Her throat is dry. She moistens her lips.

"They've gone over to Florence's for the night. They said they'd call in tomorrow. How are you feeling?"

Ellie's confused. Something has happened... not Seth and Catherine...

She shifts position so the bluish light from a neighbour's security lamp won't shine in her eyes. Something is making it come on and off: a child playing; a cat walking along the top of a wall.

"Will you close the curtains, please?"

He does it and comes back to the bed. She squeezes his hand because he looks sad.

Then it hits her, the reason everybody was in the house. More than hits her: it slams her through the bed.

She plummets through the floorboards and joists and plaster of the living room ceiling and the boards of the living room floor. She smashes through the concrete and the damp earth below that.

She flips over and is shoved face-first into the boiling hot core of the earth and is buried there.

She claws for air, gasping for breath, sweat pouring from her.

Seagulls cry in her head, crows caw, parrots screech. A vulture rasps. Every kind of piercing animal noise choruses. The sea crashes, the wind shrieks, branches break and thunder rumbles.

Eels wriggle under the dark surface of mud.

But the chaos and calamity can't drown out what has happened, nothing can.

30

Rosie

Hull, July 2000

Eliza always said, "as soon as I'm sixteen, I'll leave home." She'd often then add, "So fuck you."

Yeah, right. Only a year to go, then. As it was, since she became 'home educated' (as if Mum had any say over her) Eliza hardly ever left the house, apart from going to the library.

"It's not fair for adults to be in charge of children," was another of her war cries. Rosie was sick of them, all those things she said as if she was superior to everyone else and ought to be treated differently. Eliza had to have all the attention, and it meant the others had to try not to cause Mum any extra stress.

Rosie thought, why can't I be a normal teenager, and flounce around slamming doors? Because Eliza was the one who did that and Rosie would only get guilt laid on her. She'd have Dad ringing up, saying be kind to your mother. Yeah, like he'd been kind to Mum, sticking his thing into

'Auntie' Bryony at the pub. The place he used to take Rosie to when she was little, to give Mum a break.

Eliza had been out of school for two years.

Rosie couldn't help being jealous. There was no rational explanation for this, since she enjoyed school and had no wish to walk in Eliza's shoes, it was just that Eliza always seemed to get what she wanted. She used to spend her days at the public library researching her latest obsession. But since they'd got the computer it was easier for her to follow her interests at home. At the moment the thing she cared most about was Russia, working her way through the history and literature of the pre and post-Soviet Union. Dostoyevsky, Eliza declared, was now her favourite author, and The Idiot was her favourite book. Her favourite things changed so quickly Rosie couldn't keep up with them.

But it wasn't just history she was good at. Eliza was the world authority on current events. She'd be the first to know when there was a state of emergency in the Philippines, or Ken Livingstone became the Mayor of London. Only because she got to watch the news all the time when everybody else was at school.

Peering through the keyhole of Eliza's room, Rosie could see the Dostoyevsky library book face down on the floor, its spine broken. Ellie must be mentally calculating how much a replacement would cost.

Eliza had just had the biggest meltdown ever because of Dad.

Mum told Rosie first and asked what she thought Eliza's reaction would be. Duh?!

To be honest, though, even Rosie hadn't realised quite how bad. Now Mum had something else to feel guilty about.

"I only have one parent," Eliza was sobbing, (drama was her middle name – one of Nan-nan's sayings). Rosie had to listen carefully to make out the muffled words.

"That's not true," their mum spoke in that ultra-slow way she used when Eliza went crazy. "You still have both me and

Dad. We'll both always love you."

Rosie couldn't hear the next few words. She resumed peeping through the keyhole, saw her sister raise her head, give Mum a long look, eyes squinted. She wiped a hand under them and took a shuddering breath.

"You're saying you actually love me?"

It made Rosie want to cry too. Why did Eliza find emotion so difficult to believe?

She sank down on the floor again, back pressed against Eliza's door. Mum would want to put her arms around Eliza, but she'd be rejected if she did. Eliza had to be the one to make the first move. "Can we have a hug?" she might ask, and Rosie could understand why Mum felt each moment like that represented another fleeting opportunity for redemption. A word they'd been discussing in English.

"Of course I love you," she heard Ellie say. "Honestly, I do."

Rosie heard Eliza hiccupping. All other noise had abated now. She could picture the state the rest of the room would be in, devastation lit up by the moon shining huge and round at the large bay window. Rosie had been helping Lily with her homework in there just before it happened, while Eliza lay reading on her bed.

When Ellie came in and broke the news, Eliza went mad, hurling things around. Ellie had asked Rosie to take her youngest sister downstairs and make her a drink while she talked to Eliza.

"I don't need taking anywhere," Lily declared haughtily, through the yelling. "And I can make myself a drink, thanks. I am twelve, you know!"

"I know that, Lily Angelica," Rosie said, outside the bedroom door. Lily didn't mind when Rosie babied her. She pushed a wedge of Lily's fair hair behind one of her ears. Eliza was never a proper little sister like Lily was. "Mum just wants us out the way, as usual, so she can deal with Eliza."

One last look through the keyhole now to see what was going on. The floor around Eliza was littered with balled-up tissues. Under her eyes were violet half-circles. She looked ethereal (another great word) in the glow of the moon.

Rosie felt sorry for Lily. She never complained about having to share a room with Eliza. The times her books were ripped, her pencils scattered, the quilt thrown off her bed, she would methodically get on with tidying up after the storm was over.

"Why don't you get into bed now?" Mum's voice said to Eliza. "You know it makes you feel better after you've been crying. Tuck yourself up and I'll bring you a drink of hot chocolate."

"I didn't know we had any of that. Hot chocolate." Eliza sounded spaced-out.

Rosie put her eye closer to the keyhole. Eliza had that weird unfocussed expression she got after a rage. Mum patted her hand repeatedly but Rosie couldn't see any reaction from her sister. She wondered if she'd have to go in the room and help Mum get her into bed.

But Ellie was speaking quietly. The view through the keyhole was obscured by their lumbering figures as Eliza followed Mum robotically across the floor to her bed in the corner.

Rosie had a vague memory of Eliza screaming as a baby, the way she could be soothed by the dark interior of the charity-shop Silver Cross pram Mum used to push all three of them in together. When they went out Eliza lay between Kester's legs as he sat upright at the top end, Rosie sat on a pram seat in the middle. It had seemed a long way down to the ground from there.

She went back to her own room. Her mood had plummeted. Throwing herself on the bed she turned her iPod on and plugged the earbuds in. When Mum knocked at her door, as Rosie had known she would, she answered with a curt, "What do you want?"

Mum stepped inside and pushed the door shut behind her. She wet her lips with the tip of her tongue. It was excruciating to see her leaning on the door, hands flattened nervously against the wood behind her. Ellie spoke quickly; saying something Rosie knew she'd been planning to ask for ages (I heard you talking to Dad about it on the phone, stupid).

Rosie removed her earphones extremely slowly because it annoyed Mum.

"Would you consider swapping rooms with Eliza, do you think?" Mum blurted out. "This business with your dad and me has devastated her. I was afraid she'd take it badly and she has."

Rosie's body went taut. Mum only cared about Eliza.

Her posture didn't seem to affect Mum, or she just didn't notice, only continuing to let words run out her mouth.

"It's just that I er, thought she could use some personal space. What do you think, love?"

Nerves prickled under Rosie's skin. She settled her face into the mannequin expression she'd been cultivating recently. She saw Ellie's eyes flick over the bottles and tubes of foundation, eye shadow and lipstick on the dressing table and mentally dared her to mention the amount of make-up she wore.

"If you agree to move in with Lily, we could section the room off with some of those lovely room-dividers we saw on the Calm Your Life website, you know; the Japanese paper screens you liked."

Mum was so blinkered! Did she really think Rosie would agree to share with a twelve-year-old?

Rolling onto her stomach Rosie pushed one earphone back in and held the other ready between finger and thumb, about a centimetre away from her head.

"No," she said, rolling her eyes. "Of course not." Duh.

A level textbooks and pages of notes were strewn all over the bed. She was in sixth-form. How could Ellie even think of asking her to move rooms, to share with her baby sister?

"My needs have always been secondary to hers," she pronounced very slowly. "It's not fair. How dare you ask me to give up the one, tiny space in which I can be myself? I'm nearly eighteen, for God's sake. Don't I deserve any consideration?"

She ripped the earphone out of her ear again, flung herself upright. Papers and books slid after her onto the narrow strip of carpet by the desk.

"One baby after another, that's all you ever had. I had to be the second mother to them all. You were always stressed out, and you never had time for me."

While she spat these words out, she could see Ellie turning herself into a statue at the door. More guilt-tripping to be suffered by Rosie later.

Don't upset sensitive Mum.

"I could scream," Rosie continued. "I could scream and scream until I make myself sick and all that. But what good would it do? Getting attention that way is Eliza's department, isn't it?"

"Oh, Rosie," said Ellie, visibly gathering herself together.

"Oh, Mum," replied Rosie.

She kept her mask on while she gathered up the papers from the floor.

31

Greg

Ireland, 30 June 2013

Sweat pastes his denim shirt to his back and squelches in his armpits. Shows what an idiot he is for believing that deodorant advert. Three blasted euros that aerosol cost him. He'll stick to his usual roll-on, in future. Sweat's also dripping down his face, stinging his eyes. He wipes his brow with his forearm. Fuck it, he's taking his shirt off.

Thing is, the workshop faces an office across the street. That group of bloody women, they'll line up at the windows as usual, drinking coke, mouths falling open. Getting a bit tired of it, he is.

Anyway, isn't he a bit old for this kind of teasing?

Apparently not... The shirt comes off and the first of the women appears. She tips her head back and drinks from the ubiquitous can, lowers her chin and stares across at him, hand at her throat. Tommy McKinney's missus, that one. Sun sparkles on the glass. It's hard to identify the next one, Mary McCartney he thinks it is, shadowed by Bridget Kiernan. He'll be having a word with their husbands in the pub later, so he will.

He allows the wives a few minutes' more fun before performing an elaborate bow and turning his back on 'em. Enough's enough.

The new lad is starting this afternoon: Connor's friend. Only recently moved in to a cottage that belongs to one of them old dears up at the home. Old lady said she'd be glad of someone living in it, especially a young couple.

Greg picks up his chisel, waits for his eyes to acclimatise to the dark of the shed after the bright sunshine of the street. He's making a cabinet for the holiday cottage of a wealthy English couple. The woman wants a bit of carving around the framework of the doors, something relevant to the area. They like to show they belong, even if they live in their posh houses in London most of the time.

He's done a pattern of rolling waves for her, representing the river Shannon. The work is rhythmic and satisfying. The cabinet is the best thing he's made for a long time. Although his back aches, warmth buzzes through his muscles. It feels good to be working on something more like art than craft.

Two hours later, Greg places the chisel in the cloth with the others, takes up a soft brush and removes sawdust from the intertwined waves. He runs his finger along the curves, almost hearing the soft splashing sound of them slapping against each other. He moves over to the kitchen worktop at the far end of the shed and takes his sandwiches from the fridge underneath, lifting the kettle to check its weight and then flicking the switch. He could swear his spine creaks as he lowers himself onto his stool. Getting old, Greg. The order has to be ready by the 14th July. He glances at the calendar: 30th June.

Why does that date ring a bell?

Ah. Ellie's baby. The one she had to leave Running Hare House for. Vincent visited her after the birth, but Greg couldn't bring himself to. Things were happening in his own life. He only ever saw Ellie once after she left and that was years later. It looked like she had four children by then, unless one of them belonged to someone else.

30th June, that was when Ellie's baby was born. Vincent said she'd got depression after. But when he saw her that time in the street she looked happy again.

He wonders what she's doing today, on her daughter's birthday. She and Jonah are probably celebrating with their adult children, maybe even with grandchildren by now.

His eyes wander back to the coils of waves on the cabinet doors and he remembers the Madonna and Child sculpture made of the driftwood he and Ellie collected together, when they were so young.

32

Ellie

Beverley, 10 July 2013

Vivian's in the front pew with all of Deb's family except Catherine; she sits a few rows from the back with Seth and the rest of Ellie and Jonah's children. Except Rosie; she's with Rick in the second row. Arthur is crying noisily in Rosie's lap. His Nan-nan turns around to give him one of her stony looks and Rosie gets a book out of her bag and reads quietly to him before the service starts. Ellie can hear snatches of Percy the park-keeper (a childhood favourite of Rosie's) over the low murmur of conversation in the chapel.

Somewhere else in the room is Malachi Brown, Rosie's father-in-law. Ellie spotted him outside the chapel when they were waiting for the coffin. His wife died from cancer a few years ago. Mal looks shockingly thin. He must have been at the gathering in March but she can't remember much about it.

Ellie can't relate this older man with the memories she has of her teenage boyfriend.

Vivian had entered the building behind the coffin, Deb's arm around her. Sam Martin was one of the coffin-bearers. Vivian sits down and Ellie inspects her from behind: stiff-shouldered, dressed in black lace. Deb, in a black silk suit, looked sick as she walked down the aisle, a macabre bride to her beloved daddy. Her grief-stricken face had hardened into anger when she saw Ellie, already seated.

"What are you doing here? You never cared about Dad." She gave Ellie one of her horrible glares.

Ellie's wearing a long purple skirt. She doesn't have many clothes now she's living in the van. She scrubbed the mud from her boots and borrowed a black velvet jacket from Maria which is nipped in at the waist, it wouldn't even have fit her three months before. Sweat prickles under her arms; hopefully the lining of the jacket won't stain.

A hand rests on her back as her head droops, suddenly too heavy for her neck.

"Keep your chin up."

Jonah. She allows him to take her hand, presses his in return. He looks thin as well, thinner even than when she last saw him in March. What a year it's been.

From a Distance plays on the chapel's sound system as the stragglers at the party squash into pews, causing mourners to have to shuffle up. Ellie's not moving, she keeps her head down.

Ellie bites her lower lip when the vicar says things about her father which aren't true. Good things. Maybe they're true for Deborah and Vivian whose names keep popping up throughout the eulogy, but they aren't for her. The name Eleanor is mentioned only once or twice.

"A wonderful father and grandfather. . ." Ha.

"A loving husband. . ." as long as his wife did as she was told.

And what does love mean anyway?

Ellie's mind is wandering.

She lifts her head and stares hard at the coffin. Daddy, are you in there?

33

Eleanor

Beverley, August 1975

"Daddy." Eleanor tried another knock on the bathroom door.

Light came from underneath it.

She was dressed in her new baby-doll pyjamas and she hadn't had time to put on her slippers because she woke up to hear him calling her name. It was the sharpness of his voice that broke her sleep. You do as Daddy says or there'll be trouble. Eleanor's mind was fuggy. It was still light, just about, but the alarm clock next to her bed said it was ten o'clock. She must have only been asleep an hour.

"Daddy, are you in there?"

Deborah and Mummy were away for the night. They were staying at Grandma's because she was poorly. Eleanor would've gone too except she was doing a riding course all week. Tomorrow they were going for a hack on Beverley Westwood. She got butterflies in her tummy at the excitement.

One more time: "Daddy?"

She had a different kind of butterflies in her tummy now, or maybe they weren't butterflies at all, but moths. Why wasn't Daddy answering?

She was frightened of moths. Daddy made her sit in a room with two big moths flying around and the door shut. He said you had to learn to conquer your fears, like he did, sitting in an air-raid shelter during the bombings. But she was still scared of moths.

She let her raised hand fall and started to turn away. But there was a sound behind the bathroom door; she definitely heard it. A kind of grunt. What if there was an animal in there? It might come out and get her, too. She took several steps backwards until her ankles met with the bottom step of the upper landing. She was going to run to her room and push the cabinet against the door so the animal couldn't get in.

She lifted her foot up to place it behind her on the step as quietly as she could. Then she heard a loud sigh, long and drawn out. After a minute her father's voice: "Debbie?"

She gripped the banister. She'd never heard him call Deborah 'Debbie' before.

"It's me, Daddy, Eleanor."

There was a scramble inside the bathroom, then another period of silence. Eleanor was transfixed, she wanted to move but couldn't. What should she do now?

She waited a long time. Then she approached the bathroom door. Daddy must be hurt in there, he needed her help. She must be brave. She took two more steps.

There was no sound from the other side, pressing her ear to the door. She had to be brave. Daddy could be scary sometimes but, well, he was her father. "The only one you've got," Mummy would often say.

Without letting herself think too much about what might be happening, Eleanor put her hand on the door knob and turned it. At the same time she pushed the door open with her shoulder. She realised she'd had her eyes closed because she had to make an effort to pop them open so she could see if Daddy was alright.

At first, yellow light blinded her eyes. Then she saw Daddy. He was lying on the floor with his eyes wide open. Wide open. He wasn't moving or saying anything. A strange embarrassment came over her. She wanted to say sorry, or excuse me, because all of a sudden she really needed the toilet and she would have to get past him first. But it seemed rude to step past somebody who was lying like that with their eyes wide open and not moving or speaking, and she couldn't use the toilet with Daddy lying there on the floor.

She wished Mummy was here, even Deborah.

He stayed still, stiff on the ground.

The word 'dead' came into her mind. The digits 999 followed swiftly afterwards. You had to ring 999 if there was an accident and Daddy must have had an accident to be lying there like that.

The telephone was downstairs in the hall. Eleanor began to step backwards. Suddenly it registered with her that Daddy was naked. She ticked the facts off in her head. He was lying on the bathroom floor: not moving or speaking, with his eyes wide open and he was naked. He didn't have any clothes on. Her mind wouldn't allow her eyes to take in many details but she noticed yellowed skin and clumps of hair on his chest. There was something thick and purplish sticking straight up from a nest of hair lower down his body, at the tops of his legs, and his legs were straight and long. His toes pointed upwards.

"I need to ring 999," she reminded herself out loud. Mummy's voice came into her head, Pull yourself together, Eleanor.

She pulled the bathroom door quietly closed behind her. Her heart was knocking so hard in her chest she could hardly get down the stairs. She had to grip the banister to keep steady. It was much darker now and the shadows on the stairs always scared her; it felt like someone was coming down behind her. Monsters... there are no monsters.

She turned sideways and kept her back against the wall, but that meant she couldn't hold on to the banister. She was lowering herself onto her bottom so she could slip down each step one at a time when the bathroom door burst open above her. Yikes, it's a ghost! Light flooded out and lit her up like she was on a stage.

Maybe it's all a bad dream. She closed her eyes tightly, willed herself to wake up.

"Aha! Fooled you, Eleanor," shouted Daddy.

He made a silhouette in the bathroom doorway, standing with its arms and legs apart, and he still had no clothes on.

Half-way down the stairs, thankfully sitting on her bottom, cold water trickled down her spine. Sparkly lights lit up behind her eyes and then her skin went hot and cold at the same time. Still staring up at Daddy, her vision narrowed into two little tunnels, and she felt the relief of leaving.

"You bumped your head when you fell down the stairs, Eleanor," Daddy was saying. "Silly girl, what were you doing wandering around the house at that time of night? I went to bed early, you know, and I woke up when I heard a noise. It was you, falling. Thank goodness you didn't go all the way to the bottom."

"But I... was I?" mumbled Eleanor. Fuzzy shapes twisted around each other behind her eyes. She scrunched them closed.

"You must have been sleepwalking," Daddy said sharply. "Stupid girl. I had to carry you back up to bed."

She opened her eyes. There he was in his pyjamas and dressing gown.

"I've put a plaster on the cut on your head," he said, "but you won't be able to go horse riding tomorrow. Mummy will have to come back from Grandma's and look after you.

Deborah won't be pleased; Mummy was going to take her to that circus on the common."

"But Daddy, I. . . " Eleanor looked around her. The bedside lamp was on and she was tucked up under the sheets of her bed with her satin bedspread over the top. It was a hot night. She wanted to kick it off but Daddy was sitting in the chair next to her and she supposed he must have put the cover on. He never usually came inside her bedroom.

"Drink this, Eleanor."

It was a cloudy hot drink in a glass with a handle. It looked funny but it was sweet so she drank it down in big gulps. She was thirsty.

"Now you get off to sleep, darling."

Darling. His voice had gone soft. He wasn't her real Daddy. That one never called her darling.

She felt woozy. 'Daddy' stroked her hair.

"There, there, Debbie."

Debbie? Why was he calling her that?

It felt wrong in her tummy, like the moths had come back and she was trapped in a room with them, but she couldn't fight the sleep that was coming to get her.

Something wet smeared across her face. Huh? She prised open her eyes and in the dimness saw Daddy's tongue slithering back into his mouth, reminding her of a snake. Everything in slow motion.

She moved her head to one side on the pillow but Daddy leaned closer to the bed. He pressed his body against it, she felt the bed wobbling and it made her feel sick. He took her chin in his hand and turned her face to him. She mustn't make him cross by pulling away a second time.

"Be a good girl," he said in a gruff voice.

Trip-trap, trip-trap, who's that coming over my bridge?

She couldn't see where his other hand was but his elbow was bumping against her stomach, jab, and jab again.

Daddy had a scary grin on his face. His chair creaked and he rocked backwards and forwards.

Flutter, flutter, went the moths' wings in her tummy. Daddy licked her face again, flicking his tongue across her eyes. She tried to wriggle backwards but her body felt heavy and she was half in a dream.

Shadows flitted around the room, hid in corners. They might be bats; even scarier than moths. Daddy's elbow jerked faster, faster, hurting her stomach.

The light went out.

Everything stopped for a minute and she was sure she would drop into a dark hole. Then she heard Daddy make a funny sound. Like water draining out of the bath. Now he leant heavily on top of her. She was pinned under the bedspread, fighting to get out. She would suffocate. Panic, stark and cold, flapped in her chest.

The light came on. Daddy was leaning over her but not on her anymore. He had one hand in his dressing gown pocket, the other stroked her forehead. His hand felt clammy. In the light from the dim bulb his eyes looked sparkly.

"You've been having a dream," said Daddy. "Silly girl. I came in because I heard you crying out. You must be missing your Mummy, but don't worry, she'll be home tomorrow. Go back to sleep now."

The light went out again.

34

Ellie

10 July 2013

My Way is the music that accompanies the coffin through the curtains.

I hate you, you bastard.

She touches the tiny scar on her forehead as the coffin sails out of sight. She bores her eyes into Deb's back, wondering if she will feel it, but she doesn't turn around.

Ray Payne. I hate you.

(The family were watching a film on telly together a while after that night. There was a dead body in it, eyes staring open. Ray looked at her and laughed. She went cold all over and had to run from the room to be sick. "You're such a drama queen Eleanor," Vivian said the next morning. "Why did you have to spoil one of the few family occasions we ever have?")

"Are you alright, Mum?" Lily asks. The little worrier, always thinking about everyone else. "You look sort of green."

There is a row of stained-glass windows high in the wall of the chapel, with coloured light streaming through. It cheers the drab darkness of the mourners' clothes. Ellie's glad she wore purple.

Lily looks the most like her. She doesn't have the sharpness of Rosie's bone structure (inherited from Vivian) or the elfishness of Eliza.

"There's a plain one in every family," Vivian used to say. "In Deborah's family it's Imogen, in yours it's Lily. In ours it was you."

Of course it was.

"To me you've always been a swan," Jonah responded when she told him. Sometimes, he did everything right. "That makes our Lily all the more beautiful."

Sweat is breaking out on her forehead. Did she eat this morning? No. Tell-tale lights appear behind her eyes. She grips the back of the chair in front. You are not doing this to me now, Ray.

The congregation stand, singing Ray's favourite hymn, He Who Would Valiant Be.

But, I'm going. . . She bangs her head on the chair in front as she goes down.

35

10 July 2013

Many of the mourners are ex-colleagues of Ray's from the Council.

"Good man, your dad," someone says to Ellie as she arrives on wobbly legs.

Kester drove them from the crematorium in Ellie's van. He brings Ellie a plate of sandwiches and Catherine brings her a cup of tea.

"Get this down you, Auntie Ellie, you'll soon feel better."

She'd hit her head right on top of the scar. "You have a bruise," Catherine says. "I hope you're not concussed. You really should see a doctor."

"I'm alright." Ellie welcomes the pain.

Seth pulls over a stool, a sandwich in one hand.

"I've been thinking a lot about you since we left," he said. "When are you coming to see us in Ireland?"

She takes a sip of tea.

"I'm not sure. I'm booked into craft fairs for most of the summer and autumn."

"Well," Catherine smiles. "There's a big one in Manorhamilton in November. That's near us. Maybe you could put it in your diary?"

Ellie thinks her niece's eyes have a particular shine to them. She moves her head slowly to avoid giddiness, exchanges glances with Jonah.

"I might get a van like yours, Mum," says Kester. "What's it like for fuel?" He's currently working as a hostel manager in Venice. "I'm getting fed up of it there though. There's only so much water you want to look at. And the work's not really challenging. I'd love to travel properly, like Eliza, only in a campervan so I'd always have somewhere to stay."

"I was thinking of maybe applying for a voluntary programme overseas," contributes Lily. "I'm not enjoying being a PE teacher, the students are so competitive." She blushes when everyone looks at her. "I'd like to travel too. Life's so short, isn't it?"

They have a moment of respectful quiet. Seth suggests, "Maybe you could all come over to Ireland in November, before you all take off around the world?"

He takes another bite of his sandwich and licks a scrap of smoked salmon from the edge of his hand. "Catherine and I might have an event of our own worth travelling to by then."

He kisses Catherine. It just happens to be the moment Deb passes by with a plate of food in one hand and a drink in the other. Her shoulders hunch as she notices her daughter's behaviour. She stops, steps back a few paces until she can look Ellie in the eye.

"I'm trying to pay my respects to my father and you steal the show as always."

It's always Ellie's fault.

"Are you serious?" demands Lily, who hardly ever speaks back to anyone. "It was her father's funeral too, you know."

She goes red in the face again. Deb gives her a frightening stare.

Catherine scrambles off Seth's lap and positions herself in front of Deb. "I'm sorry about Granddad. You must be feeling terrible. It's a hard day for you."

She tries a sympathetic smile.

Deb's cheeks flare with bright spots of colour. Her breathing speeds up.

This is exactly what she used to do as a child. Why does everybody indulge her?

"Mummy," Catherine says pleadingly. "Can't we be friends again? I miss you loads."

Fury explodes in Ellie's brain. She turns to her children.

"Don't any of you ever feel you have to beg me to love you like that." She searches the eyes of each of them in turn. Especially Rosie, standing behind Jonah with a sleeping Arthur in her arms. Rosie bites her lip.

"I will always love you all, no matter what happens."

Her teacup rattles on its saucer. Lily kneels beside her. She places the cup and saucer on the floor. Ellie strokes her hair.

"I don't feel very good," she says. The fog is coming down.

"She's fainting again," she hears Lily say. "Quick, someone catch that plate before it hits the floor."

Eliza stands beside the bed.

"Your hair needs a brush," Ellie says.

"You always say that. You're not in charge of me now, you know."

"I know."

There's silence.

Eliza looks around her with interest.

"This is your old bedroom, isn't it?"

"It is." Ellie feels dazed. "Sit down, Eliza. Talk to me. Where is everyone?"

The bed sinks as Eliza parks herself on the edge of it.

"Lily stayed with you for a while but you were sleeping, so she went down. It was Dad and Kes who helped get you up here."

Ellie fingers the embroidery on the quilt. This is a double bed. Nothing from her childhood remains. She wonders if Deb's old room has stayed the same.

"What is it with Auntie Deb and you?"

Eliza leans forward. Ellie catches the wood-smoky scent of her hair. "You're sisters, what's the problem? I'd hate it if I was like that with my sisters."

Ellie pushes herself up in the bed, rubs her eyes.

"It goes way back. I think it was how our father treated us. He loved Deborah and he didn't love me."

Ought she to tell Eliza about the things Ray did to her? Perhaps not. That conversation is better saved for Deb.

Eliza is staring at her.

"Why are you looking at me like that?"

Eliza squints at her, head cocked on one side.

"You're looking at me like Jack does," says Ellie.

Eliza lowers her head, sandy lashes shielding her gaze.

"You didn't love me either." She says it calmly. The truth.

Breath leaves Ellie's lungs. No sense in lying.

"You mean when you were born?"

"Yes. . . and before that."

Eliza always had an astonishing memory. Ellie doesn't doubt she would remember back to the womb.

Memories flow out. Eliza used to feed and then push herself away from the breast. She was happiest lying in her carrycot, staring at nothing. Or that's how Ellie has chosen to remember it. But the real feelings come back now. She sees herself backing away, afraid of the way Eliza looked at her. She remembers the chaos in her head.

"You loved Kester, but you didn't love me," Eliza continues.

Kester used to cuddle at my other breast, stroking his sister's flailing arms and legs while she fed. He was a good boy.

"I'm so sorry."

A simple apology is all she can offer.

Eliza shifts on the bed. When she moves all sorts of aromas break away from her: the sea; campfires; ice, if ice has a smell. Ellie thinks it does. But the overpowering scent is water.

She shudders. The sun has moved around the house and the room feels cold, despite the fact of July. Eliza's hand is cold too, when Ellie touches it.

"It wasn't really you I didn't love. It was me. I hated myself for making such a mess of things."

"I know."

"I didn't even know who you were. But when you started to become yourself, I loved you and admired you. I still do."

"I know that, Mammy."

Ellie makes her way down with care.

"Do you know where my mother is?" she asks someone, a neighbour of her parents. The woman tells her that Vivian has closeted herself in Ray's study.

"I'm sorry about all the fainting."

Her mum is seated at Ray's desk. The sun shines in this corner of the house and the polished mahogany chest Ray kept his important papers in glows from the other side of the room.

Ellie's mother half-turns in her chair. "Are you feeling better?" She has something in her lap. Ellie realises it's the headgear Ray wore constantly in the last few years of his life. The surveillance camera winks a warning eye as Vivian fiddles with it. She endured constant observation from that thing. Why did she put up with it?

Ray was wearing the camera at the gathering in March and Ellie wonders with a sickening thump of her heart if there are tapes of the occasion somewhere. No, I don't want to know.

"I am feeling better, thanks."

It's not entirely true. She feels her way cautiously between boxes to a stool facing Vivian.

"It's the stress, I think. I'm sorry, I didn't mean. . . "

"It's okay, Eleanor. I'm not the one who thinks you were stealing the show. You must try and make your amends with Deborah though; she's more fragile than you think."

Why am I the one who has to make amends? She lets her gaze wander around the walls, finding empty patches where someone, presumably Vivian, has removed Ray's pictures; mostly of uncomfortably young girls.

"Did you mind about all that?" Ellie blurts out.

Vivian places the surveillance equipment on the desk and gets to her feet.

"It's not your place to ask."

"Why can't we talk to each other properly?"

The clock on the wall ticks.

"I don't see what there is to talk about. The past is the past."

"It might be my place to ask. . . " Ellie tries.

Her mother gives her a sharp look. She shuffles papers with restless fingers. A bird flies by outside the window, casting a shadow across the patterned wallpaper. From a corner of the ceiling a moth detaches itself, fluttering into the centre of the room. Ellie jumps up and shields the side of her face with her arm.

"Oh, for heaven's sake, Eleanor!"

The moth settles on the wallpaper. Vivian reaches across the desk, flips open the window. Then she cups her hands together and closes them around the moth. She takes it to the window and releases it.

"Thank you," Ellie breathes again. "I wish I didn't have that phobia. I have to be careful in the van at night. Once I found myself standing outside in the dark for an hour while a moth fluttered inside it. The fire had gone out by the time I was brave enough to go back in."

Vivian assesses her. "Your father tried to cure you of it once, that phobia. Do you remember?"

"Of course."

It must be the way she punches out the words that makes Vivian abandon her activity with the box on her desk and settle her hands in her lap.

"Where does your bitterness come from, Ellie?"

She's never called her that, only Eleanor. It brings a lump to Ellie's throat.

"You won't want to know."

Vivian brushes a strand of greying hair off her forehead.

"If I hadn't wanted to know, I wouldn't have asked. Now he's gone, I do."

Now he's gone.

Ellie's heart pounds painfully. Maybe she knew all along.

"Are you sure?"

Vivian draws herself up. She takes a hinged make-up mirror from the clutch bag on the desk, and produces a lipstick. After applying fresh colour to her lips she snaps the mirror closed and says yes, she is ready to hear Ellie out.

"Deborah needs to be here."

Ellie surprises herself, but realises it's true.

Vivian stands taut. Then she seems to decide. Her shoulders slacken.

"If you say so." Her eyes have darkened. "It's time you two sorted things out between you, anyway. Now your father's no longer here for you both to pivot around."

No longer here.

Vivian grasps the handle and pulls the door open.

Freya is trotting past in the hallway, followed by an older girl Ellie doesn't recognise.

Rosie's daughter peeps in the room and spots Ellie.

"Hi, Gramma,"

"Hi, Freya-Bear." She manages a smile for the darling girl, wishing she could feel those bendy plaits tickling her face. But Vivian has stepped between her and the child.

"Freya, dear, would you please fetch Auntie Deborah for me? Tell her we're in the study."

"OK, Nan-nan."

Freya shoots Ellie a heartrending grin. She has no idea how much Ellie has missed her.

36

"Why are you letting her say these things?"

Their mother switches on a lamp. A chill has settled on the room.

To Ellie, Deb says, "You're disgusting. You're only accusing him of this now because he's not here to defend himself. Why didn't you say anything before?"

Ellie meets Deb's eyes.

"I was scared."

Deb's face stays frozen, her eyes in the distance. Ellie waits for the right moment.

Then she says: "Debbie."

Deb's face collapses. She lets out a gasp and chokes. Vivian rises calmly and fetches a bottle of water from the small fridge Ray kept his beers in.

"Come on, have a drink. You'll feel better."

Deb gulps water, chokes again and starts sobbing. Vivian pushes at her shoulders.

"Sit down. For God's sake, loosen up for once. You can't hold it all in, it doesn't help."

"I can't believe you've done this to me, Ellie."

Vivian pushes a box of tissues closer and Deb blows her nose. Vivian lays a hand on her daughter's head, briefly. The golden girl.

"Today of all days." Deb is crying more quietly now. "The day they took our daddy away."

Vivian's eyes are raw. A chill settles in Ellie's stomach. She knew all along.

Ellie waits another long moment. A car starts up outside and she wonders who's leaving. A door slams within the house; children's footsteps race up the stairs. She raises her head.

"That night I told you about." No, I will not faint again. "He called me Debbie. That's how I guessed he must have done the same to you."

She touches the wet pools on her face.

"He never called you Debbie normally, it was always Deborah."

She wipes angrily at her tears and looks up to find Vivian passing the tissues. She has the weird sense they're in some kind of therapy and Vivian is the facilitator.

"He never used a special name for me. I stayed Eleanor. . . except when he thought I was Debbie."

She pictures the golden child with hair streaming down her back. Always so confident yet at the same time brittle. But the month before Deb's wedding, Mum asked me to look after her. Bile burns her throat. Florence.

Deb stops sobbing. She bunches tissues in her fists, keeps her head down. She hasn't denied it.

Vivian clears her throat.

"Was it just the. . . were there more occasions?"

"A few times he would leave the toilet door open deliberately, and I would walk in and find him. . . " She can't say it. "I tried never to be alone with him. Can you remember the other time you were going away for the night with just Deb? When Auntie Emma had her last baby and she asked you to go and help with the other children? You insisted on taking Deb with you and I begged to come too. I said I'd do all the cleaning, look after the children, anything you wanted. But you said there wouldn't be enough room for me."

Vivian supports herself with her hand on the desk.

"I remember how desperate you seemed. That's when I started to suspect he might have touched you. Or I was scared he would. I arranged for you to spend the nights with a friend instead. I got punished for that."

A hush falls over the room. Ellie struggles out of it with the two pieces of information she's just gathered: Vivian knew about pervy Ray, and she was abused by him.

"Punished?"

Deb says nothing. Her head sinks even lower.

Vivian constructs a grim smile.

"He was careful not to do it anywhere the bruises would show. Classic, I know. But where could I have gone if I'd left him?" Her eyes glitter. "Not your grandma's. She was already beginning to show signs of dementia. In those days there was no social security for the likes of me. We lived in a nice house, you girls were happy enough."

The hush wriggles between them.

Vivian cracks the silence. "I tried to protect you, that's all."

Ellie finds herself wanting to apologise, as if everything is her fault. But it isn't. Ray's to blame for the damage and he's dead.

There's a knock at the door. It's Sam.

"What have you been saying to her now?" He's straight in at Ellie. Deb starts crying again, but this time Ellie doesn't blame her.

"It's nothing to get upset at Ellie about, Sam," explains Vivian. "Things have been said that needed to be said, that's all. Deborah, darling, if you want any medicine from the bathroom cabinet, please take some. Sam will look after you now."

"Medicine?" Sam kinks his eyebrows. "I came to fetch her because I thought it was time we set off back to Bedford.

Unless you'd like us to stay?" He makes the funny movement with his eyebrows again.

"I meant for a headache, or she might like to take a sedative. The day has been very stressful."

Vivian begins to usher them both from the room. "I really would advise a sedative, darling. You can sleep in the car on the journey home. Everything will be alright, don't worry."

Sam flashes a look back at Ellie over his shoulder but Vivian is pushing him towards the stairs. "In the bathroom cabinet, Sam."

The light is on in the hall and the house seems comfortable and familiar now. But Deb turns around on the stair. Her eyes are livid.

"I'll never forgive you for this, Ellie."

For breaking up your smug fantasy. Why would she?

———

Ellie bumps into Malachi.

It's so long ago since they were childhood sweethearts, and now their children are married to each other.

Oh, Mal. You've faded since Francesca died.

"I'm looking for our granddaughter. Little minx seems to have disappeared." His forehead crinkles. "Ellie, what's going on between you and Rosie?"

"I've just got my face cleaned up after an emotional encounter with Deb," Ellie says. "I can't go into my problems with Rosie at the moment. Suffice it to say, she's angry at me, both for selling my house instead of offering it to her, and for my support of Seth and Catherine. She thinks their relationship is wrong." She pauses while she struggles for deeper honesty. "But I think it's much more to do with Eliza. When we're both up to it we need to have a proper talk. But not today."

"I'm sorry for your troubles, El." Mal's rich voice sends a quiver of sensory memory through her. She takes a closer look at him. His skin seems lighter than she remembers, as if his colour has drained away with his zest for life.

"You were the only person who called me El."

He scratches his head.

"I've been worrying about you lately. Living in a campervan. You're going to be cold in the winter." He studies her sideways as they set off up the stairs together. "You've lost a lot of weight."

"As if you haven't." Ellie pats his arm. "Maybe we both need to look after ourselves better."

They reach the upper landing, calling Freya.

"They're all staying with me tonight," Malachi says. "If you fancy driving by later it might give you a chance to have a proper conversation with Rosie?"

They discover Freya playing in Ellie's old bedroom.

"Gramma!" the child shouts, "You found me."

"We sure did."

Ellie holds out her arms.

<hr>

Rosie offers her a kiss on the cheek before leaving. Her demeanour suggests she isn't yet ready for a hug.

"We've decided to stay in Sheffield after all. We're renting a house there, if you're interested to know," she says stiffly. "We sold ours and I've started up my lingerie business."

Ellie wants to say how proud she is of her but Rosie interrupts.

"Mal tells me he's invited you to pop round later so if you're up for it, I'll maybe see you then. Say bye-bye to Gramma and Nan-nan, kids."

Rick gives his mother-in-law a sheepish wave, under strict orders from her daughter, she guesses, to keep his distance. "I'd love to take a look at that LDV of yours if you'd let me," he offers as he goes out the door in Rosie's wake. "You know, give it the once-over, check everything's alright for you."

"Thanks, Rick, I'd appreciate that. I don't know one end of an engine from the other as yet. I've been lucky nothing's gone wrong so far."

Jonah is taking most of their children back to the Boulevard house.

"I've made sure all the bedrooms are free, there's plenty of room for you, Ellie, if you want to come with us." He doesn't know what to do with his hands. "You can't drive anywhere in that van tonight."

"Jonah." They look each other in the eyes. "I don't. . . "

Vivian comes into the kitchen. She's been unusually kind since Deb left.

"Ellie can sleep in her old room, she's not driving anywhere. In fact, everyone, if you don't mind, I'd like to get the house shut up for the night. It's been a long day."

"Do you want us to take Jack with us, Mum, or is he alright in the bus?" Lily pipes up. No-one would even think of bringing him into Vivian's house.

"Oh God." Ellie flaps her hands, "I forgot about him. It's been hours."

"Shush, Mum, stop worrying. Rick and the children took him out for a walk earlier. Kester had the keys to your van. And they fed him as well. He's fine."

"Thank God," says Ellie. "My poor Jack. But you can take him back to Hull tonight. Thanks, I'll pick him up tomorrow."

There's a flurry of coat-gathering and goodbyes. Ellie feels weird, staying in her mother's house. She wishes she was going with the others.

"Here," says Jonah, throwing the Land Rover keys to Kester. "You go with Seth and pick up my wheels. I'll help Ellie get her stuff from the van."

Ellie's reluctant to spend time alone with him but he's following her out the door.

Jack's beside himself.

"It's only for one night," Ellie tells him.

Jonah looks haggard. Her arms twitch. She could put them around him; sink into him, lose herself in the old way. But no, it was a mistake letting him in. Now isn't the time to let him get to her.

She stuffs things into a bag without really thinking, stumbling as the van jerks with the slamming door.

"Jonah."

He's pressing against her.

"God, Ellie, I need you tonight."

It sounds like a line from a song. But the tell-tale ache begins in her belly anyway.

No.

"No, Jonah."

"Shit! Whaddya do that for?"

She's pushed him, hard.

Jonah rubs his hip. He's knocked it on the toilet door handle.

"Fuck, Ellie. There was no need for that. I was just being loving."

She straightens her skirt.

"That wasn't loving behaviour. You were taking what you wanted. I didn't want it."

She picks up the bag and slings it over her shoulder, determined not to be the guilty one. But she sees his eyes are brimming.

"I've changed, Ellie, I promise I have. I understand what I threw away when I had that affair. But I've never got over you, you know that."

Beyond the windows of the van, the garden is dark. Ellie hopes Jack hasn't got out onto the road.

She offers Jonah a conciliatory kiss on the cheek. They've shared as much over the past few months as in all the years they spent raising their children, but it really is too late for them, whatever her body intermittently tries to tell her. She'll just have to carry the ache with her.

"Come on, old man. I'm relying on you to look after our kids tonight. What I need more than anything is to get into bed."

At the hopeful raise of his eyebrows, she adds, "alone."

37

Heacham, Norfolk

20 September 2013

"I know, I know," Ellie says. "But you can't blame me."

The dog flops heavily onto the floor, rocking the van. He lets out a deep sigh and settles his head on his paws, keeping his eyes on her face.

"Fuck it, Jack."

Ellie hardly ever swears but his stare is unnerving. And guilt-inducing. "We were married, for Heaven's sake. For years. We had five babies. It's not that wrong."

She must be imagining it, but she'd swear he's shaking his head.

"It's not wrong. Don't judge me, okay?"

Rain lashes the windows, hammers on the roof. Damp washing, rung out as tightly as Ellie could manage, is hanging from the line strung beneath the ceiling of the van. Nearby trees whip the blank, white sky.

The van is in a layby set back from the road. There's a hedge next to the window and a footpath leads across fields into some woods. Not far beyond that is a beach. They're parked somewhere in Norfolk. She's been driving since mid-morning. If it stops raining she'll take Jack for a proper walk. Before that she has some work to catch up on.

Her skin tingles. Her bath this morning made her feel cleaner than topping and tailing in the van ever does.

The hotel Jonah booked them into was in a small castle. She tries not to think about the money he spent, it's not her concern. (The en suite bathroom was accessed by a curved staircase up a tower. It had a huge arched window with a view across formal gardens to a lake on which white swans swam in synchronicity).

Proper fairy-tale stuff.

Mist rose off the water and she expected to see a swan turn into a prince. Or something like that.

But it was Jonah.

She supposes she knew they would have sex the minute she agreed to let him take her away for the night. It was only one room after all, and the bed was enormous.

This has been bound to happen since they were in Iceland, and now it's done. You fool, Ellie, he'll never let it go.

Their candlelit dinner took place in a domed restaurant. They had a table in a corner booth shaped like a birdcage. When they returned to their room the bed had been turned down by a maid and scattered with rose petals and chocolates. There was a real fire in the grate, and their second bottle of champagne in a bucket of ice on a table near the bed.

But now she's away from the hotel, in the primal comfort of her van again, what she experienced last night feels false; almost ridiculous.

She turns her confusion into a taunt at Jack.

"You're just cross because you had to sleep in the van alone, aren't you?"

Jack lifts his head, eyes bright with interest. "Aha," says Ellie, "I'm right. I know it."

Jonah could truthfully say she's led him to believe they are 'back on' again, might even use her whispered I love you at the moment of coming as evidence against her.

Would it be so bad to try again? At least their relationship wouldn't be burdened with pregnancy and childrearing. She could travel the world with him, do her own thing wherever he is playing; see other cultures.

But no. She's promised herself she'll give her new lifestyle a chance, at least for a year or two. Promised Eliza...

And yet...But no... It's simply nostalgia she's feeling; he is the only person in the world who can understand how the past few months have felt.

"Why am I so stubborn, Jack? Ouch!"

She's pricked her finger, just to the side of the wound from two days ago.

She finds a plaster. Then she spreads the completed miniature clothes in her lap: a purple velvet skirt and jacket; a snowy blouse and a pair of long knickers. There's also a pair of felt boots. Running a finger over the fabric, she swallows a lump in her throat, but the ache spreads into her chest and stomach and she has to bend double and wind her arms around her knees until it lessens.

When she can breathe again, she feels wind buffeting the van. When the bough breaks, the cradle will fall...

She gently removes the miniature garments from her lap and lays them to one side. Rising stiffly to her feet, she stretches her back. Then she takes a few steps across the bus.

"Keep still, Jack."

Taking care not to trip over him, she raises her arms to the storage area above the cab and carefully brings down a case. She stumbles back as she lowers it.

Inside the suitcase are twenty dolls, some she has fully dressed, some whose outfits are not yet finished. The dolls are made of stretchy cotton fabric, stuffed with sheep's wool.

They have a range of flesh tones. Some have button-jointed arms and legs, mainly the baby ones.

She sculpted their faces by clever use of stitching. She sewed their eyes with different coloured embroidery thread. Their hair, made from textured yarns, looks real.

Ellie's children.

Eliza would imagine them coming alive at night. "Don't shut them in a suitcase, Mammy."

She lifts the dolls out of their padded bed, handles them one by one. She's given each doll unique features. This one has a bead sewn into her nose. That one has an elaborate hairstyle of plaits all over her head. Ellie designed and made all the outfits herself, a parody of her long-ago dreams: a miniature fashion parade. As in her real family, she's created both boys and girls.

Holding her breath, Ellie lifts out the last doll, wrapped in a square of silk cloth at the bottom of the case. She's larger than the rest. Ellie feels as though she made her in a dream. She can hardly remember running the seams through the sewing machine or pressing clean wool into the turned-out limbs and body. Was it really me? I can't remember.

The doll has long limbs and hair made from straw-coloured wool. She has no features on her face. Ellie sits on the bed and moves the case away from her. She holds the doll under its arms and gazes at its blank countenance. Maybe once she dresses her. . . it. . . Then she'll be able to bear taking a needle to its face. She cradles the doll, arranges it on her lap like a sitting child; strokes the hair repeatedly.

At least you'll let me touch you.

It's a while before she can form words.

"I'm going to get you dressed now."

But she finds herself cradling it for a longer time before she can bring herself to start putting clothes on the body.

38

Norfolk, October 2013

Ellie has money in her purse and a full tank of fuel. The cupboards are stocked with food and she's treated herself to five bags of cut logs, stowed away under the bed by the back doors. She'll have to use her axe to chop them smaller but it's a relief not to have to rely on foraging for a while. The nights are getting longer and she feels the cold in her bones.

In her bones.

Standing with Jonah at the edge of the world. Most of the waterfall fell in torrents, the edges of it bone-hard shards of frozen water, rigorised mid-fall. Everywhere was white. The landscape around riven with crevasses. Abysses. Like a cracked skull. Gullfoss. One of the waterfalls Eliza directed them to.

She tries not to think too far ahead, wondering where she'll spend her winter nights.

Maybe in the cold heart of winter she'll have to resort to her mother's, even if just to park in the garden. The prospect of the winter road is unforgiving.

Or she could stay with Seth and Catherine in Ireland. They've offered, repeatedly. There's also Jonah. Though he was hurt by her eventual rejection last month, he'd still welcome her home.

Yet if that was what I really wanted, I would have done it by now. The thing in the hotel was a goodbye. The memory of their returned closeness sometimes keeps her warm at night, but in her heart she knows it is over for good and so does Jonah.

"We're leaving Norfolk," she tells Jack, waiting for the engine to warm up. Everything is wedged or strapped down and they're ready to go.

The craft fair in Leigh-on-Sea was her biggest success yet. Children flocked to her dolls. They asked her to read from the little cards she painstakingly inscribed with the characters' stories. She imagines the toys being unwrapped on Christmas morning, falling into the arms of their new 'mothers'. They'll be safe and cherished, the ones she let go... She'd put the special doll on display, the one she loved, even though it had no face. She'd wanted to show off the fine work of the costume and the intricately sewn hair.

"This one doesn't have a price tag." A woman had examined all Ellie's dolls. "But I'm drawn to her. How much is she?"

"I'm sorry," Ellie had to say. "She's not ready to sell yet. She has no face, see?"

A sense of relief. The premonition of loss dissipating.

"But that's what I love about her," the tall woman persisted. She was immaculately groomed, hair like a lion's mane. She wore high-heeled boots.

Ellie's fingers itched to reach out and reclaim the doll.

"She's a beautiful piece of work. The lack of features is a genius touch. It gives her an enigmatic quality."

The woman looked at Ellie, hands tightening on the prize. "I'll give you two hundred pounds for her, it's a good offer."

More than twice the amount Ellie was charging for any of her other dolls.

But I'm not ready. She's not ready.

"I'm sorry," Ellie shrugged. "This one isn't for sale yet. It would be wrong of me to let her go now; I haven't quite finished with her."

The woman handed back the doll with reluctance.

"Please, take my card." The glossy rectangle she passed over had an image of a soft toy on it. "I have a doll shop up in Yorkshire, well, I sell handmade toys in general, but I specialize in dolls. Perhaps we can do business together some time."

"Thank you." Ellie noted the web address. "I'll have a look later."

The woman slipped a DollStory card from the holder at the front of the stall. She gave Ellie another green-eyed look of assessment before she turned, pulling her red coat closely around her. But halfway across the crowded floor of the hall she stopped. Her heels clicked on the laminate as she swivelled and headed again to Ellie's stall. She asked where Ellie was planning to set up next.

"Next month," Ellie told her. "I'm going over to Ireland: the fair is in a place called Manorhamilton in County Leitrim. My son lives there."

"Thank you." The woman offered her hand. "My name's Lavinia, by the way. But of course it's on my card. Lavinia Mapplethorpe. I may just see you in Ireland. That doll..." She leaned over the stall and Ellie felt a brush of energy she couldn't interpret. "There's something about that particular doll. Having no features gives her a dream-like quality. She reminds me of... oh, but it doesn't matter. I probably wouldn't have been able to bring myself to put her up for sale if I'd had her in my shop anyway. Goodbye, for now."

A faint vibration lingered in the air after she'd gone.

"We'll be going on a ferry," Ellie says as they drive away from Leigh-on-Sea. "That'll be exciting, won't it?"

She glances at the dog, sitting so alertly in the passenger seat she'd swear he's checking whether she's slowing down enough at the roundabout.

"Don't worry, Jack." She comes to a smooth stop on the white line. A few cars pass from the right. "Anyone'd think I haven't been driving this thing for months, bloody censorious dog."

All clear to the right. Third exit, she reminds herself. Which is the third exit? There. Good grief, it's a narrow lane. Feeling unsure, she changes into third gear and immediately into fourth, otherwise the van makes a horrible noise. It does.

"Don't say a word," she warns her companion. The dog gives her a sideways glance, sniffing enquiringly.

A car approaches from the opposite direction. Ellie panics. There's no way the car's going to stop, it's not even slowing down. "You stupid bitch," she shouts at the windscreen. Ellie crawls almost to a stop, crunching painfully back into first gear. The two vehicles are only about twenty feet apart when she spots a passing place on her left.

Thank God. Now, pull in carefully. Brambles scratch the side of the van. The driver of the polished silver car creeping past raises her gloved fingers in an imperious wave, her lipsticked mouth smiling grimly.

"Fuck off to you too," Ellie mutters. Damn. Some people. "Polluting your posh space, am I? With my gaudy presence?"

For some reason Vincent Mendel from Running Hare House comes into her mind. They'd have laughed at the face on that woman.

Whatever happened to Vincent? She regrets asking him not to visit again after that one time.

Checking carefully, she pulls out into the lane again. Hedges are now scratching both sides of the van. This can't be the right way. I must've taken the wrong turning.

They come to the end of the lane. At the emergence onto a wider but still rural-looking road she wonders which way to go. She curses her stupidity at not getting a Satnav. Stubborn old woman. Once again, it comes down to Eliza. She disapproves of such things.

After all, you managed to find your way around the world without one, didn't you?

Engaging the handbrake and shifting into neutral, Ellie idles at the junction. The road is deserted.

"What d'you think, Jack?"

The dog's hackles are slightly raised. Ellie suddenly realises what he's trying to tell her.

"Oh, God, I forgot. Thanks for reminding me."

Still staring hard at her, Jack begins panting. He closes his jaws but his tongue soon slips out again and his fast breathing continues.

"Stupid bloody woman, aren't I?"

Jack's ears press tightly against his head and he whines.

"What's the matter?"

No, don't tell me. I have to do this, you know I do.

She's meeting Eliza, of course. At that pub. . . that pub along. . . Now, which way is she supposed to go, right or left? Right. It's definitely right. Groaning, the van pulls out into the road.

"Did you have a nice time with Dad?" Eliza asks. She hasn't touched her drink.

The bar, like the road Ellie drove down to get here, is deserted: only the barman giving them odd glances. Eliza was waiting for her when she arrived.

The interior is dark, polished wood. They're sitting in a corner seat with mullioned windows on two sides. The wood digs into Ellie's thighs and her back hurts. Outside she can see a stretch of lawn and ducks swimming on an ornamental pond.

"Yes, it was lovely." Ellie puts on a bright voice. "A much-needed break." She takes a long sip of lemonade, ice clinking as the glass tips. She has an uncomfortable feeling. "How did you know about that?"

Eliza smiles. "I have my means. Dad really misses you, Mum. Why don't you get back together with him?"

Ellie picks up her glass and drinks again. She hasn't thought Eliza would want her and Jonah back together. In her daughter's mind, once a thing is done, it can't be reversed. So how come. . .?

Eliza's drink sits on the table untouched.

The barman returns from the other room and gives them another funny look, quizzical, examining. How rude. Ellie stares back at the man and he eventually looks away.

Jack is on the floor at Ellie's feet. He stands up, turns around several times and flops down again, tucking himself into a tight ball. He lets out a heavy sigh. He's hardly paid any attention to Eliza.

You used to love her, Jack, whenever she was home on a visit.

Under the table, Jack grunts as if reading her thoughts.

Ellie feels cold. After shaking her head she manages to make her lips work.

"If I got back with your dad it would be the end of my travelling days. He'd hate living like this. I thought you wanted me to experience a different life."

Eliza cocks her head on one side like a bird. She tugs at the flowered scarf around her neck. She hasn't brought a coat.

Ellie drinks her in.

My pretty girl, why have I never thought of her like that before? Everybody said Rosie was the pretty one.

Reaching to pick a leaf from her daughter's tangled hair, she holds it in the palm of her hand, crumpled and dry. She's staring mesmerized at it when Eliza speaks again.

"I want you to be happy, that's all. You've got to move on, Mum."

Ellie jolts. She closes her fingers on the leaf, feels it crumble into dust against her skin. Powder traces the lines of her palm. A finger of ice pokes in her chest.

"I move all the time. If this isn't moving on, what is?"

You know that's not what she means.

Eliza's eyes are like pale grey stones at the bottom of... at the bottom of... They swirl in icy waters.

Breaking through her frozen mind, Ellie hears the relentless sound of a waterfall, she feels snow crunch under her feet and the sound grows into a roaring, a deafening crescendo.

Don't think about it.

She puts her hands over her ears.

39

County Leitrim

15 December 2013

The landscape and weather form a magical Christmas card image. But Ellie's too busy negotiating the narrow road. A mountain slopes upwards on one side and a wooded gorge drops down on the other. Leafless trees tap the windscreen like skeletal fingers.

"Are you okay, Auntie Ellie?" Catherine zips her fleece-lined denim jacket higher at the neck.

Ellie nods. The scouring of twig against metal makes her wince.

She can't get warm, despite the heater on full. Since October when the woman at Leigh-on-Sea first wanted to take what she now thinks of as the Eliza-doll, a shard of ice has started build around her heart.

Since she last saw Eliza.

She can't let that doll go and nor can she bring herself to sew a face on it. Lavinia Mapplethorpe visited the fair in Manorhamilton and tried again to get Ellie to part with her.

Ellie feels like a woman under threat of losing her child.

She's staying with Seth and Catherine in their modest cottage, close to a town called Carrick-on-Shannon. The cottage has no central heating but it's dry and has a wood fire in every room. It's luxury to Ellie, who's enjoying having access to a full-sized flushing toilet and a deep bath.

"I wonder what Nana would think of this place," Catherine laughed, when Ellie arrived (she doesn't mention her mother). "Please stay with us for Christmas."

"Can't say I was looking forward to Christmas in a layby on my own," Ellie admits. "I will. Thank you for the invitation."

It's a relief to know where she'll be.

Jonah offered to host Christmas, of course, and Vivian also broached the subject (adding that she feels Deborah has to take priority, due to being depressed, and that it might cause problems if Ellie is also there).

"You do know," Ellie pointed out during their telephone conversation, "that I want to make things right with my sister, don't you? This situation has gone on too long. Deb has no reason to hate me. We ought to be supporting each other."

"I know that," Vivian agreed quietly. "Just give her some time. It's been a difficult year all round. Things will look brighter next year."

Widowhood seems good for Ellie's mum. Released from Ray's surveillance, she's joined a coffee club and is volunteering at the WI café in her local hospital. She's also enrolled on an English evening class.

Reaching their destination, Ellie steers the van into the grit-covered car park of the hall on the outskirts of Carrick-on Shannon. She parks in a big space down the side of the building and they get out. Jack makes patterns of yellow urine on the white snow. Her son and niece help her unload her wares. The interior of the van looks more like a transporter than a home now.

"Come on, Jack." Reluctantly, Jack jumps in again and she shuts the door on him, leaving a window open just enough to jam his nose through and keep track of unfamiliar scents. The cold bites through Ellie's clothes as she carries the last box inside.

In the hall, Catherine sticks with Ellie. They get off to a slow start because of being waylaid by Iris, a new friend of Ellie's.

"I'm only here temporarily," Iris tells them, busy and indispensable as she usually seems to be. "But I'll be back for the concert."

Seth's gone off to set up stall for his part-time boss.

"Seth's really looking forward to training as a joiner." Catherine returns to her favourite subject once Iris has moved on. "He enjoys working with wood so much."

Ellie's glad her youngest son has discovered another passion that might make him a living.

A record deal was always around the next corner for Jonah but it never came. Her niece chatters on while Ellie stands back to survey their work.

She places the Eliza-doll tenderly in her usual spot at the top of the arrangement of toys. She thinks back to the Manorhamilton Craft fair, particularly of Lavinia's disappointment when Ellie refused to relinquish her a second time.

Lavinia went away with a basket of Ellie's new Christmassy hares and a couple of smaller dolls. If they proved popular in her shop in York, she said, she'd be in touch to order more.

"Like this?"

Catherine has laid the folded quilt with an appliqued poppy design over the top rail of a wooden clothes airer. She finishes the display with an array of cushions on the lower rails of the airer and places a wicker basket containing finger-puppets on the floor next to it, where small children will want to play with them.

"That works very well," Ellie says. "You're good at this, thanks."

Catherine has helped her with some simple sewing as well.

Ellie's niece is singing in the concert later and Seth is playing guitar. There's a thriving community of local artists and musicians here that reminds Ellie of the Running Hare community she once belonged to.

The old woman who rented Seth and Catherine's cottage to them now lives in a residential home in Sligo where Catherine works as a part-time carer. Iris has sent her godson over there with a minibus to bring a group of the home's residents back to Carrick. They'll arrive in time for the concert.

The doors of the hall open and a crowd of people rush to get in. The air quickly fills with the buzz of conversation and footsteps. Catherine handles the sudden flood of customers on Ellie's stall, leaving her free to sit back and watch her son as he strolls back and forth behind the wooden-toys stall across the hall. The knobble of spine at the base of his neck looks so vulnerable. She can't take her eyes off him.

My last child, the eternal baby of the family.

Ellie feels a prickle on the back of her own neck, as if someone is watching her, but when she turns she can't see anyone who might be.

"Are you alright, Auntie Ellie? You look a bit pale."

"Thanks, Catherine, I'm fine," Ellie assures her for the millionth time. She arranges her scarf into a neater shape over the front of her woollen dress. "I'm going to fetch some teas if you're okay here on your own?"

"Of course, just a splash of milk in mine, please."

"I'll take one to Seth as well."

Ellie hesitates, tweaking a corner of the tablecloth.

"OK," Catherine waves a hand. "Go on, I'm fine here."

Ellie takes some steps away and pauses to look back at Catherine. The girl's cheeks are flushed, hair curls in wisps on her forehead. There's the vaguest resemblance to Eliza in Catherine's face, if Ellie studies it hard.

You've got to move on, Mum, Eliza said. Ellie thinks about their encounter at the deserted pub after she left Leigh-on-Sea. The details are dream-like, hard to keep hold of, but Eliza's voice is clear in her memory.

She waits in a queue for a cup of tea for Seth. Some spills in the saucer as she takes it over to him. When she reaches the stall she stops to examine the oiled wooden sculptures while he serves a customer. The twisted shapes of the more abstract pieces remind her of something. She runs her hands over several of them, closing her eyes. When she opens them again her gaze falls on one that resembles a hunched figure shouldering a burden; the burden is a clock face. The contorted arrangement of wood looks natural. She pictures the clock on the shelf above the sink in her van. When Seth has finished serving she asks him about it. He assures her that the artist carved it from sawn wood and has not picked it off a beach as she thought.

"It's beautiful," she says. "I think I'll buy it. Don't let anyone else have it."

Seth weighs it in his hands. He gives her an unfathomable look.

"Wait, Mum."

He takes a sheet of tissue paper and lays the clock on it. He places it on a small table behind him. "You can buy it off the artist himself, he'll be back soon."

"Well, if you insist," Ellie agrees, only half-thinking about it.

She crosses the crowded hall to the tea stall again, waits a further few minutes before collecting two cups for herself and Catherine.

She can't seem to get herself moving properly. She's standing still, tides of people moving around her stationary form as if she's a rock in a river. Sound swishes past her ears in muffled waves. She watches Catherine laying a baby doll in a little girl's arms and can almost hear the catch of the child's breath as she receives the wrapped bundle. She notices the shrug of the mother's shoulders, knowing she won't be able to resist the intensity of her daughter's desire.

She remembers Eliza's childhood happiness at her Christmas present, Rainbow; the atrocious first doll Ellie made.

I considered naming my business Rainbow Dolls when I first started it up, but you wouldn't let me steal your doll's name.

As she approaches the stall and hands Catherine her tea, Ellie is drawn as usual to the Eliza-doll. Its eyeless face seems to hold her gaze. How can that be?

Heat spreads up her spine from the base of her back, floods over her shoulders and down into her chest; the oddest feeling. The frozen waste inside her has started melting, cracking; ice breaking off, piece by piece.

She knows what she has to do with the doll's face, and she feels a terrible urgency to complete the task.

40

Ellie places her cup and saucer on a corner of the table. She stares at the Eliza-doll, afraid to touch it. Something has happened, her senses have sharpened to the point of pain. If she listens hard enough the doll will speak.

She will speak.

Ellie won't like what she has to say.

Catherine glances at her, tucks a bundle of notes into the money belt at her waist and hands some change to the customer. She leans forward and says something to the little girl with her new baby doll, then straightens and comes over to Ellie.

"Look," she says. "I know you keep saying you're alright, but I don't think you are. Why don't you drink your tea and then have a lie-down in the van?"

Ellie's beginning to feel like a burden.

She pulls her gaze away from the doll. She'll lose her soon, and then it will be over. Melted ice streams through her veins.

"I will go out to the van for a while." She tries a smile. "You seem to be managing on your own and there's something I have to do. I shouldn't be long."

She reaches for E. . . for the doll.

Catherine gives her a puzzled look.

"What about your tea?"

Ellie's already edging towards the door.

"It doesn't matter."

Catherine turns her palms outward in confusion.

Heat pulses into Ellie's cheeks.

"You drink it," she says hastily. "I can get another one in the bus."

The long skirt of her woollen dress catches on a splinter sticking out of a table and she jerks it away; notices a thread pulled loose. She's aware she's caused the stall-holder's table to sway. Items of pottery clink against each other.

"Sorry, sorry," she mouths, forcing a smile from the corner of her lips. The owner glowers at her, makes a point of picking up a china teapot and inspecting it as if for damage, but Ellie is already at the door.

Outside, the cold air's cruel. She tucks the Eliza-doll under her scarf. The doll is warm as a human against the bare skin of her neck. Snow is still falling, light as icing sugar. She thinks about the minibus full of old people Iris's godson is bringing over from Sligo, and hopes they'll all be safe.

Everything's so vulnerable.

In the van the windows are steamy from Jack's breath. He scrambles off the bed as she hauls the door open and she's glad she remembered to tuck his blanket over the bedspread before leaving him in there alone.

"Brrr, Jack." But the effort of lighting a fire seems too much. She decides to manage without.

"Steady." Jack knocks against her. She sighs. "Put that tongue away, you're drooling everywhere. Mind Eliza. . . mind, the doll."

Jack gives her a reproachful look.

She pretends not to notice.

"Where's my sewing box?"

She prays she hasn't left it back at the cottage. I need it. But no, it's in its old place in the cupboard above the bed.

Always be ready. Months of sleeping in laybys have had their effect.

She has a sudden longing for her life of solitude. The metal frame beside the stove has a few sticks of kindling in and she finds herself checking the basket under the bed for sturdier fuel. There's some dry wood, enough for an evening's fire maybe.

"Jack, we could just. . . Would you like to just take off?"

He tilts his head.

"Anywhere. It doesn't matter where we go."

That was the point of buying the van. It was Eliza's idea, surely? Ellie lays her hand on the doll. What is she doing, spending so long at Seth and Catherine's?

But her sewing machine is at the cottage, all her stock inside the hall. She can't just leave.

Jack utters a quiet whine. He prefers the constantly-burning log fires at the cottage anyway, and the special dog bed Catherine bought him.

"You're right," she says. "We did promise to stay with them over Christmas, didn't we?"

Her skin prickles. It's as if she can hear a waterfall.

It will be freezing there again now; ropes of ice, shining like diamonds in the winter sun. A rainbow across the shimmering curtain of water. I'll have to go back in summer. But not with Jonah. She'd like to see the landscape green. You've got to move on, Mum.

"Now, Ellie," she shakes her head. She must achieve the thing she came out to the van to do.

It will create an ending, a necessary one.

The Eliza-doll lies in her lap, staring blankly from its eyeless face. Ellie strokes the straw-coloured hair, her throat closing. Snow builds up in the corners of the windows. Her fingers, attempting to thread the needle, turn white from the cold inside. She struggles with the sliver of metal and the obstreperous thread; blows on her hands, giving up temporarily.

Laying everything aside, she nudges Jack with her foot.

"Shift, dog."

She goes outside again and around the rear of the van to turn on the gas. Jack leans his chin on the bed, waiting for her to appear at the back doors. A few flakes of snow settle on the coverlet when she pulls them open to access the gas bottle. When she slams them closed again, snow lands on her head with a cold shock. But it feels good on her cheeks, which are unnaturally hot. She sucks moisture from her fingers, turns her face up to the snow and puts out her tongue, remembering how she and Deb would do that as kids.

She used to encourage her own children to do it too.

Pressure builds in her chest.

Vaguely aware of a couple of vehicles turning into the car park, the rumble and silencing of their engines, Ellie doesn't want to be seen. She climbs back inside the van and drags the side door closed after her.

"It's just you and me, Jack."

With the kettle now on she warms her hands at the gas flame, settles back on the bed, legs swathed in a blanket, wriggles her fingers into fingerless gloves. It's getting dark already. She switches on the sewing light, fixed to the underside of the cupboard above her head.

"Let's try again."

Jack tips his head from side to- side, watching as she again takes up the Eliza-doll. She smooths its straw-coloured hair once more, (tangled already) cupping its face momentarily between her palms.

Take a deep breath, Ellie.

She must steady the trembling of her fingers. She winces when the now-threaded needle goes into the flesh – the fabric – of the face.

Quickly, she embroiders a mouth for the doll, using pale thread. She keeps it simple, a more or less flat line.

She can see another face in her mind, wax-coloured and still, the eyes closed.

She threads a second needle. Tears squeeze out.

Thankfully, the roll of tissue is within reach.

Ellie stiches eyelashes with light-brown thread, laying over the cheeks like feathers.

The pain in her chest is fit to burst. With the same pale thread that she used for the mouth, Ellie etches in the suggestion of closed eyelids.

The Eliza-doll is done.

41

Iceland

February 2013

They're near the end of the week of activities Eliza planned for them. Despite feeling relaxed at the Blue Lagoon yesterday, Ellie feels more tired than ever now. She can also sense the strain she's putting on Jonah. It will be over soon. Her face muscles are unbearably tense.

Today's the day they must hire a car and drive to the waterfall Eliza loves the best. Skogafoss. They eat breakfast more or less in silence and go up to the room to collect their things. One of their room-mates is in the bathroom, the other still asleep in her bunk. Ellie closes the door quietly as they leave.

It's bright and clear outside, the air sharp. Tiny grains of ice whipped up from the days-old snow blow into their faces on erratic bursts of wind. Over the harbour the sky looks like rain.

They wait at the stop opposite the statue. Three buses come and go before the number 6 arrives. They get off at the

BSI.

The young man at the car hire place is kind. He gives them a discount on the car he thinks they should have. "It's automatic," he explains. "It's a new one, just come in. You like?" Even Jonah seems to be struggling with the banter today. The car is red. Ellie can't pinpoint the memory that stirs when she sits in the passenger seat and closes the door. The interior smells clean and she suddenly wants to get out again. But when Jonah turns to her she presses her mouth into a small smile.

Traffic rushes past them on the four-lane highway out of Reykjavik, water splashing up from the wheels of hurrying vehicles. They pass a large, square lake, known as The Pond. It's mostly frozen. A cloud of geese is alighting on the small area of available water, scattering ducks and a lone seagull as they land. A stretch of parkland is hidden under snow. Ellie imagines Eliza walking across it when it was green.

Jonah drives carefully, hunched forward (everything is fragile). Speaking only when he needs to, he asks Ellie to look out for road signs: they must get onto route one.

She glances into a car stopped alongside them at traffic lights. The woman in the driving seat drinks coffee, holding the steering wheel with one hand, so relaxed.

Sitting next to him (on the wrong side of the car) Ellie has a flashback to bringing Rosie home from the hospital. That's the familiar memory. They were in a hire car then as well. Ellie sat in the back next to Rosie's carrycot, tense as she is now. On that occasion she and Jonah were also barely speaking, overwhelmed by the enormity of having brought life into the world.

They come to the roundabout. A line of traffic streams past them from the left, giving Jonah time to check the route. The road cuts cleanly through lava fields. Ellie gazes at fissures and cracks in the craggy surface, all shards and knobbles. Obscured by snow, sometimes a hint of the green velvet moss underneath is revealed. She's amazed by nature.

Tears swamp her eyes again and she presses her forehead against the glass.

Mountains surround the landscape like a curving arm. Volcanic craters, peaks and shafts stab the sky. The primeval land rushes past. As they get deeper into the mountains, Ellie spots plumes of steam rising from the slopes, dissipating into a thin mist of rain. Thick grey pipes snake over the uneven ground on either side of the road.

They cross a wide expanse of water on a thin band of road.

They stop soon afterwards, at a large town called Selfoss. Ellie's relieved to get out; it was a worrying descent on a curving, icy downward spiral.

Her legs are stiff when she gets out of the car.

"Tea?" Jonah asks.

"Thanks, yes please. I'll just go to the loo."

A coach party has also stopped for refreshments and there's a queue at the toilets. When she emerges, Jonah's already sitting at a small table by a window, both of his hands enfolding cardboard cups. He looks unguarded.

Ellie's heart pounds. She sits opposite him and he slides a cup across the table. She fiddles with the paper tag on the teabag. She can't make the tea the right colour, too much milk is already in it.

They pass several horse farms on their continuing way. Large numbers of horses, dark shapes against the snow. They huddle together or fight playfully, rearing up, the loser falling to its knees. Their coats are thick and their manes shaggy. They remind Ellie of the felt-coated plastic ponies she had as a child.

Snow blows across the road, obscuring it in places.

"Slow down. . ."

Ellie's already worrying about the drive back, it'll be getting dark, the road will freeze even more. The bright sky of morning has given way to an opaque white, shadowed by dark grey. Finally, she spots the blue sign to the waterfall and thinks only of now. Her stomach clenches.

In the stony, empty car park, they get out and pull on their gloves. They stand still beside the car, a moment's reverence.

"You should probably put your hood up," suggests Jonah.

... Over the noise. The noise! Louder than the sea, but no ebb and flow, no abatement. Relentless. Heavy. Water. Falling. Falling and falling, never to stop.

Drums and cymbals and castanets. A crashing veil, rebounding from the black river, creating a sibilant mist. The clash of water on water.

The rushing river slices through the white carpet of snow, laid out to receive them. Ellie can see a handrail running up the slope on one side, a treacherous path in this weather.

Black rocks on the insides of the open-topped cavern, stretching their arms out towards Ellie and Jonah; an encompassing womb for the waterfall.

Come in, come in.

The black rocky cliffs are covered in ice: swords and daggers hanging down, sticking out from the sheer, glassy walls. Rocks on the ground mushroom with ice, shelves of ice glisten between the ground and the high walls. It's a bewitching, mesmerising world of white and glitter. So much white. So much black.

Without realising, the fingers of her gloved hand have found Jonah's.

Her hood has blown back. Cold bites her ears. Snowflakes land on her glasses but she's led forward by Jonah's hand which fastens more firmly around hers.

We're in this together. She presses the back of her free hand to her glasses to try and clear them of snow. She slips on an icy rock but Jonah steadies her. I won't let you fall.

Don't let her fall.

Blind with snow and tears. Ellie wants to howl but it would never be heard.

They move closer. As close as they can. The closer to the water the more treacherous the icy ground. She is soaking wet; her jeans sodden, her coat drenched and her jumper damp and clammy next to her skin. Her fingers are numb in the wet woollen gloves.

She wipes her glasses again.

There's a dark cave behind the thundering curtain of water, unreachable across the churning river. Legend tells of a casket of treasure hidden there. But what use is treasure?

Ellie pushes her arm through Jonah's. They gaze at the inaccessible cave as if it might yield its secrets. Then they both tip their heads back to look up. Millions and millions of spitting drops dance along the rocky top of the waterfall. The catapulting veil of fall creates intricate looped patterns like lace, forever reweaving itself in continuous, relentless repetition.

It will keep on, keeping on.

42

County Leitrim

15 December 2013

She doesn't know how long she's been out in the van. When she looks at her watch it's stopped. It might have happened the moment she began stitching the Eliza-doll's eyes.

It can go in the silver chest with the other things.

With this in mind Ellie unstraps the watch from her wrist.

Time to move on, as Eliza said.

The kettle's boiled almost dry.

Ellie takes her gloves off and pours the remaining water from it into the sink, adding a drop of cold from the tap. She washes her face clean of the waterfall that has finally erupted from her eyes, soaking her skin with salty moisture.

Her scarf is sodden. Rifling through the remaining clothes left hanging in the van, Ellie finds a fresh one, floral, made of roughly-woven cotton. Before winding it around her neck she takes off her glasses and moisturises her face and hands with the utilitarian cream she uses. She guesses her eyes are red but she hopes her son and niece won't notice. She doesn't want to worry them any more than usual.

They're young and have a right to be absorbed in their own business, not hers.

Catherine will need to get ready for her performance. Ellie must go and resume her duties on the stall, relieve her, give Catherine a chance to warm up.

Ellie practises breathing until the shudder in each indrawn breath has been eliminated.

She doesn't realise how cold her feet have got until she steps down from the van onto the hard ground.

It would be pitch dark outside but instead, there's a glimmer from the luminescent snow. Jack jumps down behind her. He runs around the car park a few times.

"Watch out!" Ellie calls. A minibus is grinding into the car park. It turns into the space next to her van.

Jack slinks over, his body rippling ingratiatingly. The black-haired young driver gets out and opens the back. Two uniformed care workers help lower wheelchairs to the ground via a ramp.

"Nice dog you've got there," the young man says to Ellie. He bends to give Jack a fuss. "Me missus would love him. She's always on at me to get us another dog, it's a collie pup she's after. We've got this funny mixed-breed of a creature already though, Dusty, his name is. And what with the baby, I don't know. . . "

He stops talking after taking a closer look at Ellie's face. She expects her eyes are red behind the glasses but it shouldn't be too obvious in the dark.

The care workers escort the last of the minibus passengers into the hall and the lad begins to close the vehicle up.

"You alright there?" he asks, turning back to Ellie.

She realises she's been rooted to the spot. Her body tingles, oddly electrical. She stamps her feet, checks the safety of the Eliza-doll under her clean scarf; forces herself to move.

She manages a smile. He seems a nice lad, about the same age as Seth, she guesses. Must be a nice lad to have volunteered to bring a load of old people over from Sligo for the concert. Mind you, you wouldn't want to argue with Iris. She wants to ask him if he knows Seth and Catherine, assumes he does since he's Iris's godson. He mentioned a wife, a potential friend for Catherine, maybe. And the wife has a baby... the tingling starts again.

"You going inside?" he asks encouragingly. He pats Jack, who nuzzles insistently at his pocket.

"Oh, go on then," he says to the dog. "I give in." He brings some sort of treat from his pocket, allows Jack to take it from his hand. "Always keep some in there since we had the baby." He rubs Jack's head with his knuckles. "Dog's gone a bit funny, jealous, we reckon. Not quite as obedient as he was."

The baby.

She wants to ask so many questions but her lips won't move properly.

The lad stands expectantly, apparently waiting to escort her into the hall. Maybe he thinks she is one of his old people.

She jerks herself out of the paralysis that's descended on her.

"Come on, Jack," she finally manages. She taps her thigh with a frozen hand. "Get in there."

Reluctantly, Jack crawls up into the van, as if his back legs don't work properly.

"Come on, Jack. Hup! Get up there." Ellie gives his rump a shove. "Idiot dog."

Jack rolls his eyes but eventually scrambles in. He'll only withdraw his head at the last minute as Ellie drags the door nearly closed. The dog regards the young man with a sorrowful stare and lets out a whine as he slumps out of sight behind the window in the door. The lad chuckles again.

"He's a card, isn't he? Anyways, pleased to meet ya. Connor's me name."

He thrusts out his hand and Ellie makes brief contact with it. Her other hand is still pressed against the doll's body inside her cardigan.

"I'm Ellie."

"Great van you have there. My Auntie Iris used to live in one of them, she tells me. Do you live in yours? Ah, great," he says at Ellie's nod. They're walking towards the hall. Tipping her head back, Ellie glimpses stars through the tremulous veil of falling snow. When she almost loses her footing, her arm tightens around the Eliza-doll.

The lad offers a steadying hand for her other elbow.

He sees me as an old woman, she thinks, regretfully. She's aged years during her spell in the van.

43

She knows it as soon as she sees her. Not the girl standing beside Catherine but the swaddled mound on her front.

Oh, Eliza.

Not anymore.

Connor's wife has a pale, delicate face with short, dark hair curled around it. Her eyes remind Ellie of a young Twiggy, but there's also something of Mia Farrow about her. She's picked up one of Ellie's baby dolls and is smiling at it. Ellie watches the two young women giggling together. She presses the Eliza-doll closer to her chest.

Connor notices where Ellie's gaze has travelled to.

"Ah, that's me gorgeous wife, over there, Rebecca." His voice thickens. Ellie notices the way his eyes glitter.

"She's with my niece," she says.

Ellie wipes her brow with the edge of her scarf. Steam rises from her shoulders.

"Catherine's looking after my stall for me."

"Ah, so it's you is it? The doll maker. Iris was telling me about you. I'm glad me aunt's got another like-minded friend. She can leave off bossing me mam around for a bit. Have you met me mam, Sarah? You'll get on with her as well."

Amazing how easily they accept new people into their community.

Connor resumes his relentless talking as they make their way over to her stall.

"So, I've been doing some work with your boy, Seth," he carries on. "Great lad he is. Greg's thinking of taking him on full time. I work there meself, it's a good place to work."

But Ellie isn't listening.

She's approaching Catherine and the other girl through the fog of a dream.

"Oh there you are, Ellie," Catherine pipes up, slightly self-consciously. Ellie notices vaguely that she's dropped the 'Auntie'. "Did you have a nice sleep?"

Ellie hardly hears. She feels pinpricks in her fingertips and forehead, and in her heart.

Through the fuggy air of the heated hall, a ray of light shines. It pierces the fog like sun breaking through clouds.

Ellie becomes certain that Catherine is pregnant.

Deb and I are going to share a grandchild.

But her senses are singing towards Rebecca. The girl turns and meets Ellie's eyes. Rebecca's have violet shadows underneath, a sure sign of a new mother. She still has a laugh on her face from whatever she and Catherine have been talking about.

The Eliza-doll burns against Ellie's skin. Her gaze travels down Rebecca's front to the baby.

The baby. She is very new, wound into a sling, nestled against her mother.

Ellie moves forward.

"May I?"

The girl nods. Ellie curls a finger gently over the soft hair on the new-born's delicate skull. The baby stirs. She starts batting her head against her mother's chest, the tiny set of bow-lips pursing into a shape like a rosebud.

I never carried you in a sling.

"Sorry for waking her," whispers Ellie. "What's her name?"

At the sound of Ellie's voice, the baby opens her eyelids minutely. She stops rooting and stares directly at Ellie, examines her face with slits of brown eyes. Ellie feels the pain she's been carrying crack open. Seep like honey into her every molecule until she feels disembodied. The silence, that Ellie's voice mustn't have pierced, goes on forever.

Rebecca breaks it.

"Eve," she says. Then gives a small laugh. "Evelyn Iris Catriona O'Toole, to be precise. I know it's a mouthful but. . . She'll grow into it."

A miniature hand pushes its way out of the sling and fastens like a limpet to the soothing finger offered by Rebecca. Ellie is transfixed, it's the most perfect, exquisite hand, ever.

"She wanted to add Sophie to the list as well," Connor puts in, coming up behind Ellie. "Not to mention Jade. I told her we'd have to have another one to take up the extra names, I drew the line at three."

He slides his arm round Rebecca's waist, leans over her shoulder to kiss her cheek and then the top of the baby's head. Rebecca kisses him back.

"Sophie Jade," Catherine says thoughtfully. "That sounds pretty." She glances at Seth across the room.

Ellie follows her gaze distractedly through the constant motion of fair-goers and notices that the stallholder has arrived. He has his back to her, doing something at the table behind the stall. Possibly wrapping her clock, she thinks. She'll have to go over and get it later. The thoughts come like arrows flashing over her head.

Catherine moves to the other end of their table where a small cluster of people have gathered, and begins talking to a customer.

I really must get back to work.

All of it: the brief glance over at Seth, the thoughts about the clock and the customers on her own stall, the understanding that she will soon become a grandmother; the concern that there could be a problem with a baby resulting from the union of Catherine and Seth; none of it has really sunk in.

Her fleeting musings are as insubstantial as the flakes of snow drifting softly onto the windows.

It buzzes in her head, now the silence has lifted, the only real thing. The baby in the length of pink cloth wound around Rebecca's body. Making a shape as if Rebecca is still pregnant.

"When was she born?" Ellie asks, compelled to be close to the pair again. Her heartbeat pulses through the fabric of the doll on her own chest, giving it life.

"Just over a month ago."

Evelyn Iris Catriona wriggles again, struggling against the cloth that binds her.

"She wants feeding. Is there anywhere I can sit with her?"

"Of course, come over here."

The parts of Ellie that had disassembled are coming together again. She feels more whole than she has in months. And she knows what to do.

The pain has dissipated so finely now it is hardly here. She will be able to cope with it. Ice always melts when spring returns.

Catherine has gone off to a side room with Seth and the other musicians to warm up. Iris and Connor are serving the old people tea and refreshments in the dining area of the kitchen, and Ellie has started packing up the stall, though there are still a few customers around.

She puts away the quilts and cushions first. She folds up the boxes the dolls were arranged on and lays the remaining dolls carefully in their suitcase, but leaves it open in case anyone might still want to look. She arranges the last few patterned hares and the felt Christmas tree decorations and some bundles of embroidered handkerchiefs on the table to make it seem welcoming still.

But ninety per cent of her attention is focussed on Rebecca, sitting in the camping chair behind the stall feeding her baby.

The Eliza-doll waits, wrapped in a piece of red silk in Ellie's bag under the table.

Ellie can see the stallholder across the way also packing up his wares, loading the pieces into tea chests. She still hasn't been over to pay for the clock, but she doesn't want to leave Rebecca. And Seth will surely have told his employer about his mother's intended purchase. She'll sort it out when the fair is properly over.

The scrape of a violin-note escapes from the room adjoining the hall.

Stallholders who've finished packing up are helping visitors arrange chairs. After a further ten minutes, Ellie snaps the doll-suitcase shut and fastens it. She clears the remaining small objects from the table and places them in a lidded box. She folds the cloths that covered the table and squeezes them into a tote bag.

A man from the stall next door comes over and helps Ellie collapse her table.

"Did you do well today?" he asks cheerfully. "I did cracking. It was them pewter dragons I got in at the last minute." He gives Ellie a huge grin. "I nearly didn't do this fair 'coz the wife wanted us to visit her mother instead. But I decided to put me foot down. She went on her own with the bairns. Good job I stood me ground, she won't complain at today's takings."

Ellie smiles back.

"I did very well, thanks. Largely due to the help of my daughter-in-law."

It's the first time she's thought of Catherine as that instead of as her niece.

But now she shares Deb's misgivings, if not her anger, about the cousins' relationship. What if the baby. . . ?

But there's no point worrying. Seth and Catherine have managed to find happiness together; why spoil it? Happiness is precious in the face of all the grief in the world.

"That your daughter-in-law over there, with your grand-babby?"

He nods at Rebecca, slumped in the chair, almost asleep. Her winter jumper covers her breast, abandoned by the baby who has also fallen asleep, tucked into her mother's arms. Ellie wants to go and wrap one of her quilts around the pair of them.

"No," she says. "Rebecca's my..." she lets the words trail off, but the man doesn't seem to mind.

"Ah well." He rubs his hands together, glances around the hall. "Better get on with helping me buddies. What with the wife being away, y'know. I don't have to be home any time soon."

His nose is purpled by broken blood vessels. His eyes crinkle into the ample flesh of his face when he smiles at her again. He doesn't seem in a hurry to move away.

"Staying for it, are ya?"

"I am."

Ellie gazes at the coloured lights, strung across the ceiling. The people are warm and helpful. She has a new friend in Iris. Seth is settling into a job, a new family. Perhaps she could stay in Ireland, either in the bus or in a rented cottage of her own. Seth and Catherine, they might need her. A new grandchild.

Life goes on, there's evidence of that all around her. She thinks of Rosie and hopes she can improve their relationship. She looks at Rebecca and wonders if the girl has a mother who cares for her, hopes she does. But whether she does or not, she seems to be part of the eclectic family Iris seems to gather around her.

"I am staying for the concert," she repeats to the ruddy-cheeked man. "My son and daughter-in-law are performing in it, I'm very proud to say."

Ellie wakes Rebecca gently, brushing a hand over the girl's cheek. The concert is due to start and people are already taking their seats. Rebecca's eyes fly open, a hollowness in them which quickly clouds over when she registers Ellie's presence.

She clears her throat, struggles into a more upright position in the canvas chair. She keeps a hand on her baby so as not to wake her.

"Oh," she murmurs. "I thought you were... My mother used to wake me up like that when I was little."

Ellie perches on the stool next to her, their faces level.

"Your mother must be very proud of you and this little one."

"She, uhm." Rebecca makes that throat-clearing sound again. "She's dead."

"Oh. I'm so sorry," Ellie says. "That must have been hard for you. Going through all this on your own."

Rebecca straightens up further in the chair.

"I had lots of help. My half-sister came all the way from Italy to be here for the birth. Connor's wonderful, and so is Iris. My friend Sophie is coming to visit after Christmas with... with my gran and granddad. I'm lucky to have such a great family."

The main lights in the hall suddenly dim and now the fairy lights look magical, framing the stage and criss-crossing the ceiling.

"Would you do me a favour?" Rebecca asks, shifting the baby up onto her shoulder.

"Of course," says Ellie. "Whatever you want."

"Would you hold Eve for me while I go to the loo? My bladder's bursting."

44

Greg

15 December 2013

He's arrived at the Carrick fair late because of having to deliver some furniture trimmings to a store in Dublin. And, what with the weather an' all, the roads were chock-a-block in the city. Normally, Connor would lay out the stall for him. Connor's been working for him since he was a young lad. But the daft beggar agreed to drive over to Sligo, didn't he? In that ratty old council minibus. Fetch a load of old folks to the concert. Greg only hopes they have those roads well gritted and that they'll all get back safely in the dark.

Funny how he kind of thinks of Connor as a son even though the boy has a perfectly good father of his own. Mark O'Toole is Connor's dad, the fiddle player from The Shanbos.

The reason he's so fond of Connor is probably because he never sees his own son, Dylan. The lad'll be twenty-seven now, not that he's celebrated a birthday with him for years. Greg keeps on hoping Dylan will get in touch but it hasn't happened yet. Of course there's nothing stopping him making the effort...

So anyway, he asked Seth to get the stall ready instead of Connor. A nice lad, that Seth, he's been doing some part-time work at Greg's for a few months. Greg's thinking of asking him to go permanent after Christmas, might be able to get him on one of those training schemes.

The lad's happy to help with the stall, anyway; says his mother's over on a visit from England and she's also running a stall at the fair. So it'll work out well. Makes dolls, his mother does, apparently. Greg's looking forward to meeting her.

He can't help being intrigued. It's only natural. He reckons Seth's mum is single from the little Seth gives away. So, like he says, it's only natural he'll be curious. He's a single bloke; bound to wonder.

He's been on his own for years. The last partner he had, Karen, turned lesbian and went off with another woman. Rationally, he knows it doesn't work like this, but he can't help wondering if it was something he did. Maybe it was him who put her off men. He doesn't know.

But in general, he's happy on his own. He also kind of deserves it for deserting his son – well – allowing his son to be taken out of his life when the boy was only six.

Greg was thinking about all this on the drive back from Dublin.

The N4 was perfectly clear but it was getting out of the city that was the problem, he had to concentrate hard the whole time in order not to bump into the car in front as they crawled along in a traffic jam. Over the bridges, between the high buildings, along by the Liffey. The city was gridlocked in an unrelenting log-jam of traffic. Then there was the inevitable queue at the tolls.

Yeah. Greg has a family of sorts in the O'Tooles: Sarah and Mark and their three boys, and Herself, Iris Portman, that is. Connor is the O'Tooles' son and Rebecca is Iris's niece so their marriage keeps everything cosy. Greg's not sure where he fits in but, well, anyway they're all a close-knit bunch. And now they've been joined by Seth and his pretty girlfriend, Catherine, who quickly became close friends, (in this area that's as good as family) with Connor and Rebecca. Two couples equal in age (and beauty). Ah, youth.

Greg and Iris once had a bit of a fling with each other but that was a long time ago. Iris is a tough old bird and like Greg, is better suited to living on her own. But occasionally Greg still calls on his memories of sex with her. You have to picture something on your lonely-old-own, don't you? (Those lads' magazines never did anything for him). Sex born of tenderness is what he likes to imagine, soppy old bugger that he is.

Greg has to grip the steering wheel hard when the car in front of him, a fancy silver-and-black BMW, skids suddenly on a patch of ice. On a bend. The driver, give him credit, manages to right his mistake quickly but it gives Greg a jolt and makes him realise he'd better keep his wits about him. There are patches of ice you can't see.

The road straightens out again and his thoughts resume wandering.

Annoyed with himself, he hits the steering wheel with his palm and the car jerks sideways, (now who's the idiot?) causing a driver who was about to overtake him – idiot yourself, on these roads, – to toot his horn.

Oh fuck off.

Cantankerous old bastard, (that's himself). He hit the wheel because he can't understand why he's obsessing about some woman he's never even met.

The latter part of the two-hour drive is uneventful. When Greg drives into the carpark of the hall outside Carrick-on-Shannon it's about four o'clock and already dark. He backs the van into a space, turns the engine off and sits for a few moments. He rubs his cold knees with his gloved hands. Snow piles up under the hedges.

Iris pulls into the carpark shortly after him in her Land Rover, parking in the one remaining space opposite his. The back doors open and Rebecca steps down carefully, her baby strapped to her chest with that unbelievably long length of cloth he saw her wind around herself a few days earlier.

He used to carry baby Dylan in one of those stiff navy-blue creations that hung off his shoulders with straps and buckles. Rebecca's sling looks comfier, to be sure, but it's essentially a womanly design, and he can't imagine himself ever wearing one like that.

There he goes again, having weird thoughts.

Snowflakes are beginning to obscure the windscreen. Iris's door slams shut and Greg watches her squeeze out of the space between the Land Rover and the car next to it. Always parks too close, she does. Greg gets stiffly out of his van and crosses the few metres of gravel between him and the two women. He gives Rebecca a quick sideways hug and leans forward to kiss Iris on the cheek.

"Now then, how're you two? Sorry, I meant three."

Women hate it if you ignore their baby. But he doesn't dare touch it. Instead he offers a kind of admiring inspection.

"Good, good," says Iris, chivvying Rebecca along. "Our excuse for being late is we've been getting all the animals fed and bedded down for the night so we don't have to do it later. What's yours?"

She gives him one of her famous winks and follows it with a throaty laugh. He explains about his necessary trip into Dublin.

"You go in," he encourages; they appear to be waiting for him. "Don't keep that baby out in the cold. I've just got a few bits to sort out." He watches the two of them picking their way across the car park before turning back to his van to load some small objects for the fair into a box.

He's just about to prop the hall door open with his foot when he notices the van with a chimney in the far corner of the car park, almost hidden behind a wall. What the...?

A converted vehicle like that will be bound to pique Iris's interest; she's always regaling their community with tales about her days as a traveller. This vehicle has driven straight out of the peace convoy. There's a dim light burning inside but no smoke comes from the chimney. He wonders who's in it. Hmm. Perhaps he'll find out later. In fact he'll damn well go and knock on the door if it doesn't become obvious during the fair.

It's thronging inside the hall. It takes him a minute to get his bearings, the place is usually half-empty. They have village fetes here, charity fashion shows and the like. But to be fair, the Christmas concert is always full. And the concert brings in a lot of extra customers for the stalls, good news for everybody.

He finds Seth just inside the door, second stall along. Not a bad pitch, people might walk straight past the first one in their rush but they'll slow down like him, to get their bearings, once they've cleared the entrance. Seth appears to have sold about a quarter of the stock already and the fair still has another hour to run.

He congratulates the boy.

"I should leave you in charge more often." He moves behind the table to set the box he's carrying down on a chair. He stretches his back, hands pressed into his spine. He can feel sweat cooling in his armpits, but taking a surreptitious sniff he decides there's nothing to smell (good thing he went back to his old deodorant). He's wearing a new denim shirt and hopes it hasn't stained.

Straightening, he only now realises how tensely he's been holding himself throughout much of the drive. When he starts to turn back towards Seth, his eye falls on one of his prize pieces, an abstract figure shouldering a clock face. It's tucked away out of sight of the customers. Why has Seth done that?

"What's this doing over here?"

"What? Oh, that."

Seth picks it up and runs his hand over the smoothly oiled wood.

"My mum wants to buy it. I told her she should buy it off the artist himself, rather than me."

Greg's tickled pink. Seth's mum wants to buy a piece of his real artwork. Once upon a time he aspired to be up there with the Turner Prize winners, moving in gallery circles rather than craft fairs. But then there was Dylan, the responsibilities of someone else's family, and the breaking apart of all that. He moved back to his homeland for a new start and after his grandma died he got caught up with Karen. He must have forgotten about all the ambitions he once had.

But there on the table between the wooden bowls and spoons and children's toys that are his daily bread and butter, Seth set down his one genuine piece of artwork.

And Seth's mother has chosen it.

It's like a test to find the princess in a fairy tale.

And what a load of crap he's thinking today.

What the hell is the matter with him?

"There she is," Seth interrupts his thoughts. "Just coming in now."

Greg looks up in time to see the woman pass through gaps in the milling crowd. He catches the glint of the hall lights on her glasses as she turns in profile to speak to Connor while they move together into the centre of the hall. Then she stops. She stands as if rooted to the spot, while Connor goes in another direction. Seth's mum is looking towards the far end of the hall. Greg follows her gaze and he sees the lovely Catherine and the elfin Rebecca standing close together behind a colourful table that is covered in what look like soft toys. The two young women are laughing.

Greg wonders why Seth's mum is standing so still.

She's angled away from Greg so he can't see her face. But he takes in the details he can see: brown hair reaching just past her shoulders, some of it tucked into a lilac scarf with a pattern of flowers on it. The long green dress and dark grey cardigan she wears, the sturdy-looking brown boots on her feet. Her arms are folded across her front. He wonders what she's protecting with the grip of those arms.

Watching her, Antony Gormley sculptures come to mind, stoical figures planted on beaches or in underground tunnels while water sweeps around them, engulfing them and receding again, leaving them exposed and majestic, ineffable.

He feels a tickle in his belly. Ah fuck, his bloody libido is at it again. He tells himself not to be so stupid. How could he possibly get turned on by a woman whose face he can't even see?

Giving himself a mental slap across the wrist, he decides he'll have to dig out some of those memories of Iris when he gets back to his cottage. It's been too long... The sight of a new woman, the thought of her even, is enough to set his senses tingling.

Ridiculous man. He's no better than those women who ogle him from the office windows, only they're just having a bit of fun. They have someone at home to share their beds with.

He'll get busy unloading the wooden napkin rings he brought in from the van. That sort of thing sells easily around Christmas, what with people having their relatives over for dinner an' all that.

But first, he watches Seth's mother coming to life. She moves towards the young women minding her stall, and the crowd parts like the Red Sea as she walks into it.

For fuck's sake, Greg, change the record. She's probably ugly as sin. Think about something else.

There, those napkin rings and coasters are attracting attention already. Seth is selling them quicker than Greg is able to fill the spaces left on the table by the ones getting snapped up.

He might make a set of personalised coasters for each family that's having Christmas day at the O'Tooles'.

If he gets his usual invite of course. But why wouldn't he?

When he has time to look up from a rush of customers that appeared out of nowhere, he hopes to catch a proper glimpse of Seth's mother, see what she really looks like. But if she's behind her stall at all she's obscured by a group of people standing in front of it. He can just see Rebecca, off to one side, sitting in a chair with her baby.

It reminds him of an image from his past but he can't think what. Not his own son, the child's mother had enough of breastfeeding her other children. She said she'd expect him to be the one doing the night feeds if he wanted her to keep the baby.

During a lull in sales, Jim Marrows comes over. He starts to bend Greg's ear about how he's been let down by his kitchen supplier for the new apartment block he's working on. Greg gets a headache, listening to him.

"I have tried to explain this before, Jim," he finally gets out. "I don't do contracts like that. I'm essentially a one-man business, an artisan, if you like. Sorry, mate, but I can't help you with this."

Jim's mouth falls open, a blob of spittle stretching, then breaking apart and settling in one corner of his lips.

"Well." He looks indignant. "I was brought up to believe you don't look a gift-horse in the mouth, mate. Business is tough for everybody, you know. You should take it where you can find it."

He jams his flat cap down on his head with reddened hands, winds a thick woollen scarf around his equally thick neck. Rolling a cigarette he inserts it into his mouth and fits the words, "It's your loss, mate," around it. "Anyways," he adds, friendly again. "I'll be seein' you later, will I?"

Greg gives him a pat on the back and watches him shoulder his way to the door.

Folks are packing up stalls and another group are arranging chairs for the concert. It's due to start in half an hour.

Seth's gone off to tune his guitar and practice the piece he's doing with Catherine.

Greg finishes packing up the stall, but leaves the clock on the small table where Seth laid it earlier. If he isn't to pack it away with the other stuff, he'll have to pluck up his courage and personally take it to the woman.

But he doesn't have to.

She's walking across the room towards him, around the edges of the chairs, a patterned bag hanging precariously from her shoulder. Hair falls over one side of her face but she doesn't have a spare hand to push it back because her arms are full of Rebecca's baby.

He recognises this woman more easily than he might have otherwise because he's only ever seen her with a baby.

It's Ellie. Ellie from Running Hare House.

45

Ellie

15 December 2013

It takes her a moment to recognise him. She can't take it in even after she understands who he is.

Greg.

He's equally shocked to see her and the shock makes him stumble over his words.

His hands shake when he unwraps the clock. He thrusts a chair forward so she can sit down with the baby. She shakes her head when he insists the clock is a gift because he's so happy to see her again.

First the baby, and now this.

In a rush the awareness comes to Ellie that she wants to tell Greg everything, everything. Things she hasn't allowed herself to acknowledge all year. Greg. This is Greg.

But she can't speak yet. Maybe she'll invite him into her van for a chat when the show's over, talk to him like she used to.

Tell him about Eliza.

Shreds of thoughts and questions flap in deserted parts of her mind. Running Hare House, Bonnie, Greg, then. She tightens her arms and the baby stirs. She can't meet Greg's eyes though she senses him wanting to take in every detail of her. She imagines his potential touch.

Rebecca moves towards them. She reclaims the baby, snuggling Eve back inside the length of cloth she's thrown over her shoulders and tied at her waist. Ellie feels bereft at the removal but at the same time she feels the weight of Greg's hand on her shoulder, guiding her to a trio of chairs on the front row that Connor's waving them towards. Connor is playing in the concert as well, and so is Iris.

Ellie's feet must have carried her over to the row of chairs, Greg's hand loosely on her back, because she's here now, sitting down.

The main lights of the hall have been switched off and the fairy lights glow with even deeper colours. Ellie looks to her right at the baby's pursed lips, a flower within the dim nest of the sling. Ellie smiles at Rebecca and nods, but she feels numb and isn't really taking in anything that is happening.

Her breath catches with renewed understanding. Greg is sitting next to her on her left. She can hardly look but the feel of his arm against hers is warm. Years melt away and the two of them are back in the living room at Running Hare House, sipping hot chocolate, on a winter evening, baby Rosie asleep on his chest.

And then you told me about Bonnie and things were never quite the same between us again.

The concert is an emotional rollercoaster. Lately, anything can bring Ellie to tears. First the stage is filled with lively musicians performing some kind of jig on guitars, mandolins, flutes, penny whistles and fiddles. There's a lot of foot-stamping and clapping in the hall and the throbbing beat of a bodhran feels like it's coming from inside her.

Next a plaintive solo violinist threads notes into the rafters. The music is accompanied by sniffs and blown noses. Tears stream down Ellie's face and her nose becomes blocked. A penny-whistle player arrives on stage towards the end of the solo and adds a haunting harmony to the final verse and chorus of the song Ellie knows but can't name.

For a moment, Ellie sees Eliza in place of the dreadlocked whistle-player, fine hair lifting off her shoulders in the breeze she creates with the music. She taught herself to play a variety of instruments but the penny-whistle was the easiest to carry, and she busked her way across several countries with it.

Oh my girl.

Next the audience are encouraged to sing along with well-known Irish tunes including Will You Go, Lassie, Go? and When You Were Sweet Sixteen. Old people swell the melody with surprisingly strong voices.

Ellie continues to weep into a sodden hanky, keeping her sobs as quiet as possible. Now there is her Seth, settling himself on a stool with his guitar in the centre of the stage. Catherine moves towards the microphone, glancing shyly out at the audience. She looks sweet and Ellie wishes Deb could see her daughter.

Greg nudges Ellie at this moment. He smiles and offers another clean tissue. Ellie takes it, their fingers brushing. It's like a small explosion inside her. Their eyes meet but her vision is blurred by tears. She feels that he looks exactly as he did thirty years ago but this can't be true. "Thank you," she mouths, dabbing under her glasses.

Seth plays the introductory chords to From Clare to Here and Catherine begins to sing.

Ellie's hands clench. Surely Deb would be proud of how her youngest daughter's award-winning voice sounds on this stage? And yet the girl now inhabits the world unacknowledged by her mother, and Deb blames Ellie for taking her away.

Ellie would give anything to have her own trio of daughters intact. She must make things right with Rosie and cherish

Lily, the quiet one. She must try and smooth things between Catherine and Deb so they can finally all be a family.

She makes an effort to rein in her sobs and tries to even out her breathing before the final chords die down.

The concert is over.

Chairs scrape on the wooden floor and a flurry of people bustle towards the doors, wheeling baby buggies and wheelchairs through the obstacles of stacked boxes and running children. They hug and shake hands with friends and neighbours at the exit.

Ellie presses her bag against her side in a protective movement, the Eliza-doll is still inside. She means to give the doll to Rebecca.

But any suitable moment has passed. The girl is moving away, turning back only to say goodbye.

Don't go.

There hasn't been enough time.

But Rebecca is still speaking to her. Ellie catches, "when you come round for dinner," and the words, ". . . Connor's dad. . ." and "Sarah would love those quilts of yours. . . " and she understands that she will be seeing Rebecca again.

Seth materialises beside her, followed by Catherine.

"Did you enjoy yourself?"

"What did you think of. . . ?"

"Ah, I see you've already met Greg."

Greg has a puzzled look on his face when she only nods. She dimly realises that he'd expected; deserves, proper acknowledgement. Seeing the disappointment in his eyes, noting Seth's hand, poised in mid-gesture as if he's been illustrating some point or other and has suddenly noticed her lack of animation, she opens her mouth and forces out:

"Greg and I. . . we knew each other a long time ago."

———

In the van she puts the kettle on and stands with her arms folded, leans against the door to her tiny toilet room. She indicates that Greg should take a seat on the bed. There's only room for one person to sit.

"Are you sure?" he asks. At her nod, he angles his legs into the narrow floor space.

Jack presses himself against Greg's legs, his new best friend. Greg's hand runs repeatedly over the dog's back, fingers exploring the discs of his spine.

"He's a grand dog..." Greg's sentence is interrupted by a coughing fit. It sounds bad. Ellie tenses: is he ill? Is he going to die?

Don't be ridiculous Ellie, it's just a cough. Not everyone is going to slip through your fingers like. . .

Greg's lungs settle down and he gives her a wan grin. "I took up smoking for a while, not anymore, but it's taken its toll on me."

Ellie feels angry with him.

"But you used to hate it when, you know, Jonah and the others. . . "

"Aye, I did. It was Iris who got me into it though, when I first came to Leitrim. Me resistance was low, you could say. But I've packed it in now."

"I should think so too," she murmurs.

When did I get so censorious?

She loosens her fingers from their clenches.

"I'll light a fire," she says. She has to push the dog behind her and lower herself carefully to her knees. Greg tucks his legs tightly out of the way. His boots are large and take up a lot of floor.

"Should have enough wood for a while, anyway."

"Do you need any help?"

She looks up at him. "Sorry," he says. "I guess you're used to managing on your own."

There's a pause while she puts a match to the firelighter and the kindling. When it's alight she adds a chunk of log and closes the stove door.

Ellie returns to her position against the bathroom door. The van warms up quickly.

"Remember Stan?" asks Greg, suddenly. "He adored you and Rosie."

I could start again, she thinks. With Greg from Running Hare House. But for all she knows, he could have a wife at home.

Jack creeps back to his position at Greg's feet.

Ellie tries to keep her face impassive when Greg succumbs to another coughing attack.

Is he really okay?

It's just a cough.

But she worries anyway.

As they had left the hall Ellie had noticed the snow had stopped. Everything was muffled by it, the buzz of human voices and their footsteps crossing the car park. She'd liked the sense of both enclosure and freedom out there. Being in the small space with Greg begins to feel oppressive though. Her skin hurts.

"Rosie must be, what, thirty by now?"

Drinking some water has stopped Greg's coughing. "Seems impossible," he says. "What on earth is she like?" He sips again from the glass. "I only remember her as a toddler. And then you had Kester. He was a grand lad."

He peers more closely at her.

She says nothing. It's like a trickle of cold water running down her spine. She knows what's coming.

"And you were pregnant when you left."

He raises his eyebrows, meaning it as a question. She can't answer.

Greg places the empty glass by the sink. He loops his fingers under Jack's collar. The silence is uncomfortable.

"You were pregnant when you left," he repeats. "But that wasn't with your lad Seth; he's not old enough, is he? Ah, and you had a girl, I remember. I heard. . ." He notices her face. "So did you. . . how many children do you have now, Ellie?"

It's the 'now' that does it.

She locks her arms around her body but she can't stop the shaking.

"I have five. . . well, four now. . . It's a hard question to answer."

Her glasses steam up. She unlocks her arms, removes her glasses and lays them on the draining board. Greg is now a blur, which is easier.

She's making the van shake.

The kettle boils. Jack scrambles to his feet as the whistle grows louder. Greg's sitting next to the hob.

"I'll do it."

Ellie's staring hopelessly at the kettle. Greg reaches over and lifts it from the flame. The handle will be hot, but she doesn't notice him wince. But then, she can't see properly. With his other hand he turns the knob to kill the gas.

"Do you. . . ? Ah, here they are."

He gets to his feet, dipping his head slightly under the ceiling, opens the cupboard above the cooker and brings out teabags and mugs. He drops the teabags in, adds hot water.

"This'll sort you out. Might help a bit anyway, love."

He doesn't ask the reason she's sobbing, simply performs the task he's set himself, keeping his gaze away from her while she snorts and chokes. She blows her nose repeatedly, tearing tissue from the roll by the sink, then bunches the sudden squares in her hand.

Greg discovers the milk, nudging Ellie gently with the fridge door as he opens it. He hands Ellie a mug, holding the hot part so she can take the handle. He presses her hand around it for her.

"You sit on the bed, I'll take this stool."

He lifts it down from its bracket on the wall opposite the sliding door. She doesn't argue.

They sip tea, Ellie hiccupping now and again. Jack resettles in front of the now blazing woodstove. He sighs deeply and tucks his nose under his tail.

Finally Ellie puts down her mug and reaches for her glasses. She puts them on and seeks Greg's eyes. They look the same as she remembers, and it's a comfort. There was a time before. She takes a deep breath.

"My daughter died."

"Oh, dear Lord," says Greg. She sees the question in his eyes: not Rosie?

"Her name was Eliza."

How bitter the name but so sweet on her tongue. "She's who I was pregnant with when I left Running Hare House." Ellie bites the inside of her mouth. "She died early this year. February."

"Oh God, you poor girl."

Greg places his mug on the floor by his foot and presses a hand to his forehead. "I can't imagine... that's appalling. I'm so sorry, Ellie. How you must be suffering. It's the worst thing that could possibly happen."

"I'm sorry for burdening you with this," she says. "I've haven't spoken about it since it happened; I... haven't been able to accept it."

This is true. Eliza has still been alive until now.

I'll never see her again.

Greg hunches forward on the stool, hands folded in a prayer. He lifts his chin and gives her a nod.

"I kept on believing she wasn't really dead," explains Ellie. "My daughter... my... difficult girl."

His eyes crinkle at the corners.

"What happened...? Only tell me if you want to, sweet girl."

She stands up, making Jack scramble to his feet again. She pushes at the curtain on the window behind the sink and gazes out into the dark. A rich brown darkness, illumined from beneath by the thick quilt of snow on the ground.

"It's stopped snowing," she murmurs. "I need some air. Would you mind...?"

"Of course not, Ellie. Whatever you want. Let's take a walk together. There's a path, goes through those trees over there. It opens out onto a field with a stream running through it. . . ."

She pulls on her thick winter coat. It's the one she wore for her trip to Iceland. When she and Jonah went to fetch Eliza home.

Jack leaps to the ground when she drags the door open. Ellie climbs down stiffly, followed by Greg. Jack rushes about in circles, scratching deep gouges in the snow with his claws.

Greg disappears and comes back with a long woollen scarf which he is winding several times round his neck.

He glances at Ellie.

"You'll never guess who made me this?"

Ellie disturbs the crisp top layer of snow with her foot. She sees him glance quickly at her again and then away. Words build a tower in her head, a way to impart the reality of what has happened. He's the one person she wants to tell.

"Do you mind if I put me arm around you, Ellie?" Greg asks. "I know I can't make things better but if it's not too selfish of me, I'd feel better if I could do that."

She feels grateful.

"I don't mind at all."

She's as comfortable with him now as she was in the past. She remembers the long walks they took together when Rosie was a baby. Involuntarily, her body leans into his. He's something to anchor herself to while they walk. Woollen tassels tickle the side of her face when he shifts slightly to duck an overhanging branch. She girds herself to talk about something other than her overwhelming tragedy.

"Who made the scarf?"

"Bethany," he answers. "You met her once when she was very small. She's Bonnie's youngest daughter."

Her stomach lurches.

"So you're still with Bonnie, then?"

Stupid Ellie. There's no reason it should hurt. Other, much more important things have happened: Eliza is dead.

"Not with Bonnie, no," Greg is busy explaining. "Not even with Bethany any more. She did keep in touch with me for a long time afterwards, though. Bonnie and I were together until Bethany was ten. She was very close to me. I felt bad for leaving her."

"But. . . you and Bonnie split up before I left Pottersea."

She doesn't want to hear about his relationship with another woman's daughter. Her daughter is dead.

Her stomach realigns itself as she breathes.

"We did, but we got back together again. Bonnie was pregnant, you see. We had a son, Dylan."

He holds the gate to the footpath open and stands back to let Ellie through. He had a son with Bonnie. The dog bumps their legs as he shoulders between them.

"Had, did he. . . is he?"

"No, no. Oh my God. I'm sorry to put it like that, love. He's fine, Dylan. Alive and well as far as I know. We lost touch though, Ellie, me an' my boy did."

Snow plops onto her head, melts and drips down her neck. She jumps and shivers, feels Greg's arm tightening; concentrates hard on the trickle of real, actual icy water on her skin.

"I feel guilty now," Greg says. "For being such a bad father. Well, I always did, but hearing about your beautiful daughter, the baby that was inside you when I last saw you, Ellie, it makes me determined to try and put things right between my son and me."

In the cold light from the snow, Ellie sees Greg's wincing expression. Remembering Bonnie, she imagines it can't entirely have been Greg's fault that he's lost contact with his son.

"It's so odd, discovering you here."

Her brain is wide open. Greg lets go of her to push the next gate aside.

"I don't know," he says pensively. He rubs his hands together and then shoves them into the pockets of his quilted jacket, and Ellie misses the security of his arm across her back.

"You don't know?"

"I kind of knew you were coming," his Irish accent thickens, (I koind of knew).

Tilting her head to look up at his face, she glimpses moisture around the edges of his nostrils. He sniffs and pulls out a tissue. "That sounds crazy, but. I had a strong feeling about Seth's mother. I didn't know it was going to be you, but I kind of knew you were going to be important when you came."

He wipes his nose and puts the tissue back into his pocket along with his hand, which he leaves there.

The words give her a warm feeling. She concentrates on the crunch of their boots on snow, comforted by the thought of their two sets of tracks winding together behind them. They reach the middle of the field. The moon is dim but combined with the white of the snow it seems like daylight in this wide, empty space. Craggy rocks poke up out of the snow at regular intervals and rock-shaped clouds ridge the surface of the velvet-brown sky, an upside-down reflection of the mountainous landscape. Breath dissipates into the air in front of their faces.

Ellie grasps a skein of sheep's wool caught between twin rocks at the edge of the path.

She smooths the wool between her cold fingers.

Greg extracts his hand from his pocket and catches one of hers. The shock makes her twist her wrist so that the sheep's wool gets tangled in both their sets of fingers.

He gives a nervous laugh. "Like a pagan wedding."

A shudder runs through her. She wishes Eliza's voice could be at her ear again. Her and her Icelandic folk tales, she would have had something to say about these two hands tied together.

Eliza is now one of the hidden people.

Ellie keeps hold of Greg's hand, even after they've disentangled themselves from the wool. She senses he's been lonely a long time.

"Eliza died in Iceland."

Greg squeezes her hand, pulls her against him with his other arm. "Tell me all of it. Take your time, sweet girl. I'm listening."

Ellie steadies her breathing, begins the story that will go on forever.

I had another daughter, she was named Eliza, but she's gone now...

"She'd been in Iceland about six months. Before that she travelled the world, many parts of it anyway. She was a restless soul, would never settle anywhere, but I think she may have settled there."

The hot sweetness of tears blossoms and moves down her cheeks, turning cold. She allows the damp to soak into Greg's jacket. He runs his hand up and down her back in the same way he stroked Jack in the van.

"It's alright, no hurry there. Take your time, girl."

"It was the one place that suited her. While she was in Iceland, she became obsessed with its folklore, their fairy tales. There were so many. From the emails she sent us, we started to get a bit worried. She said she'd been touched on the shoulder by a. . . a woman. . . a. . . kind of fairy. One of the hidden people they believe in there. You can only see them if they choose to let you."

Ellie isn't explaining it very well. Greg remains quiet. She checks his expression; sombre and patient.

"There's a lot more to it," Ellie says. "Eliza believed she was being called to do something important. If the hidden people ask for help you should help them. They pay in luck and happiness, Eliza said. But it's not just about that." Ellie presses her ear against Greg's coat, feels the distant thud of his heartbeat beneath the layers. He gives her an encouraging squeeze and she feels safe, letting the story out little by little.

"We'd already booked our trip to Iceland when it happened. Eliza insisted on seeing us both together and we decided it was only fair to grant her request. She'd been away for years, and asked so little of us as parents."

She drags in another heaving breath.

Greg puts his hand under her chin and tilts her face up to his.

"You and Jonah."

It's not a question. But she waits a moment before answering.

"We split up twelve years ago." Pushing the memory of their night in the hotel together away. That was our goodbye. To Eliza as well as their old selves.

"Eliza was fifteen. She was devastated when we broke up. She saw things very much in black and white. She even thought she was supposed to make a choice between her parents. But she got over it, eventually, understood how we could still be Mum and Dad even though we weren't together. Jonah was actually a much better parent when I wasn't around, anyway."

She senses Greg stiffening slightly and remembers about him never seeing his own son. She gives his chest a little push with the palms of her hands, moving him slightly away, then hooks her arm through his.

"Shall we walk on?"

He nods and takes the first step.

"Steady on, there." He supports her as she stumbles over a half-buried stone. "What was she like, your Eliza?"

Their footsteps synchronise into a rhythm, the soft crunch of snow. As they move beneath a skeletal tree a light breeze showers them with a flurry of snowflakes and they both let out startled cries. Jack comes skidding towards them, tail thrashing; tongue hanging out. Ellie places her hand on his wet back as he spins away from them again, taking off across the field. He leaves a cloud of mist in the air and the rasping sound of his panting.

"I'll be honest, she wasn't an easy girl to mother," Ellie says. "I won't pretend to have understood her. She was always 'away with the fairies' if you like. I think she felt she'd found her true place in Iceland. She reckoned people she met there believed the same sort of things as she did."

Greg pulls Ellie to a standstill. He bends his head and places his mouth on her cheek. He runs a finger under her eye, readjusting her glasses on the bridge of her nose.

"You were bound to create a fairy child," he tells her.

His voice is full of emotion. She stifles a wrenching sob. Greg grasps her, drawing her closer to his chest.

"Look." He points upwards. The thick white clouds have parted and from deep within the brown velvet sky pinpoints of light prickle through. One star shines brighter than the rest.

"I don't know how to bear it, Greg," she confesses. "Tell me. How do I?"

"Just as you are," Greg says. "Just the way you are, talking about it, thinking about her. It's all you can do, lovely."

Suddenly, it's freeing to talk. Denying Eliza's death for so long hasn't helped.

She takes another deep breath and tells him more.

"She was going to look for the pot of gold at the end of the rainbow," she says. "It was that stupid."

She feels herself breaking again.

"What was that you said, love?"

Ellie reforms herself for the millionth time. She gulps, and stares up at the stars.

"Skogafoss, the waterfall is sixty foot high. Jonah and I visited it, because she wanted us to." Ellie hesitates, remembering the roaring water.

"Are you okay to go on?" Greg asks.

She nods, leaning against him. "When the sun shines on the waterfall a rainbow is created. Legend tells the story of how a chest of gold was placed behind it. Eliza told the other workers at the hostel that she was going to find the gold. The hidden people would help her."

A strangled sound fights its way out of her throat. She swallows it back down, and says the words out loud.

"She drowned, Greg. My darling girl slipped and banged her head on a rock. Then she fell into the water. She wasn't even trying to climb the path to the top."

"Oh, Ellie."

"She would've been frozen when they found her. They told her not to be silly, her friends, although she'd cut herself off from them by then. And they didn't think she would really do it. But she went in the afternoon and it would have been dark by the time she got there."

No rainbows for Eliza. This strikes Ellie as the greatest tragedy of all.

"Maybe she was planning to wait for the morning. She hitched all the way there, on her own. She told the guys who gave her a lift that she was camping with friends in the area."

"Ellie, it's so awful. . ."

"Why did they believe her, Greg? It was bloody winter. Who'd be stupid enough to camp in sub-zero temperatures?"

She breaks off for a paroxysm of sobs and coughing.

Greg waits, rock-still.

She pounds his chest with her fists. She wishes the pounding would make her hands bleed.

She subsides against him.

"She wasn't well, was she, Greg? I was her mother and I didn't know how bad it was."

Her voice freezes into silence, swords of ice on the air.

They stand together under the cold starlight for a long time. Ellie feels she ought to strip off, be as cold as Eliza must have been. She could lie down in the snow and die, it would make sense. But she won't put Greg through her madness.

"Thank you," she says finally. She pushes herself off him, turns and looks him full in the eyes.

"What for?"

"For being the one I felt safe enough to tell. For helping me get it out."

The big goon is crying. She's privileged to bear witness, as he has done.

"Ah, Ellie, me girl," he says at last. "I'm so glad to have been the one. Life is cruel, to be sure, but it's also beautiful. You don't know the gift you've given me."

She can't think what it might be. She helps him wipe away his tears. They both speak at the same time.

"Shall we go back?"

"Seth and Catherine will be wondering where I've got to."

Jack has stopped running madly from one side of the field to the other. He slinks to a rest beside Ellie, steam coming from his coat, nudges her with his nose.

"Ye poor dog, what've we done to you?" Greg asks him, passing his hand over his eyes. "Keeping you up all night."

Ellie's drained but she feels purified. Her legs have gone weak and her feet are solid-cold. Greg has to support her as they make their way back to the van. She clings to his arm, feels warmth from him eking into her cold hands.

The fire in the woodstove has gone out.

"You look exhausted," says Greg. "You're white as a sheet."

He begins stacking a new pile of kindling on a firelighter, adds a lit match.

"Get into bed, Ellie, you're shivering. It's the shock, it's understandable."

She's reminded of his tone the time Stan ripped open his paw, so long ago.

She bends forward, starts unlacing her boots. Greg closes the stove door and takes her ankle in his two hands. He leans towards her and kisses her knee in its woollen legging, then helps slide the boot off her foot as she wriggles out of it. He repeats the procedure with her other foot. She can't remember feeling more cared for at any time in her life, but she is so tired her eyelids are falling down. She's shaking again, a vibration that shimmers through the van.

"Lie down, love, that's it. Let's tuck you in." Greg leans forward again and kisses her forehead as he helps her settle in the bed. "There you go," he whispers, smoothing the quilt over her shoulders. "There you go."

It's a while since she's slept in the bus. The pillow smells musty, but that's comforting in its way. She feels loved and safe. Sleep approaches willingly, like a tame animal, and she walks into its arms with gratitude.

46

Iceland

February 2013

Before Eliza's separate requests to them both via email, Ellie hadn't seen Jonah for two years. The last time was at Arthur's christening: Rick was a churchgoer and Rosie had become one since marrying him. Jonah was hardly in Hull any more, and Ellie and Jonah had truly gone their different ways. Jonah, Lily had told her, had a girlfriend in New Jersey for a while but the relationship had ended. Ellie went on a few dates after Rosie signed her up with an online agency. "For God's sake let me cut your hair for you, Mum," Rosie insisted before the first one.

And then Eliza made that funny request, saying she wanted to see her two parents together. Sending them the itinerary for their trip. 'You owe it to me,' she'd written.

"What did she mean by it?" Ellie sobs into Jonah's chest when he arrives at the house on Somerset Street. He's already back in the country in preparation for their booked visit to Iceland, when Ellie gets the call. Ellie falls against him, all the strength gone from her bones. "Do you think she planned this? Was it the reason for our trip all along?"

"It can't have been." Jonah slumps back against the hall wall, Ellie still clinging to him. "Please God, no. Don't even think that, babe."

Ellie received the phone call from a shadow-voiced girl who explained she worked with Eliza at the hostel. "We were friends," she'd said. Were.

"But she called herself Fay," Ellie wails. "Our Eliza."

She starts to slide to the floor. Jonah takes her firmly by the shoulders and leads her into the living room where he tucks her against him on the sofa. "The girl kept saying Fay and I didn't know who she was talking about at first. I thought she'd got the wrong mother and I felt sorry for the woman who was going to get this terrible news that her daughter had died."

The double horror of it hits her again; new compassion for the poor naïve Ellie who didn't understand what the girl was telling her, along with a renewed flood for the one who suddenly did. A low moan comes out of her, or is it from Jonah? Her head is pressed to his chest so that she doesn't know whether it's her own life-force or his she hears pounding in her ears.

"That was your name for her... She called herself by the name you gave her..." Her hands seem alien as they scrabble on Jonah's chest, twisting his sweater into tortured contortions.

"Eliza Fay," murmurs Jonah. He pushes her away as he chokes, lurches up from the sofa to lean forward and retch. Nothing comes out. Ellie stands beside him and rubs his back.

(They'd reached the point when they legally had to register Eliza's birth and she still didn't have a name and so Jonah came up with Fay because she was tiny like a fairy: but at the last minute Ellie added Eliza because it had been her grandma's middle name. And Jonah said it sounded better the other way round).

It doesn't feel real. They talk and talk about Eliza but say hardly anything about the manner of her death. It's too soon.

Gradually other members of the family arrive; Lily from Newark and Rosie from Sheffield: she's left the children at home with Rick for the time being. Seth is away in Amsterdam but he's coming home. Kester gets the first available flight to Leeds from Venice. He arrives at the house mid-evening in a taxi from Hull railway station.

Ellie and Jonah are given over to comforting their children. At some point in the middle of endless rounds of tea and take-outs and another knock on the door which is Seth arriving, the phone rings again.

"It's the British Consulate in Iceland," Kester says in a cracked voice, his eyes burning within their blue-black sockets. He hands the phone to his mother. Jonah is standing next to Ellie.

The voice from the embassy apologises for the lateness of the call, explaining how their daughter's friend had requested to be the one to give them the news. The kindly man goes through the procedures they will need to follow to retrieve their daughter's body. He arranges an appointment at the embassy for them when they arrive in Iceland. "I can organise a car to be at the airport in Keflavik for you," he offers, "So it won't be necessary for you to take the public transport into Reykjavik."

But later Ellie and Jonah discuss these arrangements. They decide they would like to go ahead with Eliza's carefully-constructed itinerary for them before they go to the embassy to sort out the final journey of their girl.

"Imagine how cross Eliza would be with us if we didn't," Ellie laughs through snot. "We always did our best not to put her in a bad mood." They both chuckle, hopelessly. There's a pause, before Jonah says, "I'll call the man at the embassy back and explain the situation. We'll still be meeting her at the end of our trip, just as she planned."

Then they both have a cry.

———

On the drive home from Skogafoss, Ellie notices something flickering across the edges of her vision. She glances at Jonah, concentrating on the road, his face set into icy planes. There it is again, green flickering over his skin in the half-dark.

"Jonah." The sound of deep-grooved tires on hardened snow, no other traffic around. He doesn't hear her. "Jonah."

The sky has come alive, dancing and painting the snow green. Ellie stops breathing. Jonah pulls the car in carefully and they both get out, Ellie grabbing her gloves from the heater under the window. She draws her damp coat tightly around her and feels Jonah's arm pinning her to his side.

Coils of green streak and whip the sky; the occasional flare of gold or red, more needles of green.

The music of silence. Sheets of colour diffusing and reappearing again in fresh blasts. Come with us.

Jonah's racked breathing; her blood pulsing in her ears.

Come, come.

———

By the next day, a thorn of ice, probably snapped from a rock at the side of the waterfall, as she brushed past on her way back to the car, has embedded itself in Ellie's heart. Every now and then she presses her hand to the centre of her chest to try and thaw it but it refuses to melt.

Is this how you intend to stay with me? She can't help remembering those grey eyes of Eliza's, stones at the bottom of water, the way they stared at her when Eliza was a baby. You saved up your punishment for me.

That's an awful thing to think. But it was my fault. This is the recompense demanded for her cruelty as a mother, and Jonah, and Eliza's siblings, are having to pay too.

The hostel has refused to take any payment for their stay. It isn't the one where Eliza worked but the two are affiliated. Alicia, the girl who rang Ellie, is coming to talk to them before they go and meet Mr Johansson from the embassy. Ellie's facing the other way when the girl walks in and almost faints when she turns around. Her knees buckle. She finds a chair with her hand, her eyes fixed on the girl's face.

It's Eliza, someone made a mistake: she's not dead.

For a second her heart lifts: she's been exonerated. But then she realises the girl's eyes are blue and her skin is a slightly darker tone than Eliza's. Her fair hair is silkier and hangs level with her shoulders instead of down her back.

Ellie feels the blood drain from her head.

"Hi." The girl walks forward, her hand outstretched. Ellie recognises the lightweight voice from the phone. "I'm Alicia." Her accent might be German. She's searching Ellie's eyes with hers.

Ellie grasps her hand a bit too hard. She glances at Jonah and sees her shock reflected on his face. Alicia pulls her hand from Ellie's and offers it to Jonah. Then she gestures him to sit down next to Ellie and she settles opposite. The three of them have still not spoken by the time the receptionist brings over a tray of coffee.

Alicia's mouth is downturned at the corners. "I know," she offers, without it being mentioned. "I look like her. Fay – Eliza, I mean." Tears well in her eyes. "We were very close. Used to be, at least."

"Used to be?" Ellie finally finds her voice.

"Really close…" Alicia gives her a meaningful glance. "Until Olafur came along. He ruined everything. Sorry," she adds. "I shouldn't have said that, this is not about me."

Ellie stares at her, picturing her ethereal daughter with this equally fragile-looking girl. They could have been twins. Were they lovers? Her mind spins. And then, "Olafur?"

"He was here for a management course. Eliza fell for his stories." Alicia lets loose a sob. "She was fascinated by the folk tales. He's Icelandic and she believed everything he said. He told her he was adopted and that his real mother was one of the hidden people." She makes a swivelling signal with her finger at the side of her head. "That got her hooked. He seduced her and then he dumped her. That's when she started to go a bit weird."

"He dumped her?" Ellie says at the same time as Jonah says aggressively, "What do you mean, a bit weird?"

Alicia glances from one to the other of them. She focusses on Ellie. "He told her she was getting too clingy. Then he said he was leaving to look for the treasure behind the waterfall. He was winding her up, of course, he was like that. I'm sorry. He knew it was her favourite place, Skogafoss. Her head was completely fucked up when he went." She presses two fingers to her lips, removes them and says, "Sorry," for the third or fourth time.

Ellie shakes her head. "It's all right. So, do you think Eliza was following him?"

Alicia shrugs, fresh tears springing to her eyes.

Ellie is left stunned. In all the years Eliza's been away she's never mentioned a significant relationship. Yet in this country it seems she had two, one after the other. Ellie imagines if Eliza had come home with this girl. Alicia is more filled-out than Eliza: more in herself.

Jonah begins asking practical questions, Alicia answering as best she can. They discover that Olafur left Reykjavik on a Wednesday and Eliza became ill on the Thursday, when she realised he'd gone. "Really sick," says Alicia. "Like, you know, proper vomiting. She was saying weird stuff, things like an invisible person touched her on the shoulder. She thought it was Olafur's mother who was trying to lead her to him."

Their daughter disappeared around lunchtime on the Friday, while her friends believed she was resting on her bunk.   She was found at the bottom of the waterfall on Saturday morning after the hostel staff raised the alarm overnight, when Eliza didn't return. Jonah presses Alicia for more details. The girl's shoulders shake. "She banged her head," she offers. "They think she slipped on some ice at the edge of the water. . ."

"Stop it now, Jonah," Ellie orders.

Too many questions, when there's only one thing we both want.

"We really appreciate you coming to talk to us," she tells the shuddering girl. "I understand how hard it must have been for you."

Ellie and Jonah gather their things. The ice has spread in Ellie's chest. Jonah looks empty behind his eyes. For the first time since they heard the news, Ellie realises he's carried them both so far and has nothing left to give.

We're going to meet up with Eliza now.

She hooks her arm through his and pulls him close to her side as he did to her when the lights danced. She looks back as Jonah pulls open the door, glad to see that the couple on reception have enfolded the girl who looks like Eliza into a comforting embrace.

He explains the various courses of action they could take and hands them brochures of companies that can manage every procedure for them, recommending one in particular. "This is the one we always use. It's the company who is looking after her now, but of course, you're free to make your own decision. . ."

They are looking after her.

Ellie handles the glossy papers gingerly. Pictures of sombre-faced but beautiful models. Coffins and caskets and urns; graveyards and aeroplanes. Her fingers don't feel as if they belong to her. Jonah keeps nodding, even when the man has finished speaking.

"But as I pointed out initially," Morgan Johansson checks their faces to see if they're taking it in. "Cremation, within in this country, is really your best option from here on in." He clears his throat. "You would be able to carry her home on the plane yourselves." He coughs again, delicately. "We have a selection of receptacles for you to choose from.

Carry her home.

Silently, a howl arises in Ellie. Jonah's hands, resting straight-fingered, palms flat on his lap, are bone-white.

<hr>

There, there. Mamma's here. Eliza's eyes are closed.

You used to creep into my bed at night, it was the only time you'd let me touch you.

The cut on the side of her head is covered skilfully by her fine, flyaway hair (she would never have worn it that way).

You finally allowed someone to brush it, Eliza.

Yes, they've done a good job, here at this comfortable home. They've dressed Eliza in a purple velvet suit; a ruffled skirt with a lace-edged jacket and a white blouse. Unusual, but very Eliza. She wears dove-coloured tights on her thin legs. A silver penny-whistle is threaded into the gap between her hands and her chest.

It should have been me who dressed my child for the final time.

Ellie can barely control her anger; feels it burning in her cheeks.

"Her friend brought the outfit to us," the funeral director explains, an eyebrow crooked as if to check if this is OK with her parents. "The young lady said these were her favourite clothes. But if you'd rather..?"

Alicia knew her so much better than I did.

Ellie fights the anger down. She thinks with regret of the worn blue corduroy pinafore dress she made Eliza as a three-year-old, and her beloved patchwork coat.

Eliza's long gone from her body. Her skin's like marble. A memory comes to Ellie: one of Eliza's terrible fits of desperation and fury, when the moon shone on her skin and she looked like this.

A premonition, then.

"It was after I told her we'd split up," Ellie turns to Jonah to say, as if they're in the middle of a conversation. He stares at her a moment, in an accusatory way. It was how he used to look at her when Eliza was first born.

She knows what he must be thinking: you never wanted her in the first place.

47

Greg

15/16 December 2013

He watches her sleep. She lies on her side, the quilt loose around her. He resists the urge to tuck it securely under her chin, smooth the hair back from her face and plant another kiss on her forehead before turning out the light, the way he's done in the past with Bonnie's children and later his own boy. Ellie isn't a child. Instead he waits, folding his arms around his body and then, leaning further forward, tightening them around his knees.

His whole body aches, and it feels like his heart does, too.

At first Ellie seems relaxed, her breathing in a slow rhythm. But after about ten minutes he notices deep shudders running through her, ripples that cause a catch in each outward breath. Her trembling reverberates through the van. Ellie's face twitches and grimaces. He tries to look away but can't, feels in some way he needs to bear witness. His throat is hot and it's hard to swallow. Painful as it has been for him to lose touch with his son, he's sure it's nothing to your child dying. At least he'll always know there's a possibility of meeting Dylan again. Family members have told him Dylan is okay. It's up to him, he can do something; he's just been too lazy.

But Ellie can't meet Eliza again and never will be able to. He understands that her body needs to grieve. She's been holding it in too long.

He stands up carefully, so as not to disturb the dog, and peers down at her. In the dim light he sees dewdrops of water in the corners of her eyes.

He sits down again on the stool, feeling useless. His knees jut up either side of his folded elbows, his hands curl in on themselves.

Steepling his fingers he tries to keep his breaths deep and meditative. Both the dog and Ellie twitch in their sleep, the dog letting out small whimpers as his paws scutter on the grey carpet. The van is warm, the fire now blazing away.

Greg starts to get worried that Ellie might suffocate in her sleep. He stands up again, taking care to keep his movements steady, and pushes the skylight open. It makes a noise and jolts the van, but neither the dog nor Ellie wake up. Cool air filters in. The dog only sighs heavily, curling itself into a tighter circle, its nose jammed beneath the root of its tail.

Greg sits down again, his knees stiff. He wishes he could stretch his legs but there's no room.

He's not the sort for being inactive, wants to get up and move. But he reminds himself of the important job he's doing, bearing witness. But still... There's one dim light on, above the bed. He watches Ellie's features elongating and crumpling, listens to her breathing alter repeatedly from slow and steady to jerky and irregular. Intermittently she sobs in her sleep.

After a while Greg becomes so restless that he must do something. He fishes about in the wood box, causing Jack to growl in his sleep. The dog forces his eyes open, raises his head and stares blurrily at Greg for half a minute. Greg places his finger on his lips. The dog's eyes clear and he seems to smile at Greg, unlatching his tail and batting it on the carpet a few times. Then he lowers his head again, keeping one watchful eye open. Greg slips his hand into his jeans' pocket and pulls out a penknife. He begins whittling a small figure from the stick of firewood.

The first time he saw Ellie... hadn't she seemed too young to be a mother? She arrived one afternoon at Running Hare House with her flushed cheeks and her brand new baby. He'd used his dog to get close to her, felt a connection right from the beginning. Everything was against building the attachment with her that he craved from that first afternoon but it didn't stop him seeking out opportunities to spend time alone with her. He'd become fond of her baby, watched Rosie grow into a determined toddler. And Ellie, well. If circumstances had been different...

If Ellie hadn't got pregnant the second time... He tries to remember whether he'd colluded in the household's efforts to get Ellie and Jonah back together that first Christmas. Maybe out of a misguided sense of do-gooding inspired by Hayley or Jen or somebody, he'd agreed it was a good idea. Looking back, he guesses Bonnie was in on the scheming, she had a second sense about Greg, had expressed concern about his feelings for Ellie and he had reassured her there was nothing in it...

Those walks they used to take, he and Ellie and the baby. Sometimes he used to pretend Rosie was his.

He remembers the weight of the baby on his chest and the funny little noises she made. He remembers his jealousy whenever he witnessed Jonah's occasional displays of fatherhood. Jonah didn't deserve Rosie, or Ellie.

Was Ellie ever aware of his feelings?

He knows he's deliberately blotting out one very important element of that time – Bonnie depended on him emotionally after giving up her comfortable life in a good house with her husband. She'd chosen to be parted from her children for him.

He'd allowed her to catch him, like a moth to a flame. He could have said no when she asked him to move out to Running Hare House with her, except he felt guilty, thinking it was his fault she'd left her husband. But then, if he hadn't moved out there he would never have met Ellie, and he wouldn't be sitting in her van now, watching her sleep. There are always second chances.

Mostly.

He continues to bear witness to Ellie's troubled sleep, and keep the fire going. It's all he can do.

48

Greg

24 December 2013

On Christmas eve there's a massive party at the O'Tooles'. The usual thing it is; held in Sarah's Barn, the gallery and workshop behind the house. Half the population of Leitrim is here. These parties are legendary; they get bigger with each year of Mark and Sarah's twenty-five-year marriage. The guests include everyone local as well as clients and art students of Sarah's, anyone who happens to be passing by. The Shanbos always perform a reunion gig and even in the gaps between organised (to put it loosely) music, people will spontaneously get up and sing, play, or begin dancing or telling stories.

Greg spots Ellie huddled in a corner with Sarah, the two of them in deep conversation.

The women have bereavement in common: Sarah's beloved brother died recently. The death hit her hard. Her mother has come over from England to be with Sarah this Christmas. She's brought Sarah's sister-in-law, the widow, and Sarah's nephew and nieces. One of the girls has a boy of about four who reminds Greg of his son at the same age.

Greg's planning to take steps to resume contact with Dylan after Christmas. He's talked it over with Ellie and she says it's a good idea. Ellie has taught him not to leave things too late.

Maybe he'll even begin the process tonight, after the party.

Greg's sister has told him that his son has a Facebook account. All Greg will do at this point will be to wish the lad a happy Christmas, and say that he's missed him, but it will be a start.

More people are arriving at the party.

"Who're that lot then, do you know 'em?"

Roger McNulty from the bakery, who Greg's supposed to be chatting to (but has spent more time watching Ellie) asks.

A knot of people has just entered the barn.

There's a young woman with jet-black hair cut in a sharp line at her chin. She casts a sweeping look around the barn and he sees her eyes glide over several people before alighting on Ellie. Even from this distance, Greg senses the spark in her gaze. Next to her is a tall black man with twists of hair in neat rows on his scalp. That'll be Rick, Rosie's husband. Rick's carrying a small boy on his hip and Rosie holds her daughter's hand.

Greg's heart alters its rhythm. He can't believe this is Rosie. That little girl I knew.

The plan he and Seth worked out together has come to fruition.

Greg sees Seth hurry over to the pair, embracing his sister and scooping the little girl up in his arms.

"Your lad Seth seems to know 'em," comments Roger. "Family, are they?"

On first meeting Seth at Greg's workshop, Roger got it into his head that Seth is a relative of Greg's. He persists in this belief even though Greg has informed him otherwise. He can't be bothered to correct him anymore, it could soon be true anyway, Greg hopes. He wants Ellie's family for his own.

"That's right," he lets a smile spread over his lips. "Family. All come over to spend Christmas with us."

Greg can't take his eyes off Rosie. Ellie's description of her was accurate. He tries to connect those sculpted cheeks with the soft round baby face and wispy hair he knew. Behind the couple Greg notices another young woman, a girl. She looks like Ellie. His heart softens.

It must be Lily. The quiet one.

And that must be Kester, behind Lily. Good God.

The boy Greg heard being born, the hothouse baby. It's amazing to see him all grown up. He's strikingly similar to Seth in appearance, even has a similar haircut. Ellie's boys. He puts his hand out to Roger.

"Merry Christmas to you, mate. I'd better get over there and say hello to them all. Haven't seen them for a long time, you know."

Roger nods at him and grins.

"You can introduce me to them later, mate."

But as Greg begins to negotiate his way across the smooth wood floor that he helped Mark lay so many years ago, he sees another figure come in the door behind Kester.

It must be... it is. Oh good Lord; Jonah, still with that long hair, looks like the same stubble on his face.

Greg feels a stabbing pain in his chest. What the fuck is Jonah doing here? His presence will ruin everything, all Greg's hopes for a new start with Ellie.

It isn't as bad as he feared.

The two men slap each other on the back in as friendly a fashion as can be expected, then skirt around each other. Greg guesses that Seth has prepared his father for the situation here in Ireland. Greg realises he'll have to accept that Jonah is a valid part of these young people's lives, and Ellie's. At least he stuck around for his kids. Unlike some.

Ellie says she and Jonah are still family as far as their kids are concerned.

They're all sitting around on hay bales after the party.

Iris comes in, bringing in a waft of tobacco, or something more pungent, with her. Jonah enters a moment later. Greg glances from one to the other of them. Ah, so it's like that already.

Just as Greg's innate feelings about Ellie haven't changed, neither have the ones he has about Jonah.

"Come on, you lot," Iris calls to the remaining company in the barn. "Volunteers needed for setting up tables for Christmas dinner. It's going to be the biggest yet. I hope you Englishers have brought plenty of goodies over with you, otherwise we're going to have to kill one of my goats so we can feed everybody."

A communal groan ripples around the room.

Lily's eyes widen. She gives Greg a look of horror.

"It's okay, love," he says, smiling. Lily reminds him so much of the young Ellie. "You'll get used to Iris and her warped sense of humour. We've got plenty of food in for the occasion. Might need a bit of help cooking it, though, if you've got any talents in that department."

25 December 2013

The O'Toole kitchen is almost full already. Mark and Sarah, Greg and Ellie and Lily are all in it. Iris and Rebecca arrive next.

"Connor'll be over when he's finished doing the chickens," Rebecca explains. Greg notices Ellie's eyes lingering on the baby as she is passed from person to person. Ellie only takes her for a minute before transferring her into her daughter's arms. He wonders if holding a baby is just too painful for her, this first Christmas of her loss.

Sarah's sister-in-law, mother and nieces crowd into the room then, and there are more exclamations of delight over baby Eve.

Greg sidles out into the corridor on Mark's heels. Seth and Catherine are just pushing their way into the hall through the side door with their contingent of family guests. Greg watches Rosie's children plant themselves in front of the little boy Sarah's family have brought. Someone gets them all involved in a jigsaw puzzle.

Greg seeks out one of Mark and Sarah's boys; Riley, he thinks, but he can never tell the twins apart. Taking a risk, he says, "Now then, Riley lad. Would you happen to have a computer I could borrow for a few minutes?"

The boy turns from the red-haired girl he's talking to. Well actually, her hair's red at the top and black nearer the bottom. The youngsters are hunched over some sort of game on a handheld device. Greg wonders what his own son is into these days. Ah well, hopefully he'll soon be able to find out. He does feel ridiculously full of hope. Both the boy and the girl start laughing.

"It's Fergus, actually, Uncle Greg. This is me cousin, Angel, by the way."

"Pleased to meet you," says the girl. Angel is an odd name for someone wearing thick black eyeliner and dark lipstick.

"Pleased to meet you back," says Greg.

"Come this way, you can use the office in the hall." Fergus examines Greg doubtfully. "You do know what you're doing, don't you?"

"Aye, lad, I think I can manage."

Greg gives the boy a pat on the back. He closes the office door once Fergus has turned away.

"I left my boy a message on Facebook, wished him a happy Christmas and said I'd like to see him." Greg has been seated next to Ellie at the long row of tables in Sarah's Barn. "I kept it short." He takes his fork to his mouth and chews a morsel of turkey. Ellie lowers her chin and he watches her lips accept a nibble of the nut roast she helped Sarah make. The dish containing it sits in the centre of the line of tables, next to the huge, ravished carcass of the turkey. Greg thinks he'll help himself to a portion of the vegetarian option when there's enough space on his plate, he shouldn't have been so greedy with the turkey and trimmings. He swallows. "I apologised," he says. "For not making more of an effort with Dylan all these years."

Ellie tilts her head towards him. She gives him a look of such warmth it turns his insides to liquid.

"It's all you can do." She dabs her lips with a napkin. "You just need to be patient, now."

She loads her fork again, chewing for a few more moments.

"I made an effort, too," she says.

"You did?"

Greg waits while Ellie takes another mouthful and swallows her food. She picks up her glass and drinks some of the wine her eldest son brought over from Italy. She dabs her lips again. Every movement she makes is an act of artistry. To him, anyway. He realises he's neglecting his dinner, transfixed by her actions. She notices the intensity of his gaze and the lines already etched into her forehead deepen. Quickly, he lowers his head to his plate again.

"I rang my mum, and my sister was there," Ellie continues, "as I expected her to be."

Greg has a vague memory of Ellie's sister, a beautiful girl with long golden hair like a princess in a fairy tale. But Ellie has a difficult relationship with her, he knows from their recent conversations.

"Did you speak to your sister?"

Ellie nods and takes another mouthful of food. Greg sips his wine. Instead of fixing Ellie with his gaze he glances around the table at the assortment of guests. They all wear shining paper hats and have disassembled crackers next to their plates. He thinks again how lucky he is to be in this barn on this day, to be part of something. Not looking at Ellie only makes the prospect of seeing her again more special.

She's right beside him but the feeling of wanting... needing to be in closer contact with her is like an ache. Voices buzz around them and he feels distant, as if he's about to be sucked away.

"I did," her voice makes its way back to him through the buzz. "I said I was sorry too, for a fight we had earlier in the year, but also because of things that happened in the past. I asked if we could be friends again, or at least be civil to each other. I said that life really is too short to leave it too late. She understood that, at least."

Greg passes the salt to someone across the table. He thinks the girl is Sarah's sister-in-law's stepdaughter. Another girl with an odd name: Mariana. She looks identical to the Angel one, and is the mother of the four-year-old boy.

"I really think things might be getting better," Ellie says bravely. But he understands how much she must be hurting. It's her first Christmas as the mother of a dead child.

Glancing down the other end of the table, it suddenly hits him that Jonah has lost his daughter too.

"I'm sorry for your loss, mate."

Greg puts out his hand. After a moment's hesitation, Jonah takes it.

"Thanks," he says. Broken blood vessels outline his nose and the curve of bone beneath his eyes. "I appreciate that."

49

Ellie

25 December 2013

It's late in the afternoon before Ellie gets a chance to have a private conversation with Rebecca.

Gifts have been exchanged around the long tables and dinner is over. A purposeful team of women and men, including Ellie and, she's surprised to note, Jonah, have swept through the barn, clearing the tables and repeatedly loading the massive dishwasher hired in for the occasion.

Some of the people, including Greg, and Ellie's children and grandchildren, have gone for a walk with Jack and various other local dogs. Jonah has gone as well. He's become friendly with Iris but that's probably more to do with whatever it is they've been smoking than anything else. Then Ellie berates herself for the mean thoughts. Jonah's a nice person. Ellie feels incredibly tired, and although it's been a wonderful day so far a horrid urge to cry is swelling her throat and she tells her family she would like to have a rest.

She wants to have a meaningful interchange with Rebecca when no-one else is present.

Ellie dozes in a chair in a corner of the long living room, vaguely listening to the snippets of conversation among the young people and the low-volume, melodic music coming from a dock on the sideboard.

Finally she sees Rebecca getting up from her cushion on the floor. The girl bends down to lift her baby out of the arms of Connor's cousin, Angel. Rebecca holds the baby up and sniffs her bottom. She scrunches her face. "Won't be long."

She reaches behind the sofa for the changing bag.

Ellie pushes herself out of the chair.

I must hurry.

In the downstairs bathroom Rebecca is changing Eve. The baby wriggles on the mat laid on a low wicker chest. Rebecca kneels at the end of the chest, one hand on her daughter's stomach, the other holding a folded-over, foul-smelling nappy.

"Can I help in any way?" Ellie asks, pretending she's just passing the open doorway.

From the floor beneath the coat hooks by the side door she's collected her colourful cloth bag. The Eliza-doll has been resting in it since the concert ten days ago and now Ellie's hand feels inside the bag to touch the doll. She closes her fingers over a soft limb, leg or arm, she can't tell at first. For a moment it's hard to breathe.

Rebecca is eyeing her.

"Ah... I don't think, well, you can hand me the wipes, if you like." The girl's being generous. She lets the nappy drop from her hand into a bin. Ellie rips some wipes from the tube and hands them one by one to Rebecca.

When the job is done, Rebecca lifts Eve and hands her, tidily fastened into a fresh white stretch-suit, to Ellie while she washes her hands.

The baby's weight is pliable in Ellie's arms. Eve emits musical noises. She tips her head back to see who's holding her now, and catches Ellie's eye. Her lips fall open and she makes an 'O' shape with her mouth. Ellie can only take half a minute of this gaze before she has to bury her nose in the folds of baby neck. Tears escape from her eyes. Rebecca stands, her hands hanging loosely at her sides.

"My daughter died, you see." Ellie kisses the baby. "It may be hard for you to imagine, with Eve so small, but Eliza was my baby once."

She puts distance between her body and Eve as she starts to hand Rebecca's daughter back. She feels the pull in her guts as Rebecca takes her away.

You're not mine anymore, I know that.

But it's still hard.

"I'm sorry," Rebecca says. Her luminous eyes look scared. "It must be terrible for you."

Ellie sniffs. She moves around Rebecca to the toilet roll, threaded onto a wooden hanger fixed precariously to the wall by one screw. She plucks off a few squares and blows her nose, then drops the used tissue into the toilet bowl.

She washes her hands and moves back to her bag, hoisting it up onto her shoulder.

"I have something for you," she says.

Ellie opens her bag. With two hands she lifts out the Eliza-doll, fighting the impulse to apologise for its long incarceration in there. The expression on the doll's sewn face seems peaceful. She hopes Rebecca thinks the same.

"Well, it's for Eve, really, but you can look after it for her. Please?"

"Oh my God." Rebecca is shocked. "One of your dolls. It's so beautiful. But you can't give it to me. Don't you want to save it for... give it to one of your own grandchildren?"

Ellie gazes at the doll in her hands for a long time. Then she examines the face of Rebecca's baby, just to be sure. Eve has her eyes wide open. She stares back at Ellie.

"Not this one," Ellie says softly.

Hesitantly, Rebecca reaches out and accepts the doll. With her knee she nudges the changing mat to the floor and lowers herself to the wicker chest, settling the baby into the crook of her elbow. Eve's starfish hand waves about, trying to make contact with the doll that Rebecca holds in front of her, but she soon grows bored. She pushes her face into Rebecca's chest, makes frustrated noises.

"She's hungry," Rebecca says. "I usually feed her after she's been changed."

Ellie can tell the girl wants to be left alone.

She expected to experience a tremendous relief, a lifting sensation, when she handed the Eliza-doll over, but she only feels sad. Weightless in herself. Now it's definitely over.

Ellie turns to go, her hand on the door handle.

Rebecca fidgets. Her knee jiggles. "Wait," she says quickly.

Her movement causes Eve to gulp on her milk. She half-chokes and her mouth becomes detached from the nipple. She throws her head back and lets out a furious cry, arms and legs stiffening. Milk spurts from the abandoned breast. Colour rises in Rebecca's cheeks and she looks about to cry as she struggles to calm the baby and get her reattached.

Ellie feels guilty.

Real life goes on. It's messy and complicated. *My sorrow is my concern, not hers.*

"I'm sorry for distracting you," she says to Rebecca. *It was wrong of me to cry in front of her.* "Are you okay?"

Rebecca smiles. Eve is back in her rightful place, suckling contentedly. Ellie remembers the relief when a screaming child quietens. Rebecca strokes her baby's head, cupping it in her palm.

"It's all right," she says. "I'm fine now. I just wanted to thank you for the doll. It's truly beautiful. I can't believe you've given it to us. I'll treasure her until Eve's old enough to play with her. Thank you so much, but are you really sure?"

Now Ellie can feel the weight of her pain lifting, and at the same time her feet are planting themselves firmly on the ground.

"I'm sure," she tells Rebecca. "It's meant for Eve, I'm certain
of it."

Acknowledgements

Thanks to my sister, Dawn (RIP) for being such an inspiration. She was a fiddle-player and a free spirit. She was a member of the Peace Convoy in the early 1990s, travelling variously in an ambulance, a lorry, and in a horse-and-cart. She lived at the Women's Peace Camp at Greenham Common for a couple of years in the mid-1980s and I hitchhiked down there with her and spent a few days singing, taking part in activities and nights sleeping in a tree in the woods. The 1980s are filled with vivid memories for me, and I hope an equally poignant reflection of that time comes through in the book for others.

At the time I went with Dawn to Greenham I was living at Blackmore House in Kilnsea, East Yorkshire, a communal home on which the far more successful Running Hare House in the book is based. I had given stillbirth to the baby Ellie goes on to have (Rosie) in the book. I can't imagine what it would have been like if I'd had five children at such a young age, as she does.

Thanks also go to my son Zak for being the other familial motivator in my life, his aunt would have been proud of the travelling adventures he has undertaken from the age of sixteen onwards. It was Zak who introduced me to Iceland, a location that runs through the story of The Eliza Doll like a vein. Another location, Leitrim in Ireland, is where Dawn lived for the last seventeen years of her life and of course Hull is where I gave birth to my three sons and my daughter.

Our beloved bus-with-a-wood stove in which Phil and I travelled as much as we could is the more-or-less exact replica of Ellie's travelling home. On our first trip out in it after writing intensively about Ellie's adventures, it occurred to me how similar our van was to hers. Then I remembered that I had actually modelled her van on ours. We now have a more contemporary campervan.

In the novel, Ellie makes reference to a course she went

on which has made her better able to communicate with her family. I drew inspiration for this from the book: *How To Talk So Kids Will Listen and How To Listen So Kids Will Talk* by Adele Faber and Elaine Mazlish (Harper Perennial, Oct 1999)

Thanks to Kristin Gleason for her read through of an early draft. Also Julia Gibbs, proofreader.

Thanks, as always, to my children for my intensive mothering years, the most precious time in my life.

About the Author

Tracey-Scott-Townsend is the author of six novels — the most recent The Vagabond Mother (January 2020) and Sea Babies (May 2019) — all published by Wild Pressed Books and Inspired Quill Publishing.

Reviews often describe her novels as poetic or painterly.

She is also a poet and a visual artist. She has a Fine Art MA and a BA (Hons) Visual Studies. She has exhibited paintings throughout the UK (as Tracey Scott). She has a long career as a workshop facilitator with community groups and in schools.

Tracey is co-director of an up-and-coming small independent publisher, Wild Pressed Books, which has a growing roster of authors and poets.

Mother of four grown-up children, Tracey spends as much time as possible travelling the UK and Europe in a camper van with her husband and two dogs, writing and editing while on the road.